DENVER NOIR

EDITED BY
CYNTHIA SWANSON

BROOKLYN, NEW YORK

This collection comprises works of fiction. All names, characters, places, and incidents are the product of the authors' imaginations or used in a fictitious manner.

Published by Akashic Books
©2022 Akashic Books

Series concept by Tim McLoughlin and Johnny Temple
Denver map by Sohrab Habibion

Paperback ISBN: 978-1-63614-029-2
Hardcover ISBN: 978-1-63614-034-6
Library of Congress Control Number: 2021945695

Akashic Books
Brooklyn, New York
Instagram: AkashicBooks
Twitter: AkashicBooks
Facebook: AkashicBooks
E-mail: info@akashicbooks.com
Website: www.akashicbooks.com

ALSO IN THE AKASHIC NOIR SERIES

MIAMI NOIR, edited by LES STANDIFORD

MIAMI NOIR: THE CLASSICS,
edited by LES STANDIFORD

MILWAUKEE NOIR, edited by TIM HENNESSY

MISSISSIPPI NOIR, edited by TOM FRANKLIN

MONTANA NOIR, edited by JAMES GRADY
& KEIR GRAFF

MONTREAL NOIR (CANADA), edited by JOHN
McFETRIDGE & JACQUES FILIPPI

MOSCOW NOIR (RUSSIA),
edited by NATALIA SMIRNOVA & JULIA GOUMEN

MUMBAI NOIR (INDIA), edited by ALTAF TYREWALA

NAIROBI NOIR (KENYA), edited by PETER KIMANI

NEW HAVEN NOIR, edited by AMY BLOOM

NEW JERSEY NOIR, edited by JOYCE CAROL OATES

NEW ORLEANS NOIR, edited by JULIE SMITH

NEW ORLEANS NOIR: THE CLASSICS,
edited by JULIE SMITH

OAKLAND NOIR, edited by JERRY THOMPSON
& EDDIE MULLER

ORANGE COUNTY NOIR, edited by GARY PHILLIPS

PARIS NOIR (FRANCE), edited by AURÉLIEN MASSON

PARIS NOIR: THE SUBURBS, edited by HERVÉ
DELOUCHE

PALM SPRINGS NOIR, edited by
BARBARA DeMARCO-BARRETT

PHILADELPHIA NOIR, edited by CARLIN ROMANO

PHOENIX NOIR, edited by PATRICK MILLIKIN

PITTSBURGH NOIR, edited by KATHLEEN GEORGE

PORTLAND NOIR, edited by KEVIN SAMPSELL

PRAGUE NOIR (CZECH REPUBLIC),
edited by PAVEL MANDYS

PRISON NOIR, edited by JOYCE CAROL OATES

PROVIDENCE NOIR, edited by ANN HOOD

QUEENS NOIR, edited by ROBERT KNIGHTLY

RICHMOND NOIR, edited by ANDREW BLOSSOM,
BRIAN CASTLEBERRY & TOM DE HAVEN

RIO NOIR (BRAZIL), edited by TONY BELLOTTO

ROME NOIR (ITALY), edited by CHIARA STANGALINO
& MAXIM JAKUBOWSKI

SAN DIEGO NOIR, edited by MARYELIZABETH HART

SAN FRANCISCO NOIR, edited by PETER MARAVELIS

SAN FRANCISCO NOIR 2: THE CLASSICS,
edited by PETER MARAVELIS

SAN JUAN NOIR (PUERTO RICO),
edited by MAYRA SANTOS-FEBRES

SANTA CRUZ NOIR, edited by SUSIE BRIGHT

SANTA FE NOIR, edited by ARIEL GORE

SÃO PAULO NOIR (BRAZIL),
edited by TONY BELLOTTO

SEATTLE NOIR, edited by CURT COLBERT

SINGAPORE NOIR, edited by CHERYL LU-LIEN TAN

STATEN ISLAND NOIR, edited by PATRICIA SMITH

ST. LOUIS NOIR, edited by SCOTT PHILLIPS

STOCKHOLM NOIR (SWEDEN), edited by
NATHAN LARSON & CARL-MICHAEL EDENBORG

ST. PETERSBURG NOIR (RUSSIA), edited by
NATALIA SMIRNOVA & JULIA GOUMEN

SYDNEY NOIR (AUSTRALIA), edited by JOHN DALE

TAMPA BAY NOIR, edited by COLETTE BANCROFT

TEHRAN NOIR (IRAN), edited by SALAR ABDOH

TEL AVIV NOIR (ISRAEL), edited by ETGAR KERET
& ASSAF GAVRON

TORONTO NOIR (CANADA), edited by JANINE ARMIN
& NATHANIEL G. MOORE

TRINIDAD NOIR (TRINIDAD & TOBAGO), edited by
LISA ALLEN-AGOSTINI & JEANNE MASON

TRINIDAD NOIR: THE CLASSICS
(TRINIDAD & TOBAGO), edited by EARL LOVELACE
& ROBERT ANTONI

TWIN CITIES NOIR, edited by JULIE SCHAPER
& STEVEN HORWITZ

USA NOIR, edited by JOHNNY TEMPLE

VANCOUVER NOIR (CANADA), edited by SAM WIEBE

VENICE NOIR (ITALY), edited by MAXIM JAKUBOWSKI

WALL STREET NOIR, edited by PETER SPIEGELMAN

ZAGREB NOIR (CROATIA), edited by IVAN SRŠEN

FORTHCOMING

AUSTIN NOIR, edited by HOPETON HAY,
MOLLY ODINTZ, & SCOTT A. MONTGOMERY

CLEVELAND NOIR, edited by MIESHA HEADEN
& MICHAEL RUHLMAN

JERUSALEM NOIR (EAST),
edited by RAWYA BURBARA

JERUSALEM NOIR (WEST), edited by MAAYAN EITAN

NATIVE NOIR, edited by DAVID HESKA WANBLI WEIDEN

SOUTH CENTRAL NOIR, edited by GARY PHILLIPS

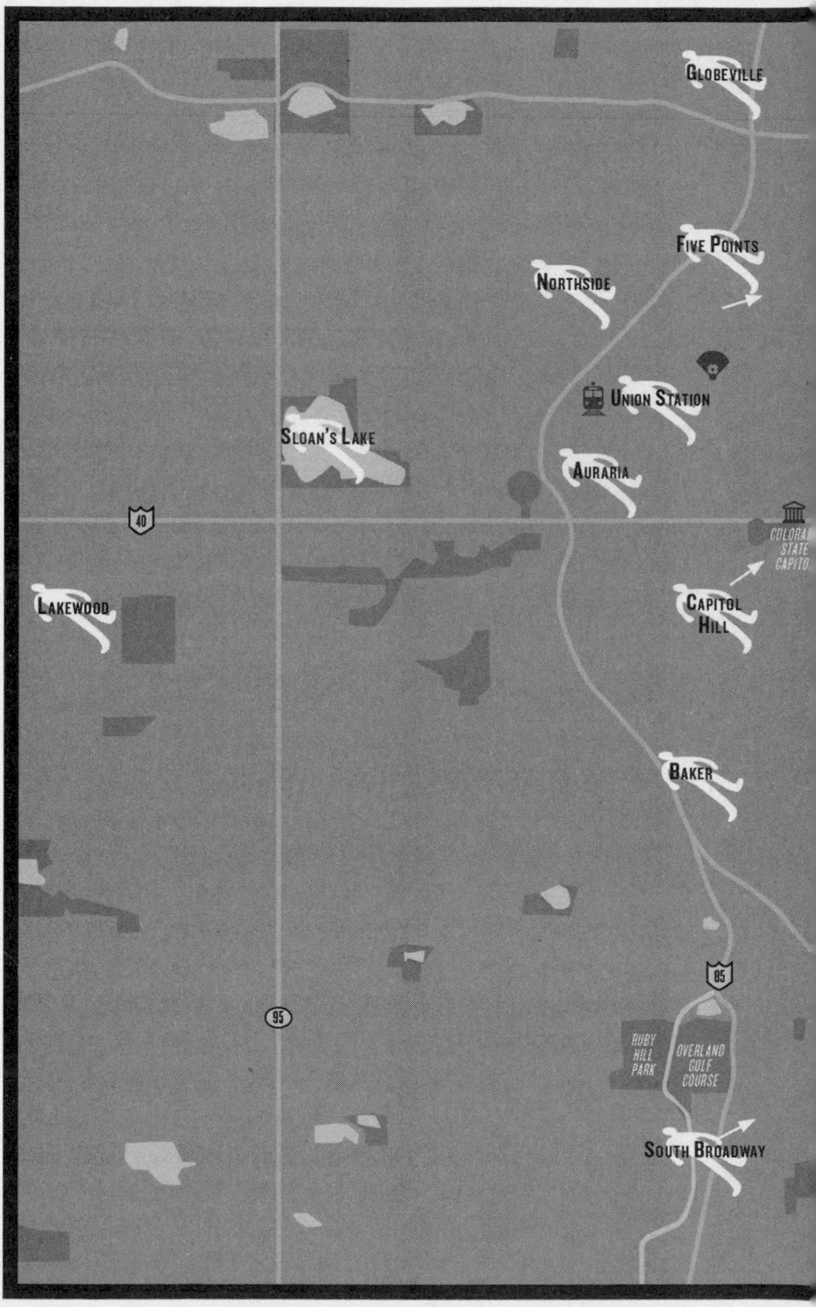
GLOBEVILLE
FIVE POINTS
NORTHSIDE
UNION STATION
SLOAN'S LAKE
AURARIA
40
COLORA
STATE
CAPITO
LAKEWOOD
CAPITOL
HILL
BAKER
85
95
RUBY
HILL
PARK
OVERLAND
GOLF
COURSE
SOUTH BROADWAY

DENVER

70

2

CITY PARK/
DENVER
ZOO

COLFAX

CHEESMAN
PARK

AURORA

GLENDALE

WASHINGTON
PARK

83

25

TABLE OF CONTENTS

PART III: THINGS TO DO IN DENVER WHEN YOU'RE YOUNG

INTRODUCTION
MILE HIGH MISGIVINGS

L ong before Sam Bates and William Greenberry Russell set their mining pans into a stream near a confluence of waterways about thirty miles east of the Rocky Mountains, the area's grassy riverbanks provided a seasonal home for the Ute, Cheyenne, and Arapaho nations. In 1851, the land was granted to the Arapaho under the Treaty of Fort Laramie, but in 1858, Bates and Russell's discovery of twenty troy ounces (620 g) of gold resulted in thousands of settlers flocking to the region to seek their fortunes. Native peoples attempted to coexist with the newcomers—until November 1864, when hundreds of Cheyenne and Arapaho were slaughtered at Sand Creek, and those who survived fled for their lives.

Even by then, Denver's forecasts as a golden promised land had begun to wane, as the area's gold prospects proved negligible while silver mines in the nearby mountains burgeoned. Still, the town of Denver, named for one-time Kansas Territory governor James W. Denver, reinvented itself as a railroad and supply hub for prospectors and pioneers alike.

The transient population inevitably led to a swell of seediness. Gamblers and guzzlers, streetwalkers and sinners—all found their place in the bustling young town. Only when barons like Horace Tabor and John Mouat began to build elegant mansions and cultural centers like the elaborate Tabor Opera House at Sixteenth and Curtis (eventually a third-rate movie house, demolished in 1964 and replaced with the brutalist Federal Reserve Branch Bank) did Denver take on a somewhat dignified air.

Following the silver bust of the 1890s, ensuing generations of Denver mayors and city planners set about beautifying their town of speculators and shopkeepers, cowhands and courtesans, by planting trees and platting parks on the area's grasslands. So successful was this effort, Denver acquired the nickname Queen City of the Plains, and a proper municipality began to take shape. During the following decades, Denver grew from a center of military activity to an oil boom-and-bust town to a technological hub. These days, it's a place of brew pubs, ballparks, culture, and community pride—and always, that view of the mountains to the west, most days showcased under a vibrant blue sky.

But even a city that boasts three hundred days of sunshine a year has its sudden, often violent storms—and writers have long taken advantage of that metaphor. Renowned authors Katherine Anne Porter, Jack Kerouac, Stephen King, Rex Burns, Robert Greer, Michael Connelly, and Kali Fajardo-Anstine—among many others—have brilliantly portrayed this picturesque but often merciless city. Today, Denver is home to a thriving literary scene, with writers of all stripes finding inspiration in its people and streets. The authors and stories featured in *Denver Noir* are no exception.

Surprising to many on their initial visit here, Denver is relatively unhilly. Make no mistake, we're not the Rocky Mountains—those appear some miles later, as you head west on I-70. Here in town, streets are lengthy and primarily gridded, similar to many Midwestern cities.

What we have and those cities don't, however, is Colfax Avenue. Allegedly dubbed "the longest, wickedest street in

America" by *Playboy*, Colfax stretches twenty-six latitudinal miles, crossing Aurora at one end and Golden at the other, nodding at the Colorado State Capitol as it passes downtown, and taking those who traverse its length on a journey of idiosyncrasy, artistry, and corruption. David Heska Wanbli Weiden opens Part I with "Colfax and Havana," in which an opponent's racism jeopardizes the prospects of a Native American attorney, pushing him toward a precipitous edge. Heartbreak is inescapable on Colfax, as Twanna LaTrice Hill's tragic heroine in "A Life of Little Consequence" discovers. Personally, in "Pieces of Everyone, Everywhere," I relished using a laborer's viewpoint to explore the 1893 exhumation of bodies that transformed a paupers' cemetery into one of Denver's most beautiful (and purportedly haunted) parks. There's no shortage of miscreants along the Mile High City's longest street, and Erika T. Wurth's PI in "Tough Girls" takes shit from none of them.

Speaking of the Mile High—a moniker that's endured long past Denver's Queen City status—Part II delves into the many ways in which Denver earns its 5,280-feet-above-sea-level nickname. Peter Heller kicks off this section with "The Lake," in which a writer-turned-paddleboarder finds his purpose in delivering justice on the water. In "A Baker's Duckling," R. Alan Brooks introduces readers to a man with deep neighborhood roots who puts his own life in jeopardy to expose a white supremacist. (But whatever you do, don't call this good neighbor a Black hipster!) In "No Gods," Amy Drayer questions the outlook for a former revolutionary, her friends and loved ones—and, indeed, the Mile High itself. Reporting from towering hotel suites and apartments with showstopping views, Mark Stevens's food critic and amateur PI in "Junk Feed" endeavors to solve the murder of a high-profile city official. Manuel Ramos's "Northside Nocturne" tells the tale of a young man willing to risk everything to save his neighborhood from gentrification.

From the earliest prospectors to today's millennials, young people have always found the innovative, frontier nature of Denver appealing. Coming-of-age noir is a subgenre all its own, and five Denver authors explore it in Part III. Barbara Nickless introduces us to a resourceful, freight-hopping runaway in "Ways of Escape." D.L. Cordero, in "Sangre," reveals the effects of 1970s-era "urban renewal" and forced dislocation on a Chicano family. In "Dreaming of Ella," Francelia Belton takes readers back to 1950s Five Points, the Harlem of the West, where a talented but naïve trumpeter discovers just how far he'll go in pursuit of his dreams of stardom. Mathangi Subramanian's college student and devoted daughter in "On Grasmere Lake" faces the consequences of fury released. Finally, Mario Acevedo closes out this volume with the foreboding tale of "El Armero"—the gunsmith—a young man who, in near-future Denver, unearths what happens when one's loyalty is pressed to the limit.

Editing *Denver Noir*, working with this talented group of writers, has been one of the highlights of my career. Fans of noir and Denver devotees alike, I invite you into this journey of our Mile High City, our home beside the mountains, our capital of sunshine and darkness, optimism and anguish.

Readers, enjoy the ride.

Cynthia Swanson
Denver, Colorado
January 2022

PART I

THE LONGEST, WICKEDEST STREET

COLFAX AND HAVANA

BY DAVID HESKA WANBLI WEIDEN

Aurora

The smell of the grease from the taquería downstairs overwhelmed me as I tried to review thirty pages of legal documents. I rented a small office—about the size of a walk-in closet—on the second floor of an old building on East Colfax in Aurora. The price was right, but my space was directly above the restaurant's trash can and oil bin.

I'd landed in Aurora because it was cheap and because that's where my clients lived. Driving under the influence, possession of narcotics, divorces, and custody actions—these cases were my bread and butter. A far cry from my dreams as a kid on the Rosebud Reservation of pursuing social justice for Native Americans, but I'd learned back in law school that a white knight job as a public interest lawyer required a trust fund or wealthy spouse, especially when your monthly student loan payments rivaled the GDP of many small countries.

But I'd made my peace with the loss of my ambitions to change society and argue Native cases at the Supreme Court. Now I focused on helping people with their legal problems so they could go on with their lives. That's what I told myself, anyway. After I negotiated plea bargains with the prosecutor, I often saw my former clients back at Las Adelitas or El Metapan, drinking and drugging again. They'd send over a shot, and I'd toast their freedom to pursue the American dream of titanic inebriation.

Yeah, Aurora suited me. This part of the sprawling suburb consisted of modest single-family homes, scores of low-rent apartment buildings that resembled army bunkers, and dozens of Mexican restaurants, bakeries, and markets. Because of my brown skin and black hair, my clients assumed I was Latino, which worked in my favor. Not to mention, in this part of town, there was little chance of running into former law school classmates with their expensive suits and cars. I didn't have to witness their barely concealed pity as they learned about my downward trajectory from Native social justice warrior to small-time street lawyer.

The directory panel in the hallway stated, *LAW FIRM OF GRIFFIN GERMAINE*, but it was only me. No receptionist, paralegal, or junior attorneys. The only extravagance in the office complex was a battered old Ricoh copier in the shared common area, for which I paid an extra twenty dollars per month, so long as I didn't make more than three hundred copies. I used my own ancient Dell laptop, tiny laser printer, and off-brand scanner. A generic K-Cup coffee machine rested on top of some old *Pacific Reporters*. My diploma from the University of Colorado Law School hung on the wall, encased in a fancy cherrywood frame, a gift from the Native American Law Student Association, of which I'd been president.

I got up and closed the small window, even though it was hot. I needed my full focus for the legal papers that had just arrived on my computer screen. My former DUI client Nestor Vega had been hit by a delivery truck while crossing Havana Street on foot, and the doctor had said he might never walk again. The driver's insurance company—known among lawyers by its nickname, Snake Farm—had refused to pay his medical bills or any pain and suffering compensation, arguing that he was intoxicated at the time of the accident and therefore responsible for his own expenses. Nestor had called me, asking if I would represent him again, and I'd jumped at the chance to handle a personal injury case.

Even though Colorado tort law was biased in favor of businesses and corporations, Nestor was looking at a million-dollar case, of which I'd collect one-third of the total settlement, more if the case went to trial. If I played my cards the right way, I'd be able to approach Snake Farm with a settlement offer by the end of the year. A payout of that size would mean that I could stop picking up small cases and volunteer for some pro bono work at the Native American Rights Fund. I could hang out at their cool office in Boulder and talk about Indian law again. Maybe even turn that into a full-time position if I did a good job on the pro bono work. Nestor's case was the break I'd been hoping for.

But Snake Farm's defense counsel—some meathead named Colt Jackson—was playing hardball, filing ridiculous motions, refusing to provide documents I requested, and not responding to my messages. There were a lot of these types in the legal profession, but this guy was one of the worst. I opened up Nestor's folder on my computer, then my cell phone started vibrating.

"Germaine Law Office."

A pause. "Griff, is that you?"

"Yes?" I didn't recognize the woman's voice.

"Hey, it's Louise. From the Zephyr?"

The bartender from the Zephyr Lounge out on Colfax and Peoria. The place where I'd drowned many sorrows when I'd first moved to Aurora a decade ago. Louise had been in her thirties, tall with light-brown hair, porcelain-white skin, and a vintage thrift store sense of style. I remembered that she wore cool cat's-eye glasses and a faux fur coat that looked like a leopard. She'd been kind to me, spotting me drinks when I didn't have any cash. We'd even had a few sodden flings after some of her shifts. But there was never any weirdness between us. I'd moved my drinking down the street and lost touch with her.

"Louise, wow. Long time. How you been doing?"

"Well, you know, I've been better. But hey, I'm glad I found your number. I still had your card in my purse. It was buried at the bottom."

Story of my life. "You still at the Zephyr?"

"Yeah," she said, "but it's not going so well. Ever since the med school opened, people don't want to drink there. I got my regulars, but they're dying off."

The University of Colorado had moved its medical school to the old Fitzsimons Army Hospital facility awhile back, ensuring that a horde of doctors, medical students, and college administrators were just a couple of blocks from the Zephyr. But those folks weren't interested in the bar's 1970s art collection and dicey clientele. I felt guilty that I hadn't been there in so long.

"Sorry to hear that. I'll stop by soon, promise."

She cleared her throat. "Actually, I was wondering if I could come by and see you."

"What's up?" I suspected she was gearing up to ask for money, but this well was dry. Bone dry.

"Well, I've got a divorce thing. So, do you still have your law degree or whatever? I mean, you're a lawyer, right? Not selling cars or mowing lawns."

This stung. "Sure am. What's going on?"

Another pause. "It's kind of embarrassing, but my ex-husband stopped paying his child support. For my daughter, Lily?"

I'd forgotten she had a daughter. I'd seen her once or twice at the bar, back in the day. A quiet little girl, sitting in one of the booths. She'd have to be a teenager by now. "Lily, right. Does he send the child support to the state office or to you directly?"

"Well, he's supposed to send it to me. But I haven't gotten a check in nine months, and I can't reach him. You know, tips are really down right now, and I can't make it without that money."

I'd heard this story too many times. Child support in Colorado was usually not disputed, as it was determined by a formula based on the parents' incomes and number of overnight stays. But the flaw in the system was collecting the money from those who were determined to dodge making their payments. A truly stubborn asshole could sometimes beat the system.

"I'm sorry to hear that," I said. "I'm guessing you need some help."

"God, yes. We're about two months from being evicted, and that bastard won't pay what he owes for his own kid. I can't even afford Internet service anymore—Lily is going crazy." Her voice was beginning to crack.

"Look," I said, "why don't you come to my office tomorrow and we can talk this over. I'm free in the morning; maybe ten a.m.? Bring all of the divorce paperwork you have."

"Yes, absolutely! I can make that. Lily will be in school and I don't work until two. Thank you, Griff. You're a good guy."

A good guy. It had been a long time since anyone had said that to me. Maybe things were changing.

The next morning, I put on my best tie and blazer and got to my office early. I threw out all of the trash, straightened the file folders on my desk, ran a dusting cloth over the books, and made sure the window was tightly closed to keep out the stink. Not perfect, but presentable.

Then I checked my email and E-filing account, hoping I'd gotten a response from opposing counsel in Nestor's case. I'd requested the defendant's insurance policy, but Colt had refused to produce it, even though this was standard procedure. I knew he was just playing games, trying to delay the case from moving forward so that Nestor would be willing to settle at a lower amount. My inbox was empty, so I decided to give Colt Jackson a call.

His office phone sent me directly to his voice mail, so I left a quick message: "Colt, this is Griff Germaine calling about the Nestor Vega case. I haven't gotten a response to my RFP and I want to touch base on the driver's policy. Are you going to send that over? Rather not bother Judge Stancil with a motion to compel. Let me know, please." Hopefully my message would spur the asshole into doing the right thing and sending the policy over.

A few minutes after ten, I heard a knock on my door. I opened it and Louise stepped inside. Her hair was different, and the cool coat and eyeglasses were gone. She looked exhausted, and I could tell that the last few years had taken a toll on her. We hugged, awkwardly, and I motioned for her to sit down.

She looked around the office. "This is . . . nice."

"Yeah, well," I said. "Don't know about nice, but it's a good location for me. Most of my clients live in Aurora; it's easy for them to get here."

"Of course. That makes sense. Hey, thanks for meeting with me." She set a tan folder on my desk. "Appreciate it."

"It's great to see you. Sorry it's under these circumstances. I've been meaning to drop by the bar, it's just that—"

"No need to explain. All good. Life goes on, right?"

"Sometimes I feel like I'm still waiting for my life to start," I said, then paused for a second. Our eyes locked, and I looked away. I picked up her folder and took out a stack of papers. "So, tell me what's going on with the child support."

"That's my bank statement on top. The last check I got from him was almost nine months ago. See the deposit for six hundred dollars? That was the last one he sent."

I took a look at the other papers in the folder. I glanced at the financial statements and noticed that they'd used the state's separation agreement template, rather than draft their own.

"You guys didn't have counsel for the divorce?" I asked.

"You mean lawyers? No, Roger said we didn't need them because we didn't own any property back then."

"Probably wasn't a good idea." I looked at the child support worksheet they'd completed. "What does he do? He work for someone?"

She shook her head. "No, he runs his own business. Handyman, some remodeling. I think he mostly gets paid in cash. You know, no receipts. I asked for his tax return, but he won't give it to me."

"What does he say about the child support? He explain why he's not paying?"

She set her cell phone down on the edge of my desk. "That's the problem. He's kind of dropped off the face of the earth. I can't reach him on his phone, and he moved from his old apartment, but never gave me his new address. I've checked on Facebook and all that, but can't find him."

"What about your daughter? Does she know where he is?"

Louise closed her eyes like she was concentrating, then started talking: "The shithead doesn't care about her. After we split, she'd go to his place and spend a weekend with him. But I guess he lost interest. She hasn't seen or talked to him for a long time."

"You know anybody who might know where he is? Mutual friends or—"

"He doesn't have any friends! Because he's an asshole."

I held up my hand. "All right, I get it. Is there anyone you can contact who might know his address?"

She shook her head. "No, I've done all that. I emailed his sister, his cousin, a couple other people. They just ignored me. I checked all the social media stuff, even bought one of those PeopleFinders searches. Cost me thirty dollars. The last address that came up was his old place. I already had that."

"Do you know if he's still in the state?"

"No clue. Although I doubt he'd leave. Where would he go? Maybe he's dead. A girl can dream, right? But I think someone would have told me."

I looked at the ex-husband's financial statement for a moment, then put it back in the folder. "Okay, here's my advice. First thing you do is contact the Colorado child support division at the Department of Human Services. They're trained to find parents who won't pay up. They can check his credit report, utilities, everything. If he's in state, they'll find him. If he left Colorado, there's the federal parent locator service. They do the same thing, nationwide."

She frowned. "Uh, how long does that take? I mean, it took me six months just to get my license plates from the DMV."

I wondered how much to tell her. The reality was that the child support division was usually overwhelmed and underfunded. "I'll be straight with you," I said. "I hear there's a pretty long lead time. It can take a year or more, but you can file for back child support when—"

"A year! I can't wait that long. I'm about to get tossed out on my ass. What am I supposed to do?"

I raised my hands up in surrender. "Look, I hear you. These things take time. But maybe they'll get lucky, find him right away."

"I can't count on luck! I'm about two shakes away from living in the motel across the street."

She meant the Dust and Wind Motel, which rented rooms by the week, day, or hour. It wasn't a place where you wanted to raise a kid.

"Louise, you know I wish there was some magic wand to wave, but if you don't know where your ex is, you're—"

She reached across the desk and grabbed my hand. "Please, Griff, isn't there some other way? To get this thing going? For old times' sake?"

I looked at Louise and remembered one night years ago when I'd been at my lowest point. I'd been on a two-day bender, convinced that my life was over because I didn't have any clients, any prospects, or enough cash to support myself. I'd felt like a true failure—the only one of my Native law school classmates who couldn't get a job at one of the good law firms. I'd stopped in at the Zephyr, and Louise saw I was in a bad way. She sat me down in one of the back booths, gave me coffee, and took me home with her when the bar closed. I spent the next day at her place, badly hungover but glad to be with another person. That time had meant a lot to me. And now she was asking for my help.

"Okay," I said, "I'll do it." I took her pile of divorce papers and put a binder clip on them. "It might be a long shot, but

I can try and find him on my own instead of waiting for the state."

"Oh, thank you, Griff!" She leaned across the desk and kissed me, which I wasn't expecting.

"You're welcome," I said, and leaned back in my chair. I felt a little dizzy.

"Look, I want to pay you," she said. "I don't have anything now, but I promise—"

"This one's on the house. Really. But remember, even if we find him, that's just the start. We'll have to file with the state, then try to get his wages garnished or his income tax return seized. No guarantees, okay?"

"I have faith in you," she responded.

I wasn't sure what to say. Any faith I had—in the government, the legal system, even myself—was long gone. If Louise believed in me, she was the last one.

For the next few days, I had to put Louise's case on the back burner so I could get ahead on Nestor's lawsuit. I'd received the results of Nestor's medical examination, and the doctor had confirmed that he'd be confined to a wheelchair for the indefinite future. This was terrible for Nestor but good for our case, as it dramatically improved our position with the defense. There was no way the driver's insurance company would take the case to trial now. Juries were immensely sympathetic to any plaintiff who entered the courtroom in a wheelchair. Nestor would never have to worry about money again. And, of course, this would mean that I could move to a decent office, buy a better car, and maybe show my face at the Colorado Indian Bar Association meetings again. I felt better than I had in a long time.

Then I heard my phone buzz.

"Germaine Law Office."

"Is this Griffin Germaine?"

"Yes, who's this?" I said.

"This is Colt Jackson. Just who the fuck do you think you are?"

It took me a second to orient myself to the call. "Sorry, what did you . . . What are you calling about?"

"That goddamn message you left on my machine! Threatening to go to Judge Stancil. For shit's sake, he and I went to Stanford Law together. You really think he'll grant a motion to compel for some nobody like you?"

I was speechless. I'd dealt with enormous assholes before, but this guy won the prize.

"Look," I said, "I don't give a gigantic turd if you went to Stanford Law and sucked off all nine judges on the Supreme Court. Just send the damn insurance policy. My client has a right to it, and that's the law."

He laughed. "You really don't know shit about torts, do you? The law is what we say it is. And you're not getting that policy. I've sent over all the docs you're going to get."

"Fine," I said. "I'll file the motion to compel. Your judge buddy denies it, I'll file a writ of mandamus with the appeals court."

"Hoo boy, you really are stupid, aren't you? You file for mandamus against the judge, you'll never win a case in his court again. My advice to you, Chief Geronimo or whatever you call yourself, is that you stick to your little criminal cases and go back to your teepee—"

I hung up. I'd reached my tolerance for racist shitheads for one day. I shut down my computer and starting walking to La Morena for some cheap beer and good tequila. It was karaoke night, and with any luck they'd play some rock and roll. I'd drink and pretend that I was on some faraway beach, safe from bigots and deadlines and doubt, just for a few hours.

The next morning, I shook off my hangover and turned to Louise's matter. She'd given me the ex-husband's name, date of birth, and last known addresses. Roger T. Haskell, formerly of Aurora, Denver, Wheat Ridge, and Commerce City. I did a Google search but didn't find anything beyond the usual outdated social media profiles, voter registration, and family history sites. The state government databases didn't yield anything useful either.

Having come up dry on the standard searches, I went to the site I saved for the most important cases. Only law firms, collection agencies, and law enforcement had access to the MegaUnion MLOxr database, but it wasn't cheap. The company could track unlisted landline phones, legal judgments, arrests and convictions, assets and licenses, as well as names and aliases. But an extensive search could run a thousand bucks or more. I wanted to help Louise, but a thousand dollars paid for two months' rent in my crappy office. Or some advertising in the *Thrifty Nickle*. Or maybe just some decent hooch and a box of Omaha Steaks. I entered Roger's name and information and hovered over the *Submit* button.

What the hell. I clicked on it, and tried to mute the voices in my head telling me I was an idiot. After a few minutes, an email appeared in my inbox from MLOxr. The report was eighty-seven pages. Ten dollars per sheet plus a processing fee. As I'd feared, I was out nearly a grand.

I downloaded the report and started to read. The first part contained his complete job history since he was eighteen, his electric, gas, and water utility history, and a list of his relatives and associates and their addresses. The next section listed his bankruptcy and lawsuit history. He'd taken a Chapter 7 bankruptcy about fifteen years ago and discharged all of his debts. Interesting. There'd also been a civil lawsuit filed against him for nonpayment of debts around the same time. His criminal history revealed a third-degree assault charge in Denver that had been dismissed. I wondered if Louise knew about all this.

The last section of the report listed the trade names he'd registered with the state for his businesses. He'd filed a new business trade name just a year ago. End Zone Construction, registered in Highlands Ranch at an address I hadn't seen anywhere else. Then I went to the list of relatives and associates, and found what I'd been looking for. The address for End Zone Construction matched the one for his associate, Sherry Chamberlain, and her name appeared on the trade name registration along with his.

It was possible that Roger had created a legit business with a new partner, but my money was on the likelihood that Sherry Chamberlain was his new girlfriend, and he was living with her and running his business from that address. Maybe he'd created the company to avoid paying child support or perhaps there was something else shady going on. Either way, I'd found him and could serve him with a motion for back child support. I'd call Louise and tell her the good news. Better yet, I'd go over to the Zephyr this afternoon and tell her in person. We'd have some celebratory drinks and toast a victory for the good guys.

Later in the day, I stuck the MegaUnion report in a folder and strolled down Colfax. It was a nice day, and I decided to walk the mile and half or so to the Zephyr Lounge. No point in driving, especially if I was going to have some drinks. First, I passed by Pasternack's giant pawn shop and looked inside the windows. A few years ago, I'd had to pawn some electronic gear when I couldn't afford groceries. Thankfully, Nestor's case would pay out soon, or I'd have to pawn even more of my stuff. Then I walked by the old Fox theater and the Weedstar cannabis dispensary, which looked to be packed as usual. I came to Havana Street where Nestor had his unfortunate accident, and made sure to look both ways before crossing. There were a couple of food trucks by the Mexican supermarket, and I could smell the tacos al pastor they were selling. I sidestepped the line of people waiting to get inside the Guadalajara Mexican Buffet, and then walked by the Golden Chalet, the swingers' motel that had been there for decades. The place had survived recessions, wars, and catastrophes—a testament to the enduring power of hook-up culture. For all of its flaws, I loved Colfax Avenue and its people. I missed the reservation, but Colfax had become my home.

Thirty-five minutes later, I made it to the Zephyr and walked inside, my eyes adjusting to the darkness. It had been a few years since I'd been there, but the décor looked to be unchanged. Lots of neon, velvet paintings of Jesus, Elvis, and Santa Claus, and old stuffed animals propped up on the stage in back. The place was empty, and I spotted Louise sitting down behind the bar, staring at her phone.

"Hello there," I said.

"Hey, stranger!" She stood up. "Are you joining me for a happy hour cocktail?"

"Why not? Pour me your favorite."

She grinned. "We don't carry my favorite booze, but I can whip up some pretty good dirty martinis."

She mixed the gin along with the other ingredients, then poured it into some old-fashioned martini glasses. We toasted and took a sip. The juniper taste of the gin complemented the saltiness of the olive juice.

"What brings you in, sir?"

"Got some good news for you. Outstanding news. I found Roger."

"You did? Already? That's so great!"

I opened the manila folder and took out the MegaUnion report. "I used one of the big skip-tracing sites to check him out. Some interesting stuff. Take a look at this." I pointed to one of the pages.

"What does that mean?" she asked.

"He took bankruptcy and got rid of his debt. All of it. You know about that?"

She shook her head. "Sure didn't. Makes sense, though. Hey, you want another round?"

"Sounds good." I turned to the next section of the report while she made the drinks. "Looks like he was arrested for assault too. He ever tell you about that?"

She finished shaking the cocktails and refilled each of our glasses. "Yeah, he mentioned it. I think he said someone owed him money. Does it say what he did?"

I took another sip of the gin. It was starting to go to my head. "No, just that it was dismissed. That tells me the DA gave him a diversion, let him wipe out the charge. But that's from a while back. Check this out—I found some new info."

She came around the bar and sat down next to me. "Yeah? Lay it on me."

"See here? He registered a new business name last year. End Zone Construction. You ever hear of that business?"

"Nope. Sounds like a name he'd pick. Big Broncos fan."

"The interesting thing is that the business address is listed in Highlands Ranch. You never lived out there, right?"

"No, we were out in Thornton. Other side of town."

"I searched the address on Google. It's not an office, it's

a house. A big one too. I'm guessing that's where he's living now."

She gulped her drink and set it down. "Highlands Ranch? He can't afford that. Doesn't make sense."

"Here's the kicker," I said. "End Zone Construction has two registered partners, and the second one owns the house." I paused. "Looks like he might be living with a woman out there and using the address for his business. That's why you couldn't find him on the Internet. It's her house. Her name is, uhh . . ." I leafed through the pages of the report, trying to find it.

"Sherry Chamberlain," she said.

I looked up and saw that Louise's face had crumpled. "Yeah, how'd you know?"

"The address—it's on Mountain View Drive, right?" she said.

"That's right, but—"

"That motherfucking bitch. No wonder she won't answer my texts. She's my best friend—well, used to be. Goddamn her." She took her martini glass and threw it across the bar. It hit the brick wall and disintegrated into jagged shards, the sound ringing across the room. "She's always been after him. Well, she can have the bastard."

She moved back behind the bar, opened a drawer with a key, and started digging around inside.

"Louise, I'm sorry, I didn't know any of this. I had no idea he—" I stopped when I saw what she'd taken from the drawer. A handgun. "Hey," I said, "what are you doing? You're not going to—"

"I'm getting what's mine." She grabbed her bag and stuck the gun in there, then started walking toward the door. "That son of a bitch owes me five thousand dollars. If he can't pay it, his rich bitch can."

I stood up. "Let me handle this. I'll file the papers on him tomorrow, all right?"

She walked out and headed to the parking lot. I watched her fumble for the keys to her car. I could see her hands were shaking.

"Louise, stop! There's nothing you can—"

And she was gone. I watched her pull out onto Colfax and head for the highway. She'd left the bar wide open. I pulled out my phone and called her. No answer.

I wondered what to do. I could call the cops and warn them, but that would only make matters worse. I realized I had two choices: drive all the way out to Highlands Ranch and try to settle things down, or go back inside the Zephyr and help myself to some free booze. I stared inside at the liquor bottles. Whiskey, vodka, tequila. I could get good and drunk and forget about everything. I felt bad for Louise, but nothing good would result from a confrontation with her ex-husband. Learning that Roger had taken up with her former best friend must have been the last straw after years of struggling to support her daughter. Her breaking point.

I remembered my own father's breaking point, decades ago. Jobs were scarce on the Rosebud Reservation, and he'd been forced to travel to Nebraska to work for a local mechanic, sacrificing his health as he repaired hundreds of cars, trucks, and farm vehicles. His lower back pained him so badly that he couldn't walk at times, couldn't even make it to the bathroom. And then he got fired. His boss had said that there wasn't enough business, but my dad knew the real reason. Some of the racists in Nebraska didn't want an Indian working on their vehicle. I remembered that night, when he sat at our little kitchen table and wept. He didn't know if he'd be able to provide for his family again, and the indignities of reservation life fell upon him all at once. He found another job after a time, but he was never the same. The father I'd known was gone, never to return.

I stared up at the sky for a moment, then walked back inside the bar and grabbed the folder with Roger's address. I shut the bar door and started running back to my car. People stared at me as I made my way down the sidewalks, past the restaurants and liquor stores and pawn shops and motels. I ran as fast as I could.

Even going at top speed, it took over twenty minutes to make it back to my vehicle. I bent over and caught my breath, then tossed the folder on the passenger seat. I glanced at the clock. Six p.m.—the height of rush hour. The highway would be jammed. I tried calling Louise one more time, but she still didn't answer. I wiped the sweat off my forehead and started the car.

As I'd feared, the traffic was terrible, and it took a full hour to get to the outskirts of Highlands Ranch, one of the outermost Denver suburbs. The GPS on my phone directed me to Santa Fe Boulevard and informed me that I was five minutes from my destination. My plan was to try to settle Louise down and broker a compromise. Perhaps I could get Roger to agree to an installment plan or a lump-sum payment. I'd appeal to his sense of fatherhood, if any of that was left.

The houses became larger and spaced farther apart. The lawns and bushes were immaculate. I took a right turn and pulled into a cul-de-sac. Then I saw them. Five police cars, the reds and blues flashing.

I was too late.

I parked halfway down the block and walked to the front door of the large house. Two police officers were chatting on the porch.

"What happened?" I asked.

"Sorry, crime scene. Need you to move back."

I tried to look inside but couldn't see anything. "I'm an attorney, here for Louise Hoffman."

"You're her lawyer?" the officer asked.

"Yes. Can you tell me what's going on?"

The two cops looked at each other. "She took a shot at the owner of the house. Didn't hit anyone."

"No one got hurt?"

"Looks that way."

Thank God. Maybe it wasn't as bad as I'd thought. "Where is she?"

"On her way to County. You just missed her."

I knew it would take hours for the police to finish taking statements and even longer for Louise to be processed at the jail in Castle Rock, so there was no point in sticking around. I stared at the mountains off in the distance. They seemed so close here, majestic and severe. After a moment, I turned back and headed home.

The next day, I was able to reach the assistant district attorney, who briefed me on what had happened in Highlands Ranch. Apparently, Louise had burst into the home owned by Sherry Chamberlain. As I'd suspected, Roger Haskell was living there, but he hadn't been home when Louise had stormed in. Louise had yelled at Sherry and tried to shoot her, but had—thankfully—missed by a large margin. Sherry had run out of the house screaming, and neighbors had called the police. Louise had confessed to everything, which destroyed any chance she had of defending the charges against her.

The prosecutor told me that they'd be filing charges of attempted first-degree murder, felony menacing, and several firearms counts. My heart sank when I heard this. I knew how plea bargains worked, and I realized that the best Louise could get would be a reduction to second-degree attempted murder and the other charges dismissed. Second-degree attempted murder was a class 3 felony with a minimum sentence of ten years. That meant that, with good behavior, she'd serve no less than seven years in prison and probably more. She'd never see her daughter Lily grow up, and most likely, Lily would go live with her father, who didn't appear to have much interest in parenting. If he wouldn't take her, she'd enter the child welfare system.

I realized the scale of my failure to help Louise. I'd tried to do a good deed, and now my friend was headed for prison. Her family was destroyed, and Roger—the bad guy in all this—had come out unscathed. Everything I'd tried to do to help Louise had only made matters worse. Yeah, I'd made a mess of things, but maybe I could still help on the margins. I'd keep an eye out for Lily, and would even use some of the payout from Nestor's case to help her. The least I could do.

So, it was time to get back to work. My DUI cases had dried up, but I still had Nestor's personal injury lawsuit. That case was the best piece of luck I'd had in a long time. As I booted up my computer, I could sense that things were about to turn around for me. A new day, and a chance to finally get the respect I deserved.

My cell phone vibrated. I looked down and saw there had been five attempts to call me and one voice message. I picked it up and hit the button.

"Griff, it's Nestor. Nestor Vega. Anyway, I been trying to call but can't get hold of you. So I guess I gotta leave this message, hope that's okay. Yeah, so, I wanna let you know that I hired another lawyer. I mean, you're great and everything, but this guy Colt called me and said you're not doing so well with my case. Like, totally messing it up. You know, I can't work no more cause of my accident, and I really need that money. So I called that lawyer on TV—you know, the guy who calls himself the Big Fist, and I went ahead and signed the papers with him. Uh, yeah, I just wanna thank you for the work you done. That's it. Later."

I heard a rushing sound in my ears and the walls began to waver. A fury overcame me and rose up through my spine. That racist Colt Jackson had fucked me over royally. Never mind that he'd broken every norm of professional ethics—he realized he could screw me and get away with it.

I knew what I had to do. I kept a baseball bat under my desk for emergency situations. I'd take it and show him not to mess with a Native warrior. I pushed my chair back, reached under the desk, and grabbed the bat. It felt good in my hands, and I thought about what it would be like to take Colt out, inflicting some street justice on a jerk who deserved it.

Then I saw my reflection in the window—kneeling down on one leg, grasping the bat like a rifle. I realized that I looked like the famous photo of Geronimo, the one where he's holding his weapon upright and scowling at the camera. Geronimo, whose real name was Goyahkla, the last Native warrior to surrender to the US military; he spent his final years in an army prison, only being released to appear in Wild West shows where he was trotted out as a curio for the spectators. Natives believed he had the power to foresee incidents that would occur in the future, even though he was unable to change or influence those events. I wondered if he'd been able to predict what was in store for him—the years of imprisonment, the demise of Native traditions, the loss of his culture. On his deathbed, Geronimo said to his nephew, "I should have never surrendered. I should have fought until I was the last man alive."

I pondered what my future would hold if I beat the crap out of Colt with the bat. Would I be upholding my honor and paying tribute to the spirit of Geronimo?

And then I felt foolish. It was ridiculous to fantasize about taking revenge on the asshole defense lawyer. I'd only end up in jail, where I'd experience the criminal justice system from the other side. I'd be validating everything that Colt and other racists had probably said about me and every other indigenous person.

I tossed the bat on the floor. As it rolled across the room, I realized that there was nothing left for me here, that I'd never ascend to the legal heights of which I'd once dreamed. The respect of my peers, the chance to win some courtroom victories, working for the causes I cared about—these things were beyond my grasp, and there was no longer any reason to keep fighting. Like Geronimo, it was time to surrender.

I grabbed my keys and started walking. I'd need to get a job, a real one, and I knew there was an opening at the Zephyr.

A LIFE OF LITTLE CONSEQUENCE

BY TWANNA LaTRICE HILL

Capitol Hill

B y the time LaVonda returned from setting the table, the two men had nearly traversed the length of her block. She had watched them for over an hour and now it was dusk. As they approached her walkway, she closed her book and rose from her chair.

"You'd best come in," she said, before either of them could speak. She ignored the screech of her screen and turned back into her apartment, settling herself in the middle of her slate-gray sectional. Even though she was wearing jeans, she crossed her legs delicately at the ankle.

The taller of the two men mounted the porch and stopped at the screen door. He was a large man, blond, with close-cropped hair that marked him as ex-military, but the fleshiness of his face and the protuberance of his gut told her that had been some years ago.

"We're with the Denver Police Department," he said, holding up the badge around his neck.

Don't be nervous, LaVonda thought. She filled one of the coffee mugs from the carafe on her coffee table. "Black, or do you take sugar and cream?"

"I'm Detective Niedermeyer and this is my partner, Detective Delgado," he said, inclining his head toward the other man, who followed him into the apartment. "Um, black is fine."

"And you?" she asked the younger detective as she handed a cup of coffee to Niedermeyer.

Detective Delgado glanced at his partner before sitting on the chaise at the opposite end of the couch. "If there's sugar, I'll take some."

LaVonda hoped her hands didn't tremble as she filled the second cup. Delgado was maybe forty, with thick black hair and a neatly trimmed mustache above full lips. Dark tendrils curled above his collar. Thin trails of sweat trickled down his neck and his long-sleeved shirt clung wetly to his body. The tang of his musk teased her nostrils as he leaned forward and took the mug from LaVonda's hands. She felt a slight quivering between her legs. *Don't get carried away*, she thought to herself.

"We were hoping you might look at a picture for us," Niedermeyer said.

Detective Delgado set his coffee on the tray, slid a piece of paper from the clipboard on his knees, and held it out to her. "Do you recognize this man?"

Don't stare at him, she thought, turning her attention from the detective to the flyer in his outstretched hand. She took it and studied it for several seconds. An image, captured in black-and-white, looked back at her. The picture was a few years old and grainy, but the drawn face with the furrowed brow beneath an untidy Afro was clearly recognizable.

"Yes," she said. "That's Ronnie. But this looks like an old picture. He's much older now."

Niedermeyer flipped open his notebook and began writing on a large yellow legal pad. "How do you know him?"

How did she know Ronnie? He wasn't a friend, not really. But he was more than an acquaintance. "He just hangs around the neighborhood," she said. "Why? What happened?"

"He's dead," said Niedermeyer.

LaVonda pressed her fingers to her mouth and stared down at the picture. "Oh my. He's dead. Really? But how?"

"Somebody killed him," said Delgado as he took back the flyer. "Dumped his body in the schoolyard. Since he lived down the block, we're just canvasing the neighborhood."

LaVonda looked from one detective to the other. "But when? I just saw him yesterday."

Yesterday, he had been with Toby, the live-in boyfriend of her upstairs neighbor, Allie. In the wee hours, when the pain in her back had forced her from her bed, LaVonda had gone to sit outside in the dark and had seen them, Ronnie and Toby, skulking about, getting into only god knows what kind of trouble. Toby spent more time with Ronnie than he did with Allie.

"Do you know who he associates with?" Niedermeyer asked.

LaVonda shrugged. "Ronnie knows everybody."

"And you saw him yesterday?"

LaVonda nodded.

"Did you see him with anyone in particular?"

"Well," she said, "sometimes he hangs out with Toby. My neighbor. Well, sort of neighbor. Toby lives upstairs with Allie. He and Ronnie hang out together sometimes."

Niedermeyer stood. "So, we can find this Toby upstairs?"

LaVonda shook her head. "I doubt it. At least, not right now. He doesn't have a regular gig but he gets those day jobs—you know, where you show up for same-day work. He's basically a temp."

"And his girlfriend—your neighbor—is named Allie?"

LaVonda nodded. "She works full-time. She's a few years older than Toby, in her thirties."

Niedermeyer wrote steadily on his legal pad.

LaVonda turned to Delgado. "Ronnie wasn't really a bad guy. I wish I knew more."

Both detectives pulled business cards from their pockets, and LaVonda took them. "In case you hear anything," Delgado said.

"We can see ourselves out," said Niedermeyer, turning toward the door.

Delgado took a last swig from his coffee, then stood. LaVonda held out her hand. He clasped it and LaVonda squeezed. It was warm and slightly moist; his grip was firm. She realized he was looking beyond her, at the pictures on the wall of her with friends, most of whom she hadn't spoken to for the better part of a decade. She released his hand and followed the men to the door.

"You both have a nice evening," she said as they made their way down the weathered steps of her porch. She stared at Detective Delgado's back.

Turn around, she thought. *If he turns around, it means he's thinking of me.*

LaVonda watched as the two men left her yard. They headed toward the end of the block without turning around.

LaVonda tossed Niedermeyer's card on the coffee table. She brought Delgado's card to her nose and inhaled deeply. Her stomach fluttered. She hadn't been this excited since the regular UPS driver had gone on vacation and his replacement had brought a package to her door. She had been entranced by his hazel eyes, his 1970s 'stache, the way the muscles in his arms rippled. For weeks, she had yearned for his body, longed to feel his touch. Now she had a new man to fantasize about.

In her mind's eye, she could see Delgado's hands—those

large hands, covered with a layer of smooth black hair. Hands that should be holding her, touching her. She needed to attract his attention, but how? Maybe if she had some key information about Ronnie's murder, she could call him and he might come back to see her. But what if he didn't come alone, or worse, asked her to go downtown to make a statement? She had learned from watching dozens of true crime shows that it was rarely wise to inject yourself into an investigation. And this wasn't some TV show, this was real. Someone was dead—murdered. Someone she knew.

LaVonda burrowed into her stash, which she kept hidden in a small alcove in her dining room, and retrieved her bottle of pills. She struggled momentarily with the childproof cap, pressing and turning until the lid popped off in her hands. Her back was screaming. She knew it was best to try to stay ahead of the pain but she had delayed taking her meds for a couple of hours—hours spent sitting on the porch in a straight-backed wooden chair, watching folks meander by, taking little heed of the eclectic architecture that marked this community. Victorian mansions over a century old reigned, though many had been converted into office buildings or multifamily dwellings. They retained their majesty despite being nestled between twenty-first-century apartment buildings and overlooked by ever-invading condominiums that deigned to scrape the sky.

LaVonda lived in a historic house that had been subdivided into four family units. It had been affordable while she was working, but her settlement couldn't cover the annual rent increases forever. Nonetheless, she couldn't imagine living anywhere else. The apartment had three bedrooms, a dining room and living room, a cavernous kitchen with minimal counter space, a good-sized bathroom, and laundry facilities in the basement. She had access to a small garage in the back—which she cherished, as street parking was practically nonexistent. She lived just off Thirteenth Avenue, so she was far enough south to see young professionals jogging or out walking their dogs, but close enough to East Colfax that a few people living on the streets shambled by each day. A decade ago, the city got serious about cleaning up Colfax and tried to shunt most of the transients away from the Hill, but LaVonda felt they were more than part of the local color—it was their neighborhood as much as hers.

East Colfax had once been a haven for prostitutes and drug dealers—and it still had its share of those—but now Denver's main drag also featured ethnic eateries, trendy boutiques, and even a recreation center. Coffee shops, restaurants, and a couple of clubs were all within walking distance. But it wasn't the shops that made Capitol Hill what it was—it was the people. The neighborhood was filled with young people, sharing apartments and group homes; urban professionals who enjoyed the easy commute to downtown; lovers of every gender and shade who entwined their hands as they crossed each crack in the sidewalks. It was a place for bohemians, for the colorful and the eccentric, the shady and the urbane, the lovers and the lost.

What you didn't see here on the Hill were women pushing fifty, alone and barely getting by. Women like her.

LaVonda placed one tablet of oxycodone on her tongue and washed it down with a flat Diet Coke that had been sitting out since morning. She hadn't gotten these pills from Ronnie, but from the pharmacy a few blocks east. There had been a short while when she had turned to Ronnie. Her pain-management doctor had suddenly closed his practice and it had taken her a few weeks to find a new one. Ronnie had sold pot before it was legalized and now dabbled in opiates. She hadn't thought of Ronnie as her dealer, just a friend of Toby's who was able to help her out in a time of need.

Toby, was, well, he was little more than a boy, and not a particularly bright one. Her maternal urges kicked in whenever she saw him. He was nice and well mannered, in his midtwenties, with unruly hair and a crooked smile. He was one of those kids who needed to wake-and-bake just to face the day. He was also a cigarette smoker, and even though she had quit five years ago, LaVonda looked forward to his visits and the few drags he let her take from his Camel Lights.

In her bedroom, LaVonda closed the blinds, then unzipped her jeans, shimmied out of them, and unrolled her Spanx. She felt an almost instant sense of relief as her belly fell free. Now she could breathe. She removed her blouse and unclasped her bra. As she reached for her shift, she caught sight of herself in the freestanding mirror. Her stomach wasn't huge, but it was soft, flabby, and lined with stretch marks from the days when she was more than seventy pounds heavier. Even though her breasts were small, gravity had done its damage and, without support, they sagged. She stood in front of the mirror naked, examining her body. The ever-present pain she endured had ruined her appetite, and at first she had been thrilled to lose so much weight. She had not anticipated how much her body would change. She was no longer curvy, at least not in the right places. Her ass, once high and round and firm, was now flat and wrinkled. Her stomach was marked by a fifteen-year-old hysterectomy scar. It had been a bikini cut, but it had still created a line on her stomach, creasing it unattractively. Her thighs were dimpled and the flesh beneath her arms jiggled. She averted her gaze. *Who could possibly want me?* she thought.

She made her way down the hall, straightening one of the several diplomas and accolades that were hung there as she

walked past. They were reminders of her life before the accident. She kept these artifacts free of dust, even though there
was no one to notice them. No one really came by. At least,
not anymore. As she passed through the living room, she retrieved the detectives' half-empty cups and dropped them in
the kitchen. A few lunch dishes remained, but they would
have to wait. Right now, she needed to lie down.

LaVonda tightened the belt of her robe and stretched
out on the couch, berating herself for spending all day on the
porch like some little old lady. She was forty-six. It had been
ten years since an SUV had barreled through an intersection
near the Cherry Creek Mall and T-boned her, leaving her with
a twisted spine and extensive nerve damage. The settlement
had been adequate, it paid the rent, and for a long time she
had thought she would never work again. But next week, she
would start her new gig with a crisis line, taking calls from
those who were reaching out for some kind of help. Some
might call it volunteering; she considered it nonsalaried employment. She would matter again.

LaVonda flipped through the TV channels, waiting for
her meds to kick in. She settled on *Forensic Files*.

The pounding at her door startled LaVonda, who was dozing
lightly in front of the television. It was late—much too late for
visitors. LaVonda crept to the front door in her bare feet and
looked through the peephole. It was Toby.

She unlocked the door. He leaned his head against her
chest. LaVonda pulled him into her and hugged him hard.

"I heard about Ronnie," she said, as she stroked his back.
"I'm really sorry."

Toby looked up at her. He was handsome in an unkempt
kind of way. His hair was too long, and when he didn't wash it,

he tied it back with a rubber band. His face was long and oval, his eyes spaced wide, his lips a little thin, but they, like his cheeks, blazed red. He was only about five foot six and he was soft—too soft. His hands were smooth and almost doughy, revealing a man who'd never done a day of hard work. Still, he went down to temp agencies on most days and usually ended up with some kind of gig. He was charming and that went a long way.

Toby pulled a crumpled pack of smokes from his pocket and waved them in front of her. LaVonda looked at the clock, then followed him onto the porch. He placed a cigarette between his lips and lit it, then passed it to her. LaVonda inhaled deeply, the smoke filling her lungs. Her entire body seemed alive. As she exhaled, a sense of relaxation coursed through her.

They smoked together silently for several moments. Toby let her have the last drag.

"Okay," she said as she stamped the cigarette out in an ashtray on the railing, "it's really late. You need to go home to Allie."

"Wait. Hear me out."

"Toby . . ."

"LaVonda, please." He dropped his head and looked up at her through a veil of shaggy hair. "I have to talk to you."

LaVonda let him take her by the hand and lead her back into the apartment. She nestled into a corner of the couch and drew her knees beneath her. "Well?"

Toby produced what looked like a fat cigar from his front pocket. He inhaled as he passed it under his nose, then proffered it to LaVonda.

She tightened her robe. "I don't think so."

"Come on," Toby said, kneeling before her. "It'll help you sleep. Just one toke."

LaVonda sighed and shook her head. This was ridiculous—but it might help her sleep. "One toke. That's all."

Toby lit the blunt and LaVonda inhaled. Almost instantly, she felt warm. Her extremities began to tingle; her shoulders relaxed and her breathing deepened. She stretched out on the couch, next to the chaise where Delgado had sat, and rested her head back on her arm.

"Okay, Toby. What do you want to talk about?"

He exhaled a thick cloud of blue-gray smoke. "The cops are after me."

"What do you mean?"

"They've been over to a couple of my friends' houses. They even left a card upstairs for Allie. She won't turn me in, though."

LaVonda shook her head, thinking of how Allie clung to Toby as to a life raft. She was not love-smitten, she was just a woman trying to hang on to a younger man by buying his clothes and making him breakfast. Allie couldn't understand that Toby would never love her, could never love her. He was hustling, always hustling. Allie was just a sugar momma.

"The cops were here too," LaVonda said. "They had a picture of Ronnie."

Toby sat beside her on the edge of the couch. "I still can't believe it. Why'd they come to see you?"

"I think they were just canvasing the neighborhood."

Toby stood and began stalking around the apartment. "So, what did you tell them?"

"I told them that you two were friends."

Toby turned on his heel. "Why would you tell them that?"

"Toby, it's no secret that you two hang together."

"Yeah, yeah," he said, squeezing next to her on the couch. "Yeah, I saw Ronnie early yesterday evening. I went over to his place, smoked a couple of blunts. Watched something loud on TV. He was fine when I left him."

LaVonda leaned back on the couch. "Yeah, I saw you two late last night."

"What do you mean, late last night?"

"Late. Really late," she said. "My back was bad, so I went out to sit on the porch. It must have been after—"

Toby shook his head. "No. That's not right. I left his house at eight. I didn't go out with Ronnie last night."

"Are you sure? I'm positive I saw—"

"Is that what you told the cops?"

"No. I mean, I said I saw you two together yesterday."

"Well, after I left Ronnie's place at eight, I was in with Allie all night. Just ask her."

LaVonda stared at Toby for a long moment. If he wasn't the man she saw with Ronnie, who was? *The killer.* She shuddered.

"Oh, LaVonda, what am I going to do?" He leaned over on his side and laid his head in her lap, burrowing into the fabric of her gown.

"If you didn't do anything, I'm sure everything will be fine." LaVonda felt completely relaxed. She toyed with his hair, brushing it back behind his ears, smoothing it across his forehead. She scraped her nails along his scalp. She pressed her fingers against his temples, rubbing them in firm circles.

"That's nice," he said, nestling his head deeper against her thighs. "That feels really nice." He placed one hand on her knee.

She removed it. "Get a grip, Toby. I'm old enough to be your mother."

"So?" he said, looking up her. "Maybe I like that."

LaVonda's mouth went dry. *What does he want? I could*

never think of him that way. She gently pushed him from her lap and stood. "You'd best get upstairs to Allie."

"But what if they come back?"

"There's no point in you hiding from the police. Just answer their questions and be done with it." She grabbed him by both hands and pulled him to his feet. "Time for you to go home, Toby."

He encircled her waist with his hands. Suddenly, he dropped to his knees and pulled her gown over his head.

LaVonda's pulse quickened. "What the hell are you doing?" she asked, pulling away.

"You'll see." She felt his hands on her thighs, rubbing them, parting them. Felt his mouth kissing the tender spot by her knee, then moving upward.

LaVonda tried to twist away, but Toby moved with her. He was nibbling her now, tiny little bites that tickled her flesh. She felt herself relenting, and her hands relaxed on his shoulders. Then she dug her thumbs in near his collarbone and pushed hard. "Wait! Wait!"

Toby sat on his ankles, continuing to caress her calves. "What?"

"Toby," she whispered, "I haven't even showered."

He laughed. "You don't have to." He scrambled back under her gown. Then he was pulling down her panties and before she could object, his mouth was on her pussy, his tongue darting about, doing delightful things that hadn't been done to LaVonda in a long time.

She fell back against the wall as Toby's mouth became greedy and insistent. She closed her eyes, and found herself thinking of Detective Delgado. It was *his* scent that she breathed into her body, *his* hands that were kneading her thighs, *his* tongue that was dipping inside her.

"You like that, huh?" Toby's voice interrupted her reverie. She clutched at his hair, forced him back between her legs. Waves of warmth spread throughout her body. She wasn't sure she understood what was happening. She just knew that she didn't care.

LaVonda was hot. She kicked at the sheets that entangled her feet until her lower legs were free. Toby lay beside her. Even in the darkness, she could see the pale skin of his hairless back. She was unused to sharing her bed, and he had left her very little room to maneuver. She was also lying in the wet spot. She rolled away from him and off the edge of the bed. She crawled around until she found her nightgown and robe where she'd dropped them on the floor. She clutched them to her chest and silently made her escape.

LaVonda headed to the alcove in the dining room. The room was dark, brightened only by the ambient light from streetlamps that filtered in through her windows. Still, she easily found her pills. She had never mastered the art of swallowing the tablets dry, so she wended her way to the bathroom, closed the door, and turned on the light. She popped an oxy, then hunkered down over the sink and drank deeply from the spigot. Water trickled from her lips and she swiped at her mouth with her sleeve. Her hands gripped the sides of the sink and she stared at herself in the mirrored medicine cabinet. She turned her face first to one side, then the other. It was still mostly unlined, except when she laughed. She pressed her fingers to her temple and cheek, tugging at her skin until it was taut. That was better. When she removed her hands, her face went slack. There were faint hollows under her eyes. She thought she saw a gray hair and looked closely at her scalp; it could have been a trick of the light. *I look okay but I look my age*, she thought.

Parts of her body still tingled from her interlude with Toby. He had been patient and had gone down on her for a long time until her body began to convulse. They had stumbled to the bedroom. He'd grabbed the back of her head and crushed her mouth with his. She'd felt dizzy as he'd pulled her night-gown over her head. His hands roved over her body. They were so soft and warm against her skin, skin that hadn't been touched like this in so long. She'd fallen back onto the bed and he'd shucked off his clothes and climbed on top of her. Their bodies had fit comfortably. She was still limber enough to wrap her legs around his back as he nuzzled and suckled and kissed her repeatedly. She'd quickly felt herself coming again and she could just make out the smug smile on his face. He had come then too, as if he had been holding back, wait-ing for her to come first. *He really is a nice boy,* she thought.

Now she curled up on the couch in her living room, turned the volume of the TV on low, and flipped through the chan-nels. Even as images flashed on the screen, she closed her eyes and replayed the night in her mind. Part of her felt awakened and alive, another part felt something akin to shame.

Why had she slept with Toby? He was certainly no De-tective Delgado. He had caught her unawares but she had immediately surrendered. It had been so long since a man had touched her in a way that made her feel desirable. She may have been forty-six and past her prime, but she was still a woman, goddamnit. He had made her feel like one—twice. And yet, the mildest hint of disgust lingered. He was barely in his twenties, he was lazy, he let himself be supported by women. She hoped he wasn't lining her up to be next. *I'm not that desperate,* she thought. *Besides, he doesn't really want me. Does he?*

* * *

"Come back to bed," Toby said.

LaVonda opened her eyes. Toby sat beside her on the couch. He pulled her feet into his lap.

"Let's have a smoke," she said.

Toby pressed his thumbs into the bottom of her foot. "We smoked the last one."

LaVonda draped her arm over her face and sighed softly. "Damn. That would have been nice."

"I'll go get some," he said, as he tugged gently at each of her toes.

LaVonda sat up. "Really? At this time of night?"

"The 7-Eleven is only a couple of blocks away." Toby massaged her calf in long, languid strokes. "But I don't have any cash on me."

Her breathing became more shallow as Toby's hands moved farther up her leg. "I do," she said. "Do you really want to go?"

"Sure." He laid her leg down on the couch and smoothed her gown around her ankles. "I guess I should put some clothes on."

Toby disappeared into the bedroom and returned holding a small bundle of clothes. He stepped into his pants, then knelt beside her.

"Hey, why don't you come with me?"

LaVonda laughed. "It's almost three o'clock in the morning."

"It'll be good to get some air."

"But that convenience store is like thug central. Nothing legit happens there this time of night."

"It'll be fine," he said, tugging at her arms. "Come on."

LaVonda let herself be pulled up from the couch. In the bedroom, she dressed in a pair of baggy jeans and a dark hoodie, tightening its strings beneath her chin.

"You look like some kind of hoodlum," Toby said.

"Good, I'll fit right in."

The store, on Colfax, was notorious for prostitutes plying their trade and dealers pedaling their wares. LaVonda rarely went there. Even in daylight, she was afraid she'd step on somebody's works. "I'm not so sure this is a good idea," she said.

Toby laughed. "It'll be fine." He grasped her hand and led her out of the apartment.

LaVonda could hear traffic noise from East Colfax, even at this time of night. She noticed the occasional lighted apartment, but the street itself was decidedly empty. As they walked, LaVonda threaded her arm in his. He squeezed her hand.

We actually look like a couple, she thought. But LaVonda knew they weren't. *Maybe we just needed each other.*

They turned into the alley that ran alongside the store. As they neared the back of the store, Toby stopped.

"What is it?" LaVonda asked.

Smiling, Toby walked her backward until her body was pressed against the brick wall. He kissed her, his tongue deep inside her mouth, and squeezed her ass with one hand.

"Not here," she said. "It's filthy."

Toby chuckled, then kissed her again. She wrapped her arms around his back, holding him tighter. She hadn't thrown on a bra, and her hoodie brushed deliciously against her hardened nipples.

After a long moment, Toby pulled back from her. He looked at the ground and kicked at a broken chunk of glass. "You know what's funny?" he said. "If Ronnie had died back here, no one would have thought anything of it. They'd just think it was related to all the other shady shit going on around here."

LaVonda took his face in both hands. "Stop thinking about it. At least for right now." She leaned forward to kiss him.

"Maybe then the cops wouldn't be after me."

LaVonda leaned back against the wall. "They're not after you. They just want to talk to you. You and Ronnie were tight. Besides, you walk along the edge of a dark world. Anything could happen."

With his fingers, Toby traced the length of her nose, the line of her jaw. He parted her lips and slid his finger into her mouth. LaVonda closed her eyes, moving her mouth up and down on his finger. It tasted of sweat and cigarettes. He placed his open hand over her face. She licked his palm and gently bit at the pad of flesh at the base of his thumb. He cupped his hand over her mouth.

Suddenly, her body stiffened. She inhaled sharply as Toby pushed his body harder into her. Pain flared in her side. She tried to pull away but he held her head tight against his chest, his fingers tangled in her hair. LaVonda's knees gave way and she slid down the length of his body.

She pressed her palm to her side. Her hand felt wet, sticky. She looked up at Toby, watched as he closed the knife with a soft *snick* and tucked it into his waistband.

LaVonda slid sideways onto the ground. Her mouth was open, her lips moving. Toby bent low, his ear to her mouth.

"Why?" she whispered, then began to choke and sputter.

"I really wish you hadn't seen us when you came out on your porch last night. It's a shame. I've always really liked you. But Allie will say I was in all night last night. Just like tonight."

LaVonda's eyes widened. "You . . . Ronnie . . . Why?" She coughed.

Toby shrugged. "He thought I was his bitch. I find all the

customers for a few bags of weed? I deserved a serious percentage. Just a few dollars for everyone I brought in. He didn't want to give it up."

The coppery taste of blood was strong in the back of her throat. She still tried to talk. "But then, why did you . . . why did we . . ."

Toby nuzzled his face against her cheek, then pressed his lips to her ear. "You wanted it."

LaVonda felt the knife against her throat. Tears slid from her eyes. *I shouldn't have slept with him.*

But it was far too late for that thought.

Toby's face filled her field of vision. Weakly, LaVonda pressed her thighs together. She knew that even though she'd washed herself, part of Toby was still inside her.

Good. She closed her eyes, tilted her head back, and arched her neck up to the sky.

PIECES OF EVERYONE, EVERYWHERE

BY Cynthia Swanson
Cheesman Park

Digging graves is straightforward labor, involving little more than brute strength and a sufficiently sharp blade. The job can be done with relative ease by even the most doltish of common workhands.

But here's something many do not know: *exhuming* graves, by contrast, is art. One cannot simply thrust one's spade in the ground, hack around until one hits upon some solid object, then mercilessly subtract shovelful after shovelful of raw earth until the grave's remains, treasure-like, are exposed. Nor can one wrest such treasure from the ground, haphazardly tossing fragments to the surface and flinging them into any vessel conveniently nearby.

No. Such practices would be immoral. Moreover, they would, as my Uncle August said, invite misfortune. August believed, as do I, that regardless of circumstances, the dead deserve to lie peacefully. They should be disturbed only in the most dire of situations. If a body *must* be moved, it should be done properly and with reverence.

"There's no cause to uproot them, Sam," Uncle August told me. "If you have to do it, you better have a damn good reason. And you better treat them with respect."

I had, and continue to have, no argument with that. All

bodies, in my belief—both the dead and the living—should be treated with respect.

Uncle August and I had this conversation last year while standing in an Iowa cornfield. Plowing a new field, we encountered a shallow grave under a meager scattering of stones. We found no coffin, no shroud, not even a scrap of clothing—just a full, adult human skeleton set into the thick Midwest soil, all flesh that once graced the bones returned entirely to the earth. That the grave was unviolated by an animal was nothing short of providence.

No one besides our family had ever homesteaded that land, so the skeleton was either an Indian's or perhaps belonged to some white man who, decades earlier, had been making his way west and died en route. Uncle August said his money was on the latter, because Indians are smarter than that—they don't leave their dead lying about like so much rubbish. I suspect he's right.

Either way, Uncle August said we were obliged to move the body appropriately. We returned to the barn and hammered together a solid though simple coffin. We lugged it to the field and eased the bones into place, carefully reassembling those separated from their neighbors. Then we moved the entire affair under a willow tree—where it should have been all along, as was obvious to both of us—and ensured the box was set accurately, buried deeply. The task cost us nearly a full day of plowing, but we accomplished it with respect.

Well. What would Uncle August say about my first job in my new city of Denver, Colorado? What would he say about the merciless, hack-job labor into which I had embroiled myself?

I choose not to think about it. When such thoughts enter my mind, I hang my head in shame.

* * *

Upon arriving in Denver, I'd spied the undertaker's notices all over town. Posters were tacked to trees; advertisements took space in the local papers. *Gravediggers needed for extensive exhumation project. Apply in person, E.P. McGovern, Undertaking and Embalming, 549 Larimer St. Strong white men only.*

Inspecting one such sign, I inquired of a bystander how to find Larimer Street.

He glowered. "Cursed Tammany crooks. Think you're free of them out here in the west? Think again, son."

I shook my head. "Sir?"

"Mayor's out of town," the man explained. "Acting mayor is in deep with the local Tammany Hall cronies. Crooks pushed through a downright pointless contract to relocate those graves." He shook his fist. "It's nothing but taxpayer money lining wicked pockets, son."

None of this made the least bit of sense to me. I asked again for directions to the funeral home.

"God'll smite me, aiding such sinful jobbery." He looked me up and down, appraising my shabby hat and coat. "But I can see you need the work."

Indeed, I did. When the gentleman gave me directions, I thanked him and hurried away.

Applying for the job at McGovern's funeral home, I was given a brief account of the situation. The graveyard in question, named City Cemetery, was located east of the Capitol and just a few blocks south of Colfax Avenue. For a time, this area had been the outskirts of Denver proper. As the city grew, a larger and more remote cemetery, Riverside, was established some miles north. At that point, City Cemetery was essentially abandoned—the graves uncared for, the tombstones crumbling, the entirety of it an eyesore. Now, the city intended to transform it into a park. The land would, as it was explained to me, become a green, grassy setting, intended for the leisure of those who lived nearby.

The next morning, upon arrival at City Cemetery, I glanced around at the nearby homes. They were nothing short of mansions, each larger and more elaborate than the next, positioned like well-trimmed rosebushes along the cemetery's perimeter. No surprise that well-heeled homeowners were loath to gaze upon an unsightly public space.

The crew that assembled that day numbered approximately thirty, each stronger than the next. It was a warm spring morning—the type of day that, upon other circumstances, might inspire hope within the soul. In outlying cottonwood trees, sparrows chirped. Closer by, robins pecked for worms, and sunlight-seeking wildflowers broke through the dry earth. Along the boundary of the cemetery, curious onlookers gathered, arranged in a muddle that reminded me of the disorganized shelves at the unkempt country store back home.

The laborer next to me grinned. "What sport," he said, striking the blade of his shovel into the scrub grass, where it met, clanging, against a rock. "What d'ya think we'll find under there, lad?" He clapped me on the shoulder. "Nothing but thieves and degenerates, I hear. Bastards gettin' what they deserve."

Not entirely convinced of this, but disinclined to engage in argument within my first few moments on the job, I dipped my head just enough for my gesture to be recognizable as a nod.

In some areas of the soon-to-be-erstwhile City Cemetery, graves had already been exhumed. Long before undertaker McGovern was hired to finish the job, city officials had put out notices that any Denverite who had relatives at City Cemetery would be wise to have them removed to Riverside. The Jewish graves on the hill were relocated, every one of them, carefully and with respect, by families and synagogues. The Catholics negotiated a deal with the city to purchase their parcel of the graveyard, leaving those who had worshipped both God and the pope to continue peacefully resting in their current locale.

The remaining section of City Cemetery—"the Boneyard," as I learned it was called—was where paupers, thieves, and unclaimed, disease-ridden bodies were buried. No surprise, then, that most of these bodies were unspoken for. Who'd speak for them?

Wagonful after wagonful of rudimentary caskets were brought forth and unloaded. "Dig," the foreman—a bulky, weather-beaten fellow named Rudiman—instructed us. He told us not to attempt salvaging any containers we encountered; most, he said, would be cheap construction, not worth the cut-rate lumber comprising them. Instead, we were told to put the bodies in the delivered caskets, mark them with the identifying tags provided, and keep going.

"There are thousands of bodies in this soil!" Rudiman shouted to the assemblage. "You'll be paid for each one you tag. The faster you dig, the more money you make. Have at it, men!"

Someone let out a holler: "Let's do this, boys!" Enthusiastic spades were raised, and piles of dirt and rubble soon began to dot the landscape. Less inclined to revelry but nevertheless eager to demonstrate my strong work ethic, I grasped my shovel and began to dig.

"Respect them."

I looked up. An elderly woman, threadbare shawl over her head and shoulders, had quit the onlookers and was making her way among the workingmen.

"Respect them, I say," she told the laborers. "Say a prayer

for each man's soul as you raise him. Treat his body with tenderness—for tomorrow, it will be your own."

They brushed her off. "Go away, old woman," one man growled, raising his shovel in a half threat toward her. "Leave us to our toil."

Across the clumps of earth, the woman's eyes met mine. She hobbled over, gripping my shoulder, pulling my head toward hers.

"These men are unwise. But *you* possess prudence," she whispered in my ear. "Do right by them, girl."

She knew. *How* did she know? I'd hidden it so well—or so I'd believed.

Before I left Iowa, Uncle August had been the one who'd shorn my hair, handfuls of my rich dark locks stuffed into a bag for me to tote on my journey, in hopes of selling it at some future date. August loaned me britches, a belt, and two work shirts, one to wear and one for a spare. He handed me a long cotton cloth and told me to bind my—providentially small, anyway—breasts.

"You're safer this way, Samantha," he said.

I eyed him. How could I—whether dressed as woman or disguised as man—feel more threatened elsewhere than I was in my own home?

Three nights earlier, August had discovered my father at me. August did his best to haul Father away while I lay helplessly, my eyes filled with terror. August cursed and yelled and took the blows that blackened both eyes.

Only a few weeks prior, Uncle August and I had mourned the loss of my mother, who'd contracted influenza in early February. Before then, she'd done all she could to keep Father from me. So did August, once he knew. But like his sister and like me, August had no power over that man, who dwarfed him. Father had Uncle August by close to a foot and more than seventy pounds.

I'd inherited my father's coarse facial features and his height, but not his girth. I was gawky and thin-limbed, my strength stringy at best. I could not fight off my father.

A disguise, on the other hand, I could manage.

And so it was Uncle August who helped me prepare for my journey—my mother dead and my father drunk and snoring in the barn. Harmless then, but he wouldn't stay that way; we both knew it.

"Join me," I said to August.

He shook his head. "You know I can't, Sam. Not with what I owe him. He'd come after me—and where would that leave us?"

Father had paid for August's passage from England—and paid, as well, the hefty gambling debt that caught August in Chicago, before he made his way west to our homestead. "I'll keep working, pay off my debt. Then I'll come to Denver, if I can," August assured me. Gently, he touched my cheek. "I can pay your train fare and put a few dollars in your pocket. After that, you're on your own. I'm sorry, Samantha. I'd do more, if I were able."

"I know you would." I nodded. "Thank you, Uncle."

He reached into the pack beside his cot, the canvas knapsack he'd toted across the Atlantic, in which he kept all his worldly possessions. "I did set aside a small sum for this."

Into my hands Uncle August pressed a slim volume— *Poems: Second Series* by Emily Dickinson.

I opened to the title page: *Robert Brothers, Boston, 1892.*

"Hot off the press, just last year," Uncle August said. "I know you love your words, Sam." In the lamplight, his eyes dimmed. "I wish things were different. You should've had the opportunity to continue your education. You should . . ." He drifted off, turning away from me.

I laid a hand on his shoulder. "It's all right. This gift means everything to me."

I thumbed through the beginning of the volume. Several pages in, I stopped. Over my shoulder, Uncle August read, as well.

> We play at paste,
> Till qualified for pearl,
> Then drop the paste,
> And deem ourself a fool.
> The shapes, though, were similar,
> And our new hands
> Learned gem-tactics
> Practising sands.

I looked up at Uncle August. "Thank you," was all I could manage to whisper.

He gathered me into his arms. "You're the pearl, Samantha," he said. "You're the pearl."

I nodded at the old woman, who nodded back and left my side. I gripped my shovel's handle, contemplating the humble tombstone at my feet. *Ernest Smith*, it read. *1855–1872*.

No other words. Nothing indicating how young Ernest— aged seventeen at time of death, precisely my own age—had met his fate.

I bent to the ground, with my index finger tracing letters on stone. "What happened to you, Ernest?" I whispered. "What happened?"

The foreman, striding among the headstones, spotted me. "Get up," he said.

I stood, shovel in hand.

Rudiman considered me. His eyes beheld my shorn, capped head, then took in my smooth cheeks and jaw. His gaze lingered at my collarbone, where the top button of my shirt was unfastened against the warmth of the day. From there, his eyes roamed the length of my body and came to rest on my long, booted feet.

He gazed upward, meeting my eye. "Get to work, boy," he growled.

I took up my spade. My arms, in Uncle August's shirt, were wiry. Plain of face, with no brothers to assume the field-work and no prospects for leaving my father's homestead and becoming some other farmer's wife, I'd left school at fourteen and taken my place in the fields. There, I'd been paid nothing for my work. But here on this rubbled turf, laborers would earn twenty-five cents for each body we removed from the ground and transferred to a new casket. Undertaker McGovern, I suspected, was being paid many times that amount by the city. Rudiman, self-importantly stomping amongst the workers, likely also received a healthy cut.

But I would earn nothing unless I started to dig.

Nonetheless, I was careful. I removed dirt from Ernest's grave, the mound piling up until I encountered a rotting wooden box, sunk in the middle and exposing a skeleton's torso.

Ernest had lain here for over twenty years, almost as long as the cemetery existed. What had he done? How had he died?

Gently, I shoveled my way around the decrepit box. When enough of the ramshackle casket was exposed to begin raising it, I set aside my spade and bent to the earth.

"Need a hand?"

A fellow laborer, young and handsome, smiled at me. I admired the well-defined shoulder muscles I discerned through his faded cotton shirt. His beard was full and neatly trimmed. I had to resist an impulse to touch it.

We each took one end of Ernest's crumbling coffin. As we raised it, the bottom collapsed. A stench erupted, and I covered my nose with my neckerchief. The corpse, primarily skeleton but for a few persistent scraps of flesh, tumbled to the earth.

I fell to my knees. "I'm so sorry," I whispered to Ernest Smith's remains. "I should have been more cautious."

My associate knelt beside me. "It's all right," he said. "You did your best."

We looked at one another, and without a word folded our hands in prayer.

"May God have mercy on this dear, departed soul," my companion said.

"Amen," I finished. "Amen."

On the second day, we sat amongst the dead eating our noontime sandwiches. I had my Dickinson with me, and I read beneath the shade of a cottonwood.

> *And so, upon this wise I prayed,—*
> *Great Spirit, give to me*
> *A heaven not so large as yours,*
> *But large enough for me.*

"Rise, you men!" Rudiman shouted. "Cease your loafing and get yourselves unloading."

I looked up. A fresh shipment of caskets had arrived. Tucking the book into my knapsack, I got to my feet.

Hauling coffins from wagon to ground, we noticed something portentous.

Someone spoke. "Sir," he said to Rudiman, "these caskets are mighty small."

Shielding my eyes from the noonday sun, I observed that the man who spoke was none other than yesterday's fellow precant over Ernest Smith's remains. Again, my fingers itched to stroke the smooth hair along his jaw.

Rudiman approached, joined by our employer, E.P. McGovern. "What's your name, man?" McGovern asked.

"Walter Perry," came the reply.

McGovern lowered his hat over his brow. "Well, Perry, I don't see as how it's your place to ask questions. But as you ask, these caskets are all I was able to get on short notice." He held up his hands in a gesture of helplessness. "You hear about the accident at that mining site out in Utah? Can't tell you how many dead, but every remaining full-sized casket in Denver has been shipped west. Can't find one to save your life—much less theirs." McGovern waved a hand dismissively at the graves, then shook a finger in Perry's face. "Way I see it, sir, you got two choices: either you find a way to fit these bodies in the caskets provided, or you set aside your shovel and leave the work to those who have the stomach for it."

McGovern and Rudiman waited. Walter Perry eyed one man, then the other. Then he stuck his shovel in the ground and crossed the field. Exiting the cemetery, he broke through the assembled onlookers and disappeared.

The undertaker and foreman exchanged chuckles. "Anyone else?" McGovern called out. "Or are the rest of you *real* men?" He looked around the decaying field. "Your decision, gents."

I felt my shoulders stiffen. I saw no possibility that a grown man's body could fit into so small a casket. And yet, I lacked the courage to do what Walter Perry had just done—simply walk away.

My dilemma seemed to elude the others. Indeed, it appeared that they relished the task ahead. With fresh enthusiasm, shovels were raised. Skeletons were hacked apart—torso, upper limbs, pelvis, and lower limbs separated with the swift strike of metal on bone. Skulls were carelessly cracked from the rounded bone at the pinnacle of the spine. All of these bones were then crammed into tiny caskets, intended for children who left this world before their third birthdays.

Naturally, most of the disconnected frames did not fit, no matter how valiantly the men—at first—attempted ramming them into the miniature boxes. The remains of these unfortunate souls were, instead, distributed to secondary and sometimes tertiary caskets. "All the better," one worker said. "We're being paid by the casket, right?"

Overhearing him, McGovern grinned. "That we are, mister."

Something else happened then too. Perhaps the men had exceedingly enjoyed the contents of their whiskey flasks during the noon hour. Or perhaps it was simply that the notion of what was being asked of them, the notion of dismantling and cramming adult skeletons into diminutive caskets, brought out something animallike in the workers.

I can't say what it was. Regardless of the reason, tactics became increasingly macabre. Men warmed to the task, and their inhibitions, if they had any, loosened. They worked faster and rougher, gleefully shouting obscenities at one another and at the cemetery's remains.

Then began the looting. Laborers examined bodies for jewelry. Cigar boxes filled with treasured possessions, buried alongside some of the deceased, were opened and rifled through. Anything of worth was stuffed into laborers' pockets.

I glanced about. The old woman was nowhere to be seen, but I could hear her words in my head: *Respect them.*

I nearly put up my blade. How could I go on? How could I, recalling young Ernest Smith's decomposed body, continue this mockery of a job that McGovern and his henchman Rudiman required? How could I—remembering my first exhumation, the one in an Iowa cornfield, remembering my uncle's kind eyes and warm words—how could I, under these circumstances, attempt to transform such gruesome work into art?

But I needed the work. Afraid to try my luck at a boardinghouse, fearful my secret would be revealed, I'd been spending my nights in a bedroll, curled up in an alley off Colfax Avenue, all night slapping my palm against the dry dirt to ward off the rats who scurried and sniffed nearby.

My plan was to save up sufficient funds to take off my mantle of maleness. Using what I earned from this repugnant job, combined with what I could get for the mounds of hair stuffed in my knapsack, I'd buy myself a frock or two. Then I'd figure out what, in this new life of mine, came next.

And so I hoisted my shovel and commenced exhuming the next grave in my path. Trying, as best I could, to disassemble the corpse slowly and carefully—and then fit it like puzzle pieces into a juvenile casket.

I left the jobsite at dusk that evening, walking north on Franklin Street and turning west onto Colfax. My pack over my shoulder, I focused my eyes ahead, taking in the tableau of the under-construction Colorado State Capitol building and the setting sun dropping behind the Rocky Mountains.

Despite the ghastliness of my first job here, my sense of

Denver was that it was a city of opportunity. In such an environment, one might achieve success—or better yet, happiness. Provided, of course, that one was able to find one's footing.

As I breathed in the combined scent of horse droppings in the road, refuse in the alleys, and frying meat in the boardinghouses, I heard the clomping of boots behind me. Prickly, I forced myself not to turn my head, hoping that in refusing to acknowledge whoever trailed me, I might will them away.

The footfalls came closer, and hands grabbed both my arms. I twisted my neck, coming face-to-face with Rudiman and McGovern.

"You, *boy*," McGovern sneered. "You work for me, don't you?"

Swallowing hard, I nodded. "Please, sirs," I said, in my practiced gruff voice, "take your hands off me."

"We will not," the undertaker replied. "Not until you explain yourself."

I shook my head, feigning ignorance. "Sir?"

Placing a hand on the small of my back, McGovern thrust me into the closest alleyway, shoving me behind a wooden barrel beside a brick wall. My pack tumbled from my shoulder and rolled across the dirt.

McGovern nodded at Rudiman, who pressed on my shoulders until I sank to the ground. "You work too slowly," Rudiman said. "You're not man enough to be on this crew." He pushed me backward, and my head snapped against the bricks. My eyes closed, then opened again, trying to focus on Rudiman's jeering face. "But then again, you're not *man* enough for anything—are you?"

"I'm sure I don't know what you mean," I croaked.

"You know exactly what I mean." Rudiman took one hand off my shoulder and gripped my chin, tilting it toward the twilit sky. "Such smooth skin," he said, and his voice bore nearly the softness one might use when addressing a lover.

"Please," I begged.

He shook my jaw from side to side.

Arms akimbo, McGovern eyed me. "You're fired, *boy*."

Jerking my head, attempting to release myself from Rudiman's grasp, I said, "You owe me for two days' work."

"Such cheek," McGovern snapped. "I owe you nothing. You deceived us—and liars deserve no wages."

I stared him down. "Please tell your henchman to unhand me, sir."

Rudiman chuckled. Grinning up at McGovern, he said, "Whad'ya think, boss? Let's have some fun, eh?"

I opened my mouth to scream, but Rudiman clamped his hand over it.

McGovern shrugged. "I don't get into any of that business." He turned on his heel. "I've said all I have to say on the matter. What happens from here is of no concern to me." He exited the alley.

Rudiman watched him go, then turned back to me. "Try to make fools of us," he said. "I'll show you a fool."

He tightened his hand over my mouth. Forearm pressed to my collarbone, he snaked my belt from around my waist and tore at my britches until my body lay bare and exposed beneath him.

Afterward—after he buttoned his pants and left me lying in the dirt—I tried to catch my breath, half-naked and crumpled on my side.

In my mind, I played the prior moments back, wishing I'd had a knife or a gun. Or even a stick to poke in his eye.

Anything. Any object to make me feel less vulnerable than this.

Fumbling in the dark, I pulled on my tattered clothing and reached for my pack. I patted it, assuring myself that its humble contents—my bedroll, a flannel cloth to wipe my laborer's brow, a shirt that had at one time been my uncle's and at one time had been clean, and most importantly, my hair and my poems were safe and intact.

I doubted Rudiman would come back, but just in case, I made my way to a different alley. Was one safer than another? Likely not, but I had to take my chances.

There would be no sleep for me that night. Once the moon rose, I read by its faint glow.

> Through the straight pass of suffering
> The martyrs even trod,
> Their feet upon temptation,
> Their faces upon God.

Determined, I looked up at the sky.
I would be no such martyr.

The offices of the *Denver Republican* were two stories tall, composed of brick, with heavy cornerstones and a wide oak door. They'd be imposing to one who had fear.

But I no longer had fear.

Upon that morning, and every day of my life thereafter, this is what I stored in my heart: when we are filled with fear, no others fear us. But when the chin a man grasps becomes the chin tilted high and proud, above a neck long, upon shoulders squared, fear dissipates like a blown-over cloud.

"I wish to speak to the editor in chief, please." Before the clerk seated at his desk could respond, I went on, "I have a scoop for him. I believe he will be most interested."

* * *

Seventeen years later, on a warm day in the spring of 1910, I stood pencil and pad in hand amongst the crowd at the newly christened Cheesman Park. As each speaker took the podium, I scribbled notes for my story about the dedication of the park's neoclassical marble pavilion. A thing of glory, the pavilion stood in the east portion of the park and over-saw the lush green lawns that last century's city elders had envisioned—those green lawns that the Tammany politicians, now long gone, were unwilling to lay over paupers' graves.

And yet, exactly that happened. After the *Denver Republican* broke the story—"The Work of Ghouls!" ran the headline—the city immediately shut down McGovern's horrific opera-tion. For a time, nothing else happened; the graves remained opened, pieces of everyone everywhere. Eventually, Denver's first bipartisan mayor was elected, and a different company was hired to set the skeletal fragments into the earth from whence they came. At that point, properly reassembling corpses was impossible. Bones were transported as they were into the exhumed graves, covered and tamped down. Folks say the poor, restless souls still wander the park, especially by cover of night. I don't doubt it.

After they followed my lead and scooped the story before any of the other papers got wind of it, I talked my way into a job as the *Republican*'s first female cub reporter. My initial stories were trivial, many of them relating to ladies' charitable activities. Eventually, Ellis Meredith, suffragist and reporter for the *Rocky Mountain News*, took note of my work, finding in my stories the lyricism and authenticity I pursued regardless of subject matter. Ellis took me under her wing and helped me get hired on at the *News* as a beat reporter covering civic issues—a position I hold to this day.

I never saw Walter Perry again. I kept an eye out for him, but if he was still in Denver, our paths failed to cross. Perhaps because no other man I met had Walter's integrity—or perhaps simply because my lifestyle is incongruous with it—I chose never to marry. It's a decision I've yet to regret.

In 1896, three years after I left Iowa, I heard from Uncle August that my father had died. Threshing accident it was, terrible shame—apparently, someone had emptied the water from the steam thresher's tank, causing an explosion when the machine was fired up. Father, standing nearby, was effectively blown to bits.

No one besides August knew my whereabouts, and since he was not a blood relation, Father's homestead passed to distant relatives in Cedar Rapids. Then August joined me in Denver. Our reunion was a delightful one, although he only stayed a few months before marrying a young widow and moving with her and her children to California.

And Rudiman? That lecherous soul was not difficult to locate. The day after the city fired McGovern, the undertaker dismissed the laborers and left Rudiman alone to close up the City Cemetery jobsite. The wretch did so in near darkness, swilling from a flask as he went about collecting pickaxes and shovels.

This time, I was prepared. As night fell, I selected from the discarded shovels the heaviest and sharpest one I could find.

Approaching Rudiman from behind, I swung with all my might and all my care—ensuring that when his head split open and his body collapsed, it did so into an empty, waiting, desecrated grave.

TOUGH GIRLS

BY ERIKA T. WURTH

Lakewood

Entering the White Horse was like entering a dream. A dream of the past. My mother's past. She had grown up here—in Denver, on Colfax, like a million other Indians, like her own mother. Now I was back to solve a crime. Another Indian woman dead, like so many others in our communities, no one but her mom giving a shit. Not the cops. Not her dad, who hadn't been seen in a decade. No one else but me, a woman whose face, though allowed to grow much more cynical with age, so resembled hers.

"Naiche? Naiche Becente . . . of Apache PI?"

I nodded. "That's me."

"Thank the Creator!" The woman swiveled toward me on the old leather barstool. She looked to be in her early thirties, her eyes bloodshot with what I had to assume was lack of sleep.

I smiled cryptically. I had agreed to take her case, but that didn't mean I was going to be able to solve it.

God, I needed a smoke.

The bartender was the only one in there besides me and my client—Betty was her name—and his eyes were riveted, fixed on the screen, the wild, colorful images of Fox News flashing, the sound turned all the way off, the jukebox blaring CCR's "Up around the Bend."

I sat down next to Betty and shook her hand loosely, and

she thanked me profusely for coming, for agreeing to do the work for just the cost of travel and hotel.

"It's fine. I got plenty," I said. Which was nearly true. I made a decent living in Albuquerque where I had my practice, and I liked to do pro bono for other Natives. I loved Albuquerque—the original homeland of my people. Plus, rent was cheap, and I roomed where I worked, in a building downtown, a few doors from Java Joe's.

"Nick!" Betty said, turning to the bartender, an edge to her voice.

It took him a minute to extricate himself, but he turned, a friendly smile on his face, his blue eyes the color of a small butterfly. "Beer for your pretty friend?" he asked.

I scoffed, and pulled my black motorcycle jacket closer, hooked my biker boots onto the metal of the stool.

Betty nodded and wiped at her brow. Took the last slug of her Bud, pushed it forward.

Nick swept it off the counter and replaced it with two more, settling back in front of the television.

"So," I said, pulling my pack of cigarettes out of my pocket and packing it, hard, into my left hand. It helped me think. "Your daughter disappeared a month ago?"

Betty nodded. "Yes! And she's sixteen, and a good girl. She doesn't do nothing but stay at home and do her homework."

"You said though that you suspected her friend . . . Macina Begay, she might know more than she's saying?"

"Yeah, I told her to get that Macina out of her life. She's a bad influence. I smelled alcohol on her breath more than once." Betty sat back, crossed her arms over her chest.

"Huh." I'd heard this kind of thing before. Mom sure that her girl was an angel being dragged down by some devilish friend. Turns out, it's the other way around, but the parent just doesn't want to see it. I'd been making some calls on my way up. Her girl—Jonnie—liked to party.

"I made some calls—school, where you said she likes to hang out. There's been an older gentleman hanging around her, you know that?" I asked.

She sucked in breath. Then, "No."

"You think of anyone that could be?"

She went silent, her dark green eyes moving rapidly. "My brother, he lives with us, he says he got some weird phone calls while I been at work. Says he don't know for sure, but he thinks it's my ex."

"Why he think that?" I took a swig of my beer, wishing it was whiskey. I'd had a breakup of sorts a few days ago, and though it was another in a string of married men, this one had stung a little. More than a little.

"He says he can feel it. They were tight, back in the day."

"Go on."

"He picks up, it's nothing but silence, then whoever it is hangs up."

"You don't think this is your daughter?"

"Started happening before Jonnie went missing." She finished her beer in one quick swallow and sighed, heavy. I could tell she wanted another but was embarrassed to drink more in front of me. I ordered a whiskey for myself, a beer for her.

"You didn't think to bring this up to me on the phone?" I asked, unhooking my boots.

"Well, I didn't because there ain't no proof. It's just something my brother thinks. But then again," she said, squinting, "it would be just like my ex. George Labont. He grew up near me, near the Fond du Lac rez, where my grandparents were from. When I was pregnant with Jonnie, George kept saying he couldn't handle taking care of a kid, but he couldn't handle not being in its life. He went on like that, getting drunk and disappearing for days, until finally he was gone for good. I'm lucky I had my brother, Michael. Would've been lost without him."

"You mind if I ask your brother? What's his last name?"

"Michael. Michael Cloud." She peeled the label off the beer with a dark-brown finger.

"Mind if I ask Michael some questions?"

"Sure. Here's his number." She wrote it on a cocktail napkin. "He and Jonnie were close—been like a dad to her. He's all broken up about it, says he wants to do anything to help."

"Email me anything you got on your ex. Any pictures, old letters, anything. I'll figure out if he's back in town."

"I bet it is him," she said. "He was so screwed up. Maybe he kidnapped her. That bastard." The shadow of old wounds gathered in her eyes.

"I'll find out," I said, not bothering to argue with her.

She dried her eyes, thanked me again, and I left her to drink alone. The White Horse was just my kind of bar, with its old booths, red-glassed chandeliers over aging pool tables, and various pictures of 1970s-style white horses everywhere, but I could tell she needed her space.

So did I.

Thing was, I already had a lead. A strong one.

And shit, I needed a smoke.

Honestly, if Judd—Jonnie's reputed boyfriend—wasn't sixteen, I'd have happily beat his ass.

"Like, I don't know where she is?" he said, absentmindedly wiping at his nose. "The cops already asked me." His expression was one of pure derision. He wouldn't look me in the eyes.

"Uh-huh," I said. I was rapidly losing patience.

The girl beside him snickered. I flit my eyes over to her. She was no other than Jonnie's buddy, Macina Begay, who was looking at me beneath her long, straight, black eyelashes with a mixture of fear and hatred.

I'd been to Jonnie's school before I met with Betty, and a number of kids had told me that Jonnie had been partying for a while with this kid—Judd. Even his T-shirt annoyed me. It was a Metallica T-shirt, and when I'd first approached him with "Cool shirt," he'd merely squinted quizzically.

They were in the alleyway between the 7-Eleven and the diner, right where their friends had said they'd be. When they'd heard me, they scrambled to put a number of certainly highly illegal substances into their pockets.

"Yeah, I think you know more than you're saying," I said. "And you're going to tell me what it is right now."

Macina snickered again and leaned back on the chain-link fence.

I closed my eyes for a moment, centered myself. Remembered that these two were young, poor—that Macina was just a Diné kid trying to make it in a highly unfriendly city—and changed tacks.

"Look. If someone threatened you? I can make sure they're the ones who feel threatened."

Judd scoffed, and whipped his long, greasy-brown locks over his forehead in one small motion. "Yeah, right."

That right there told me something. Someone *had* threatened them.

"Aren't you worried about your friend?"

They looked at one another, Judd turning away then, Macina's glance moving down to her shoes.

I was getting closer.

"Whoever threatened you? I can take care of it," I said, glancing around and then showing them what was under my jacket—a Ruger .327. It was new. Shiny. "I've made a lot of men regret a lot of things."

Macina's eyes grew wide, and a speck of admiration began to creep into them.

"And I know how to keep them quiet," I said. "I do it for a living."

Macina opened her mouth.

"No! Don't," Judd said to her, wiping at his nose again, the skin of his short white fingers wrecked with cleaning chemicals.

"She's scary. And I'm worried about Jonnie. I think . . ." Macina trailed off.

"Don't say that!" Judd rasped, a teary edge to his voice.

"Lady, you promise if we tell you what we know, we're not the next ones to go missing?" Macina adjusted herself against the chain-link fence.

"Yes," I said. "Believe me. Men are scared of me."

Judd still seemed unsure, but I could tell my gun had impressed them both.

Macina sighed deeply. "We was here with Jonnie before she disappeared. And some older Indian guy—older than you—he come over here and started barreling her way. We hang out together in this spot all the time, party. We're tight."

I nodded. I didn't want to break her flow.

"He was grabbing her arm, yelling at her, she was fighting him. Judd and me—well, we were telling him he better leave her alone or we'd call the cops. He laughed. He said—" Macina stopped, her voice breaking.

"He said," Judd started, "that he was her dad and that there was nothing we could do. That he had a legal right to do whatever he wanted with her."

God, hearing that made me sick. But it confirmed my suspicions.

"Yeah, and," Macina began again, apparently recovered, "I guess we figured that was true. But still, Jonnie didn't want to go with him, said, 'You're not even my dad!'"

I nodded. That made sense. If he'd come around after all these years, especially considering what a deadbeat he seemed to be, there was no way Jonnie would've gone with him easy.

"He told her then," Macina continued, "that she better go with him or there'd be consequences for her mother. And that she better shut up about everything."

That was odd.

"Mind if I smoke?" Macina asked.

I pulled my pack out, lit one for myself, then offered Judd and Macina one. I guess that meant I was contributing to the delinquency of minors, but these two seemed to know what they were doing with their lives. And who was I to judge? I'd started smoking at twelve. So had my mother. And hers.

Macina closed her eyes, and it was clear the cigarette was working its cancer-like magic, as she looked better, refreshed, a quick, hot line of smoke shooting out the left side of her mouth. I understood. I wanted to quit—was always quitting— but then the damn things would pull me back in.

"Then he told us he'd call the cops on us if we told any- body about what had happened."

"You see her after that?" I asked, removing a stone from the bottom of my left boot—another gift from my latest sort- of-ex. He was gone. But the boots? Those I'd love forever.

"No," Macina said. "Nobody did."

I got a description of the guy from them then. Tall. Medium-brown. Short hair, hazel eyes. "Pretty Indian-looking," Macina said.

"Gotcha. He indicate at all where he might be taking her?" I asked.

They both went silent. "All he said was he was taking her home," Macina finally said.

Also odd. But perhaps that was his logic. After this, I was planning on running his name through the system—but I had a friend at Fond Du Lac, and reservations were small, tight communities. If George was there—or had made the mistake of telling a friend or relative about his whereabouts—I'd find out.

When I talked to Betty on the phone, she confirmed that the description fit her ex, George—except for the eyes. But they could've gotten that wrong. Heat of the moment. I also asked if he'd been abusive in any way. She had to admit that no, he hadn't—but that his drinking had stepped up hard during her pregnancy, before he disappeared, and his angst over the kid so wild, that it made sense.

"One minute he'd be talking about how he was too young for all of this. How he just needed to get away. And the next, weeping over the idea of my ever being with anyone else, the idea of anyone else raising our kid. Kept talking about how blood ties don't break."

Sounds like a man, I thought, but didn't say.

I was sitting in my hotel on Colfax, not far from the White Horse, thinking about giving up for the day and going over for a drink, when my phone rang.

I put my stale cup of coffee down and picked up.

"You wanted to know about George Labont?" It was my buddy. He was also an ex—one from many years ago who'd come through Albuquerque for long enough to hook up with me, before he decided he needed to go back home. We'd kept it cool, though.

I sat straight up. "I do."

"Got a number for you."

"Hello?"

My heart was beating like a rabbit's. I'd called the number a few times, though nothing but straight to voice mail. He was either busy or he didn't want to talk to nobody. I'd gone over to the White Horse for a beer—after a stop at a Mexican restaurant called Asaderos Mexican for a quick dinner. Nick the bartender was pleased to see me. Had been talking me up about all of the Natives that used to grace his doors, years ago. It was mainly a dead joint now—cats wandering in and out, occasionally jumping on the bar, looking for a treat or a pet.

Jonnie's dad had finally picked up.

"Who is this?" I could hear heavy breathing on the other end.

"It's me," I said, my voice breathy, low.

"Who?" he asked, softening.

I giggled. "You don't remember? How could you forget?" I asked, my tone dulcet. "I know I couldn't."

"I—"

"That night," I said, and sighed. I rolled my eyes and walked out for a smoke. The night was cloudy, no stars. I could see the lights of the Burger King next to me flickering.

"What was your name?" he asked.

"Cindy. I can't believe you don't remember the sound of my voice," I said, mock-angrily, ending with another giggle.

"I'm sorry."

"I was just . . . you know," I said, lighting up, taking a puff, "hoping we could get together again for a drink, now that I heard you were back in town."

A long silence.

"You are in Denver, right?"

Another silence. My heart sped up again.

"I . . . this must'a been a long time ago. I haven't had a drink in fifteen years, um—what you say your name was?"

"Cindy," I replied, listening hard. It didn't seem like he was lying, but some men were good.

"And Denver, you know, I got a kid there, and an angry ex, to tell you the truth. And I ain't been back there in, well . . ." I could hear him light up, the flame struggling to move, "over ten years. Though I been thinking about it."

"That's too bad," I said. Shit. Shit. Shit. I'd call around, but this guy—unless he was serial-killer good—wasn't lying. "Well, you know where to find me." I hung up, hoping he wouldn't call back. It was a burner phone anyway.

I finished my cigarette, and it began to rain.

I was back to square one, and I didn't like it one bit.

Sitting in Betty's living room in Lakewood was like sitting in my mom's or one of my aunties' houses on Colfax. My mom had left Denver after a breakup, telling her sisters that she was done with this city, ready to go back to the Chiricahua homeland in Albuquerque—though as far as I understood it, my family was originally from northern Mexico. But we'd always come back to Denver, back to Colfax, back to Lakewood, to Aurora. Back to the same large, sweeping T.C. Cannon and R.C. Gorman prints that were on the walls over the couch in front of me—the Indians gray-haired, old and beautiful, crows at their shoulders, their braids moving down their necks like living things. The couch was beige and rough, ancient multicolored afghans covering it, old powwow-bought blankets draped over the cracked leather La-Z-Boy.

And the great thing was, I could smoke indoors.

We were drinking coffee—Betty'd told me she'd just brewed a fresh carafe—and waiting for her brother. I'd wanted to ask him some questions—but he'd never showed. I'd made some more calls, and it turned out that George had been living in Minneapolis for the past ten years. That he was sober—he'd been telling the truth about that. I'd even gotten it on good authority that he was on the job—he'd become a mechanic— at the time that Jonnie was being accosted by the man outside the 7-Eleven. But Betty was having none of it. She was sure it was him. A little too sure.

Something had been poking at me.

I asked if I could see Jonnie's room, and she told me of course, but not to feel disappointed if I didn't find anything— that her baby had been an open book, and that even if there had been anything to find, she and the police had gone through it thoroughly, a few days after Jonnie had disappeared.

She followed me down the hallway, but at the doorway to the girl's room, I told her that I worked better alone. She frowned, but acquiesced.

I waited for the sound of her footsteps to diminish completely before I went in. On the door was a handmade sign that stated, *GET OUT!!!!* Huh. That didn't sound like Jonnie was an "open book." It sounded like Jonnie—like most teenagers—wanted to be left the fuck alone. But though she was sixteen, and certainly at an age where drama was high, there was something about the plain black marker, the four exclamation marks.

The bed was little and covered in a bright-yellow and red star quilt. God, had I coveted those when I was a kid. Shit, I coveted them now. The walls were covered in posters of hip-hop stars—Lil Yachty, Young Thug, Playboi Carti—and one retro Lil' Kim, in all of her leopard-print glory.

I sat down on Jonnie's bed, closed my eyes. Unbidden, an image of my ex came to mind, his long, lithe brown body, his sensitive eyes. His expression of sadness when I cut him off, after I found out he had kids.

I shook my head.

"Let's try this again," I whispered. I thought of the pictures of Jonnie that Betty had let me borrow—her long brown eyes, her shy-but-bold smile.

My eyes snapped open.

I went over to her dresser, which she had painted black. There were pictures everywhere—her mother, even an old one of her dad, I had to guess—and friends—there was Judd and Macina—and baby pictures of herself, clearly. And cutouts of hearts, all black, pasted or taped to each picture. I opened the first drawer and slid my hand along. No. Then the second, third, the fourth and last—still no. I shut it, disappointed. My instincts were usually so on-point.

Wait.

I hunkered down on the old red-carpeted floor, some of the white hair from the cat I'd seen earlier sticking to me. I scooted. Ran my hand along the underside of the dresser. Bingo! It was duct-taped to the bottom. I pulled, and it came off, out.

I opened the journal, which was gold—but had more black hearts taped to it—and gasped. I'd been right. That poor kid . . .

My eyes narrowed in anger.

I was going to get that fucker.

"Hey there, Michael," I said. I'd been waiting outside the restaurant for a while, smoking one cig after another, making sure I had every part of how this was going to go down lined up. It was a nice, breezy spring day, only a few clouds lining the horizon.

"Who are you?" His voice was drenched in suspicion, irritation.

I took a hit, put the smoke out in the dirt. But I didn't move from my position leaning against the brick—I didn't want this excuse for a human being to know that I was a threat, not just yet.

"Name's Naiche. I'm a friend of your sister's—and of Jonnie's," I said, watching him flinch.

"Jonnie's been kidnapped by her dad." His mouth was soft, his eyes brown—light brown—and he moved his tall frame like a snake. He was just about the same color as Jonnie's father. Medium-brown. Just a shade darker than me. I'd wondered briefly about how Judd, and especially Macina, hadn't seen Uncle Michael before—wasn't Macina Jonnie's best friend? But then I thought back to the girl in my high school who, come to find out, was being molested by her father—how she never let anyone spend time at her house. I had to assume that either Michael had banned guests, afraid they'd find out, or that Jonnie hadn't wanted anyone else to get diddled by her nasty uncle.

He worked at a Mexican restaurant, not far from the one I'd eaten at only days ago. He wiped his hands down his apron, then pulled it off, exposing his stained blue work pants, and folded the apron up and slipped it into his pocket.

"Yeah, that's what Betty thinks."

"And she's right," he said, his eyes narrowing. "That piece of shit was never good for nothing. I was glad he left."

I nodded. Then, "You didn't show the other night. Your sister said that you and Jonnie were tight. That you were real broken up about her disappearance. That you'd do anything to help."

He cocked his head. "You got another one of those?" He pointed to the pocket I'd shoved my smokes in.

"Sure," I said, pulling it out, shaking one out for him.

I could see he was sweating. All I had to do was reel him in, slowly.

He took a hit, the smoke piling out in a nice, neat line.

"Work ran late," he said, smiling, his lips a thin, neat, purple dash.

"Thing about that is, I called here. They said work didn't run late."

"They're lying," he responded, too quick. He took another hit, his hand shaking.

We smoked in silence for moment.

"You Apache, right?" he asked.

"I am. Chiricahua."

He sniggered. "Figures. I dated an Apache girl once— White Mountain though. Real tall. And a real bitch. You got the same black eyes as her."

"I *am* a real bitch, Michael."

He glared at me.

I continued: "The other thing is, did you know Jonnie had a journal?"

He was silent now, the sweat on his brow growing more profuse.

"I found it," I said, lighting another smoke for myself, squinting hard. "There sure is some awful shit about you in there."

"She was like a daughter to me."

Was. Past tense. This motherfucker. I had to assume Jonnie was dead. I already had, but this confirmed it.

"That's a pretty nasty way to treat your daughter, Michael. Men go to jail for treating their daughters like that."

His eyes narrowed again, almost to slits. "I ain't got time for this," he said, turning.

"Ah-ah-ah, I wouldn't do that."

"Fuck you, cunt," he said.

I pulled my gun out, and he stopped.

"Thing is, some friends of Jonnie's saw you take her the other day. And they can ID you. And when you add what I found in Jonnie's journal—you molesting piece of shit—I'm guessing that wherever you go, the cops, this time, will pay attention to the evidence that's finally right in front of their eyes, and they'll find you. And Jonnie's body."

"Fuck you!" he said, turning to run. I'd hoped he do that.

I squinted. I was a great shot. My mom said that all Apaches had great aim. I wasn't sure about that, but I knew I was good.

"Fuck!" He stopped in his tracks, clapping one hand over his right arm.

"I'm good at this. I clipped you on purpose—like a bird who's about to spend his life in a cage. Your wings ain't good for flying anymore. I'd stop now, or the next shot? Well, let's just say that I'm debating: balls or heart? Of which you got neither, so it's not like it'll be a loss either way."

"You fucking bitch!" he screamed, and bolted into the alley.

"Mother*fucker*," I said, and went after him.

He was fleet of foot, I'd give the ballsack that, and gaining ground, turning one corner after another, until—fuck!—I'd lost him.

My God, this piece-of-shit man, this piece-of-shit life. I couldn't let him get away with it, I just couldn't. Jonnie's journal had hurt me to my core. Year after year of it, him coming into her room at night, telling her to be a good girl, to be quiet—or he'd kill her mother. Until finally, one day, she'd had it. Had made the mistake of telling him that she was going to tell her mom—that's when she'd disappeared. It had been her last entry. And I was sure as anything that when he hadn't been able to persuade her to shut up, he'd killed her.

And now I was failing her, just like I'd failed so much in this life, never going after the right men, always in trouble with the police in Albuquerque for getting in their way—shit. I might as well give up, go home. He was gone, and Betty seemed determined to believe that her ex was behind this. Wasn't it better to let the truth die?

I thought of Jonnie's young brown face again—the love that her mother had for her. The fact that Jonnie was Betty's only child. How she'd told me she lived for Jonnie. The fact that this man had taken this from her.

Fuck him.

I closed my eyes, went clear, then opened them

"I know you're behind that dumpster, you shit-for-brains. There's no other way out of this alleyway. You don't come out? I'll just shoot both your balls and your heart."

He crawled out from behind it, scowling. "You're just making things worse, you know that?"

I was silent.

"Betty's already lost her child—I'm all she has left. Think about that."

It was true.

"She wanted it," he said. "I know she did. Always looking at me in that slutty way." He chuckled. "Some girls are just born slutty."

She had been eight when it had started—that was in her journal.

I wanted to kill him with everything I was.

I took a deep breath and called the cops.

* * *

Betty arrived with them. I guessed they'd called her.

I explained what I'd found, handed them her journal—told them I'd be happy to come to the station with them.

"I'm going to press charges!" Michael screamed as they cuffed him, put him in the car. "I didn't do nothing to that kid!"

"He didn't do it," Betty said, the cops nodding. "I'm sure she just imagined things—kids do that. She loves her uncle!" She started sobbing then, great, jagged, near-hysterical sobs. "It's white men who rape us, not Indian men!"

I closed my eyes. White men did rape Indian women, and the law was just beginning to shift to make them have to suffer the consequences for that. But Indian men raped Indian women too. They killed Indian women too. I knew, because I dealt with cases like this all the time in Albuquerque—the great violences brought upon all of our ancestors echoing in our souls, each generation seeing just enough incremental change to make me hope for an eventual avalanche of change.

"Betty, I read the journal. He raped her. He's been coming into her room since she was eight years old—and he threatened you, that's why she said nothing. But she was going to tell you. That's when he snapped," I explained.

She was silent.

"I'm sorry, Betty." I ran my hand down the length of my dark hair. "I texted the kids who saw Jonnie the day she disappeared—they've ID'd your brother. He's the one who threatened her—and I'm telling you, he killed her."

Her lip trembled. "You whore!" she screamed. She chucked her purse at my head.

I ducked, picked it up, tried to give it back to her. She merely batted violently at my hand.

"I never should've called you!"

I nodded. This was why I always asked for half of my fee up front.

I walked over to my beat-up Honda and shut the rusting door. I wondered if and when they'd find the body. I thought again of Jonnie's sweet face. I stared at myself in the rearview mirror, wiped at the mascara and eyeliner that had melted during the day, images of my ex floating into my mind. He was also a liar. I'd met him in the Anodyne, I'd been playing pool when he'd made his way over to me, told me he liked my biker jacket—said he liked tough girls. I'd come up smiling but cautious, shrugged out of my jacket, exposing my shoulders, the wind from the open doors grazing them. He'd told me he was getting a divorce. No kids though, he said. Good, I'd told him, I don't do kids.

I put the car into drive. I was headed for the White Horse. Then home. Thank the Creator for home. There was always, at least, that.

PART II

5,280'

THE LAKE

BY PETER HELLER

Sloan's Lake

I live on a lake on the west side of Denver. Sloan's. Three miles around with an island in the middle. I live in a small 1950s blond-brick ranch house whose walls are cracking because the water table is high and there is a stream running through my crawl space. But I wouldn't trade it. I look out the window and I see grass, water, trees, mountains. The long escarpment of the Continental Divide. I'm really in the middle of a city but it doesn't seem that way.

I am a novelist, with a lot of free time and not a ton of direction. I mean, I write. I drink coffee, and I spend a lot of my day outside. My debut thriller was a surprise best seller. I wrote it after I got fired from my job as editor of a national gym equipment trade magazine, where I'd been spending way too much time fantasizing about the ways I would kill the association's communications director—a treadmill gone haywire was one of the most satisfying. Anyway, the book took off, but the three novels since have notched steadily diminishing sales. I am sensing that my publisher and I are about to part ways.

Kara is a pharmacist who works ten-hour shifts, so we try to see each other for coffee in the morning and at dinner.

I love where I live but here's a confession: I have never really known what I was supposed to do in my life. Or whom I should listen to. Should I listen to myself? I always seemed to get in trouble that way. It seemed I could aim higher. God? How do you do it? I have tried praying, but I never get a clear message back. My wife? My friend Ted, who is a cop? Good compromises, but I noticed that when I listen to other people all the time, I begin to lose whatever sense of true north I still possess.

This not knowing is a little like tinnitus, a ringing in the ears that never ceases. I can still function and nobody knows I live with a constant drone, but . . . how clear and relaxed would life be without it? I discovered long ago that the best balm is to be outside and be physical. For a little while I forget.

What I do is: I carry my paddleboard across two hundred yards of grass and I launch where there is a gap in the willows and they have dug granite blocks into the bank and they make two high steps which are also great to sit on. I used to paddle in the evening. There are always a lot of birds—ducks and geese on the water, pelicans in summer, osprey hunting—but I got tired of the motorboats with wakeboarders kicking up waves and all the strollers on the bike path which follows the shore. Also there is a homeless couple under the pedestrian bridge at the lake's outlet and sometimes they fight and yell. I have seen him strike her with a closed fist more than once, and seen her buckle and lie on the rocks sobbing. I called the cops twice. I saw an officer I recognized on the bike path later and he said she never talks, never testifies, always goes back to the man. Then I didn't see her anymore.

I like it more quiet. So I started going in the morning. Motorheads tend to be partiers. They're always blasting music as they tear by, and holding up plastic cups which I'd bet money are not filled with Hawaiian Punch, and so I imagine they are hungover a lot and they tend to sleep in. In the morning, except for the early dog walkers and joggers, I mostly have the lake to myself. Me, the muskrats carving their quiet wakes, the birds. I love it out there. As soon as I step on the paddleboard and am buoyant and free of the shore, all the normal, pedestrian laws of nature fall away and are replaced by a different rhythm, a different sense of gravity. And somehow I forget that I don't know what I am supposed to do.

And I began to go earlier and earlier. Just at daybreak, when the sky is a crimson flush behind the Dickensian brick chimneys of the middle school; then I really am alone. There might be one or two runners. But if I go even earlier, in the dark, there is no one.

I walk across. Say it's June. The dew on the grass wets my toes and I hear a night heron croaking on the shore and smell the sediment in the water. The water will be icy from the snowmelt in the tiny creek that flows under the pedestrian bridge at the west end, and as I get closer I can feel the chill. Most of the water in the lake, though, comes from a spring. That's the legend. The legend is that this was farmland back in the 1800s and the farmer came out to dig a well and hit an artesian gusher and in a few days his cornfield was gone and he had a lake. Maybe it's true. I like the idea. I like the idea that the lake bore herself into this world and that below the surface calm is a powerful animus of self-expression.

I push through the gap in the willow thicket and sit on the granite boulder. I let the short paddleboard rest on the ground beside me. The heron has ceased, but a redwing blackbird wheezes from a nest somewhere in the branches. No moon, good. Oh, there is one, a slender crescent hanging like a sinking boat over the jaws of the Divide, sallow and lost. Lights along the bike path on the other side of the lake, maybe a quarter mile across, but no movement. I can tell the water is very still and smooth because the ropes of light that extend across barely waver. The murmur of a duck, somewhere close. Are those shadows geese? Probably. They drift without sound. No pale shapes of the white pelicans that migrate here every summer to breed; they must be bedded down on the little island. I breathe. The lake breathes. It seems the wet silt and stone and algae at my feet, and the expanse of dark water, all exhale and I inhale them in. In this way we exchange breath. In this way I gain a little strength . . .

The only problem with going so early is that I miss Kara for our morning coffee. After a few days I got a note: *I don't know what's gotten into you. All your spare time is on the damn lake! Miss you. XO.* After a few more days she seemed angry when we met at night. She wouldn't talk about it. I guess I was going out in the evenings too, and had missed a couple of dinners. She rolled away from me in bed when I tried to touch her.

Well, the lake is dependable. She always floats and rocks me, always has something new to say. If there is a wind before sunset and I paddle into it she sprays me happily as I hit each little whitecap. If there is a fog at dawn she embraces and covers me. Always.

Why is there fog? It was June, as I said. The nights were still cold but the water should have been colder. Makes no sense. But why would I ask? I love to get lost in it.

So that first morning of thick fog, I was alone at dawn, happily paddling blind. I felt disembodied in the mist as if I were paddling through outer space with no real up or down, and the fog parted a little before me, and on the glass of dark water there was a sudden suffusion, a glow, and then I clearly saw a man reclined, bearded, under . . . under a bridge. The picture pulsed once and was replaced by a figure, the same man, striking and striking a woman, until she buckled and fell. And then, like the shadow of a sudden cloud, the black water coalesced into kind of a cloak and blotted out the man.

I must not have been breathing then. I was shocked that a life might end with the toss of a cloak. That it *should* end. The image on the water looked exactly like the homeless man who slept under the bridge at the east end. For the first time in my life I knew exactly what I was supposed to do.

I am not a geologist. But I know that under a lot of this country lies a bedrock of limestone. That would explain a lot. Limestone tends to be full of water. Pockets, reservoirs, streams, rivers. It erodes easily and can be riddled with tunnels. And so the story of the farmer and his well makes sense. Also the Vanishing Point. What I call it. I noticed in my years living here—nine now—that in cold winters when the lake froze, there was almost always a spot clear of ice in front of my house. The size varied, but almost never got smaller than the area of a couple of tennis courts. Of course that's where all the water birds congregated. The only open water for miles and it would be full of mergansers and shovelers, geese, canvasbacks, seagulls. My favorite are the green-winged teal. Who could have put all those colors together and made them sing? The burnished-cinnamon head with its swoop of emerald. Slate-gray sides with jaunty white shoulder stripe. Flash of jewel-green in the wing, yellow in the tail. Oh so elegant. Whenever I meet one I tell him that there has never been a thing more gorgeous and I swear he gets the gist.

The pair of bald eagles that winter here even have enough water to fish, and they plummet through the floating flocks and ignite an explosion of alarmed waterfowl. At first, I thought the opening in the ice was where the artesian spring welled up. But then, paddling my board on calm evenings when the sun dropped below the mountains and the lake glassed off, I noticed that twigs, lost fishing bobbers, errant soccer balls, tended to drift toward the spot and congregate like trash in the Pacific Gyre. If the spring flowed up here, I would think that flotsam would be gently pushed away. That's when I decided that it was harder for ice to form because there was a subtle current drawing down—into some sort of limestone drain.

The lake was full of mysteries.

That morning after seeing the scene on the water, I dug the paddle in, pivoted the board, and paddled back toward the east end of the lake. I was in thick fog. But as I passed the hazard buoys that mark the rocks near the bridge, I was close enough to see the man sleeping. He lay curled on his side, with only the back of his head and thick mat of long hair outside his sleeping bag. He had been there for months. He had a little camp, a ten-tin kerosene stove, a rolling trash bin on wheels, a heap of clothing and tarps. I paddled in quietly, slowed, bumped a chunk of granite, hopped off, reached down for a rock the size of a softball, and bashed the back of the man's head. He jerked, groaned, writhed, I swung again, harder, and he was still. Blood seeped onto the rocks.

Moving very fast, as if I'd done this a hundred times, I unbuckled a cam strap between two D rings on the front of my board and ran it through two rusted ten-pound barbell weights he had leaning against a cooler, and I tied them off. I set the weights on the back of the board, looped a clove hitch around the man's neck, and dragged him into the water. I towed him out to the spot I figured had the Vanishing

Point—I could tell where it was because there was a little island of floating trash—and I just shoved the weights off the end of the board with my paddle.

Down he went. I thought, *What the hell*, and paddled back to the bridge and used one of his old pots to wash down the rocks. Then I paddled home.

The next morning, I was out on the water even earlier, and wherever I paddled the lake trailed me with a faint wake of pulsing pink and blue. I am no hero. Definitely no hero. But I felt appreciated and . . . loved, I guess. I had done a good thing and gotten rid of a bad man.

Well. In the following days I watched for the body to resurface, because I hear they can do that, even with weight, but there was nothing. And so in the next months, as summer turned to fall—the autumn fog is the thickest, though darkness is the only cover I really need—I felt renewed, energized . . . purposeful. One cool morning in September I saw a man who came down at dawn some days to fish. He always brought his dog, a black Lab mix. I always waved at him but he never waved back. I got the sense he thought I was scaring his fish, how stupid. So that morning I was paddling easily by and I saw his dog grab a catfish out of the bucket and the man yelled and beat the poor thing without mercy. He used a stick. I will never forget the yelps of pain. And on the water, again, was this suffusion of light and moving shadows which flowed into the figure of a man striking a dog. It's incredible to know what you are supposed to do. To know with certainty. To be told by this . . . this spirit of the lake. This angel, I guess.

It was early, it was foggy, so I landed up the shore, out of sight behind an outcrop of willows, and I beached the board on the rocks, picked one up, and snuck up behind the man and beaned him. Now I always carried rusted old barbell weights on the front of my board under my life vest. I got them at yard sales. I strapped them to his neck, as before, towed him out to the Vanishing Point, and sent him down.

And again, I felt completely at home with my world. How novel. I breathed in huge drafts of air that smelled like water, mineral and clean—and the air seemed to be the grateful, intimate outbreath of the lake. Inhale, exhale.

We weren't often home at the same time, but when we were, Kara began to look at me with a wary expression, almost afraid, which stung. She started sleeping in the guest room. Angry, I guess, for my increasing absence. Sometimes I would catch her near me, nostrils flared, as if she were snagging a bad smell, and I realized it was me. She thought I was unappetizing, maybe disgusting. I tried to talk to her but I opened my mouth and had no words. I could feel myself wanting to weep. So I turned on my heels and went out the door . . . to you know where. Where I can fully breathe. Where I am always accepted with open arms.

One morning, Ted and I were having coffee on my porch and he said that there was a curious missing persons case in District One—which is here. He said they'd found a camp chair, a fishing rod, and a barking dog just across the lake, but no man. Curious. The man had a history of mental illness and so their best hunch was that he'd wandered off, maybe hitched a ride out of town.

"What happened to the dog?" I said.

"He got adopted by my corporal, Ricardo. A great dog. He loves fish, go figure."

"Go figure."

We watched mist curl on the water like smoke. "I don't see

the homeless guy under the bridge anymore," I said. "The one who used to beat his partner."

"Yeah, he left too. Probably moved down to the Platte. Good riddance."

Good riddance.

"Got more coffee?" he said.

In October Kara left. She moved in with an old friend of mine.

I know we have been more and more distant lately, and that it was I, mostly, who stepped away. But damn it hurts. I can't stop thinking about the two of them together. Imagining them in bed is bad—especially her straddling him, I don't know why—but even more horrible is picturing them strolling down Tennyson with ice-cream cones, hand in hand, and the way she tilts her face up to his and looks so happy—it kills me. Sometimes it is so painful I don't know how I will get through the next five minutes. I miss her terribly. The worn old song is surely true—you don't know what you've got until it's gone. The What Ifs and If Onlys and Maybe Ifs circle so relentlessly in my head they have incised a groove I am afraid I shall never escape.

So I can't sleep. Not a chance. So now I go out with the board at all times of night. Someone snipped the wire at the base of the streetlight on the bike path near my launch spot so if there is no moon it is very very dark. I wear black workout tights, a black nylon shirt, the board is navy blue so we are blended. Before I launch I sit on the granite block and breathe the scents which I know as intimately as any on earth. It calms me. I study the water. Body of water. Maybe there will be a faint spreading glow, a pulse almost like a heartbeat, and maybe in the flush there will be a moving image. I hope so. I pray so. I am listening hard, and I hear the scuffing cadence of footfall, a night runner who I'm guessing can't sleep either.

Is the runner good or bad? I don't know yet. Tonight one pulse of light will be enough.

THAT'S LIKE *ME* SAYING:

"SPEAKING OF WHITE FOLKS, MY MECHANIC IS ONE OF YOU."

AT THAT POINT, THEY AIN'T REALLY SEEING YOU AS A *PERSON*--

SO, Y'KNOW, LIKE-- I *UNDERSTAND*...

--JUST AS A SYMBOL OF WHATEVER THEIR FANTASY IS ABOUT BLACK PEOPLE.

IN THESE CASES, I LIKE TO SAY SOMETHING ABSURD--

--*AUDACIOUS* AS *FUCK*--

--TO SHOCK THEM *OUTTA* THAT SHIT.

SO-- --YOU'RE SAYING YOU LIKE BLACK *DADDIES*?

UM...

SEE--

WHEN SOMEONE DOESN'T FULLY RECOGNIZE YOUR *HUMANITY*--

--THEY'RE MORE LIKELY TO BELIEVE IN SOME TYPE OF BLACK *MYSTIQUE*--

--WHICH MEANS THEY'RE TRYING TO FULFILL A *FANTASY.*

AND, I'M *NOBODY'S* FANTASY.

HEH.

OH.

HA! HA!

I EMBARRASSED HIM IN FRONT OF HIS SISTER.

I *REALLY* NEED TO KEEP MY DISTANCE.

BUT IF I *PROVOKED* HIM HARD ENOUGH--

-- HE'S WONDERING HOW I KNEW ABOUT HIM.

AND *THIS* WAS THE FIRST PLACE HE RAN TO.

LIKE, AFTER TALKING TO *ME*--

--HE WANTED TO MAKE SURE NO ONE HAD FOUND HIS *SHIT*.

BUT AS SOON AS HE LEAVES--

--I'MMA FIND HIS SHIT.

ABOUT WHAT I EXPECTED.

BUT, THIS CHECK...

IT'S FROM THAT *PROSECUTOR*--

--THE ONE FROM THE ARTICLE MARNIE TEXTED--
--TRYING TO SEND THEIR FRIEND TO PRISON.

HOW DOES HE KNOW BRUNO? WHAT'S HE *PAYING* BRUNO FOR?

AND HOW DOES THAT ALL FIT WITH HELENA AND MARNIE'S TROUBLES?

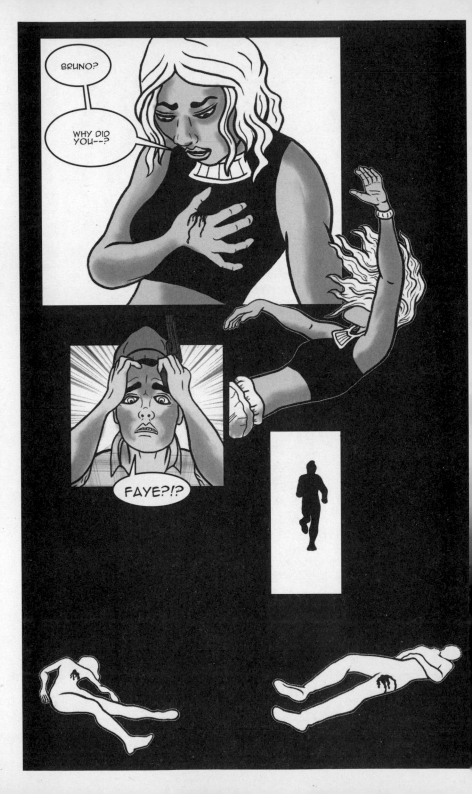

NO GODS

BY AMY DRAYER

South Broadway

There are two bars in my neighborhood that aren't terrible. Aren't full of hipsters and liars, mostly lying to themselves but still not worth the goddamn words you're wasting on them. I always walk to the bars, right up Broadway. If you can't walk to the bar you shouldn't go because you shouldn't drive drunk. And if you're at a bar and you're not drunk, what the fuck are you doing? I mean, just what the fuck are you doing? I know what I'm doing and it's not wasting my time in bars I haven't been in before and driving around drunk. Jesus Christ.

Black Crown and BJ's Carousel. One's pretending to be new and going to die soon, and one's old and dies next week. Even South Broadway is on the slate to get overrun by dog-loving craft beer drinkers, but you can still find pockets where you can get a good gay pour. But two bars, that's where I go. Alternate nights. They're both full of queens but they leave me alone. What the hell would they do with a drunk old lesbian?

In Denver there's the Detour for lesbians, but I wouldn't be caught dead there. Christ no. The only thing worse than all the queers in my bars are the dykes at the Detour. Washed-up assholes who think they're tough, but what a bunch of pretenders. Used to be right on Colfax and ten years ago when I lived on Capitol Hill I'd drink there. I moved sometime around 9/11 and so did they. Now it's to hell and gone all the way out on West Colfax. Shit. If I walked out there I'd be dead by morning.

Now as soon as I say this, of course, I get a call from Jackie. I'm sitting at home minding my own, but she's all fired up about it being Friday night at the Detour because they're going to have a *draaag* show. Not a drag show, but a *draaag* show, she says, because she's excited. It's kings, though, she says. Kings! What the fuck am I going to do with a woman dressed up like a man? Jesus Christ, now the baby dykes pretend to be men to get attention. I spend the best fifty years of my life trying to get it through our thick heads that men aren't role models, and this is what it comes to.

But I never could do anything about Jackie. She's a magpie and there's always something sparkling somewhere. Used to be me, but Christ, that's been a decade or more.

"Kings!" she proclaims. "Cheryl, you'll love it. I know you will. They're just so handsome. And they lip-sync, dance around, you know. The music is wonderful. Like drag queens—"

"What the fuck business do I have with any of it? And I assume the gestapo is still up our ass about smoking inside. Do these kings do their thing on the patio? No? Then fuck off."

"I'll give you a ride," Jackie replies, because she doesn't know how to listen. No one knows how to listen. "I don't drink anymore, you know, but I'm just so excited for the show."

"No. You don't drink anymore, and you can't stop telling me about it. Now you smoke that damn douche flute, and I can't stand it. Why the hell do you want to suck strawberry weed out of a mini dildo? Jesus Christ, Jackie."

"Well, you're clearly drunk, but it's no use arguing about it. Eat something and I'll come by and pick you up in a couple hours. I want you to come, Cheryl. It'll be fun."

* * *

The Detour used to be fun. It used to be perfect. God, what a place. Full of women who knew what they were about and not even the bar was pretending to be something it wasn't. It doesn't take an expensive logo or a lot of light to drink whiskey, and a lesbian who's drinking anything other than beer or whiskey should just piss off. Dark wood everywhere, neon too, of course. Casting a nice glow over things. You could see the pool tables and the bar and the door all at the same time. Drinks were cheap, food was cheap, you didn't have to watch every goddamn word that came out of your mouth. New girls knew to sit down and shut up for a while and they didn't get their panties in a bunch because you looked at them wrong.

They got gentrified out of the original spot, and now it's West Colfax and drag kings and gray Formica tables and a drop ceiling in BFE. The neon feels like a communist hospital on a bad trip and the whole thing reminds me of drinking in the sales room of my greasy cousin Rick's used-car lot in Greeley.

But I go on Friday because it's Jackie. And then, who walks through the door of the Detour Friday night, but Lisa Ward. Can you believe I used to have a crush on that woman? God. I had the biggest crush on her. We'd lie around on the couches for hours at the Women to Women bookstore talking about how the world was going to be someday when we were—what? Liberated? What a crock of shit. We were kids. But she only ever had eyes for Sandy Rook, and they *married*, for Chrissake. Well, not really of course, that's off-limits— thank Christ. Eleven years into the twenty-first-century AD with the walls coming down around us, but fuck if we let the gays marry. Yet those girls still put on the whole hetero show. Even fucking *registered*. Few years later, Sandy got cancer and died. And now Lisa's with some other woman and it doesn't take brains to see it's not like it was, but lesbians are so damn codependent.

"Cheryl!" Lisa calls out. "Cheryl Russo. It's been an age and a day at least. Wow, it's good to see you. Let me buy you a drink. You here for the kings?"

Who the hell is this old broad? I ask myself. Lisa's thick blond hair's all silver and white now. She used to have the sharpest blue eyes like lasers, and I loved that. No bullshit in them. Now they're watery and kind. Christ. Lisa Ward with old, kind eyes.

"I'm here because Jackie dragged me," I reply. "And no thank you. I buy my own drinks. But if you want to talk, I'm outside."

"You haven't changed at all, Cheryl. Give me a minute. I'll be out." Lisa smiles at me. People are always smiling like they mean it. She's got a mouthful of implants now, looks like. Wonder what happened. Her teeth were always good, and I suppose she knew it. White and straight as pickets and when she smiled it did get to you. But time's a bastard.

Lisa sits down at my rickety table on the patio and launches right in, because would it have been too damn much to ask to just take each other in for a minute? It would, because people hate silence. Terrified of it, more than hate it, is more like.

She's off to the races: "It's so good to see you. So good. Do you remember, Cheryl . . ." I fade out when Lisa starts there—here we go down memory lane. The old queens do it too. "When we both worked in the movement? We thought we had the world by the tits, didn't we? I'd just love to walk into Women to Women one more time."

"Well." I consider my Scotch and light a Lucky. "There were a hell of a lot more tits but it didn't do a good goddamn.

But I do miss it, Lisa-girl. All of us fired up like we were going to do something that mattered. I'll give you a remember-when. Remember when equality was a four-letter word? We were talking about *liberation*! Never have to hear a minute of hand-wringing over 'but what about the men.' We cared about women back then. No one cares about women anymore."

"I do." Lisa looks back over her shoulder, through the propped-open patio door at the show about to start. Some baby dyke with an eyeliner mustache and glitter stars on her nips is roaming the crowd, warming it up and urging women to put dollars into sock-stuffed red Jockey briefs.

"Bullshit." I slam my hand on the table and everything, everyone, jumps.

"Then here's to bullshit." Lisa holds up her glass and we're toasting the goddamn Hindenburg.

We sit quietly for a minute. Finally. And in that moment we're back in the bookstore together. Not just a bookstore, a *women's* bookstore. I can feel what we felt then, the pull to freedom and each other. God, the struggle was glorious.

Lisa looks again to the shit show inside.

"You don't have to stay out here." I offer her a fucking way out. Just like always. "What is this, pity?"

"No, Cheryl. It's an old friend wanting to catch up."

"Then let's catch up. You still with what's-her-face?"

"Sandy? She passed eight years ago. Cancer—"

"No. Christ. I'm not dumb. That new one. The nice one."

"Gloria? Yes."

"You love her as much as Sandy?"

"We make each other happy."

"That's not what I asked." I drill my finger into the table for emphasis. People are squirrelly as hell. "Do you love her as much as Sandy?"

Lisa considers me with those watery blue eyes. There's flint way down, still. But no fire. "You know, Cheryl, you always had a way of seeing through the bullshit, the sexist propaganda. No one had the insight you did. But you always turned it on your own. I know you hated Sandy, but it didn't make me love you." She pauses and look out, someone's got something profound to say. "I always wondered how you and Kathy ended up together. And more than that, why someone that good would stay with you. No one deserves to die that way, but at least she was free of you."

"Well, I'm sure she and Sandy are fucking in the great beyond, so don't feel too sorry for her." Maybe I was wrong about that fire. Maybe I can forgive myself for wanting Lisa when lust didn't feel like a waste of time.

"You really haven't changed, have you?" she says.

I don't take the bait this time and she wanders off. Christ. I told Jackie I didn't want to come here, and can you see why, now? Goddamn that woman. Where is she? Probably clapping at some girl waving fake balls in her face. What happened to us? I mean, what the fuck happened to us?

That twit Taylor Swift is cranked all the way to twelve and it's too goddamn much. I walk into the bar to call for a ride home. The airhead behind it only shrugs at me when the cab company says they're booked two hours out. I have no goddamn idea how far it is from Sappho's last stand here to my house, but even death is better than this circus. I turn toward the door and what do you know. Here comes Jackie out of the bathroom.

"Made room for more," she jokes, and orders another Diet Coke. "I'll buy your next one, Cheryl. Then we can go home."

By the stage, the lesbians are losing their fucking minds over some asshole dressed up like a cop-stripper. One more time in case you missed that. A cop-stripper. A rapist and an opportunist. Like I said. Fifty years of my life and it's come to this.

I want to talk about Faven. Jackie won't listen to me talk about her. But now it's gotten so I can't *not* talk about her, even if it's muttering to my goddamn self like an asshole while I'm walking down the street. People give me space when I talk to myself and that's a real goddamn plus for the half an hour it takes to get to work. The library's named after a woman, a real fireball. Sarah Decker got what she wanted out of this life and then some. Outlasted three husbands and I'm sure you can guess she really got going after she stopped giving the best of what she was to a man. We don't think women ever did anything because no one bothers to tell us about it, but can you vote today even if your driver's license has an *F* on it? You sure can, and you can thank her and the rest of the suffragists for it. Thank her for your national park and your local library too. The branch in Platt Park named after her does the woman some justice, at least. The place is wonderful, and I've never been unhappy a day of my life there. It's not that assholes don't use libraries, but at least they've picked up a damn book in their life. Now we lend out all kinds of crap that doesn't belong in a library, but that's progress. Shit, I'm up to my neck in progress.

The walk up Logan is nice. In spring, the eight blocks feel like you're strolling through God's vagina if the snow hasn't snuffed out all the blossoms. I take my time on my way home in autumn and stop in Platt Park. Fall in the park, the grass is still green but smells dusty, it's sunny and warm enough, and it feels like death's always tomorrow but today's just fine, thanks. I'll sit on a picnic bench under the big rusty purple maple by the playground, all the kids screaming but it fits, and I'll have a Lucky and think, it's all going to die in a couple weeks, but now—now, where no one wants anything from me and I can pretend women aren't getting beaten to shit in houses all across the city—now is good. Now is good.

Half an hour walk and I'm shelving books and talking to people who want to learn things. Best is when they bring their kids. We don't have a big section like they do in some of the other branches, but I always manage to find the right something for the kids. Last year I fell in love, I mean absolutely in love, with this eight-year-old girl who came in with her mother all the time. Her dark-brown eyes were just light itself. She always wore pants with a dress over, her mom insisted she wear a dress but Faven knew what was up, I'm telling you. Eight and you could see in this girl's eyes she's going to light shit on fire and kick ass and take names and not swallow a second of the shit our culture feeds us.

"Excuse me, miss. Do you have any books about gardening?" This was Faven's first question to me, and she asked it boldly. Not hiding in her mother's skirts, not mumbling or vague. Brass set on her out of the gate!

"I do. Where are you planting this garden?"

"Eritrea. My big brother farms there and I want to do what he does."

"I see. I think." I cast her a friendly sidelong glance, just to test her out and see if she'd pay off down the line. She held that glance and I knew we were in business. "Just what are you planning to grow in your garden?"

She replies quick and smart as a whip: "Mama says Jemal grows wheat, so I want to grow wheat."

"All right then, that clears it right up. Follow me."

I'm not sure if her mother, Mariam's her name I learned

later, expected me to take the kid at face value. She's a good woman is how I ended up figuring her after a while, but honest to God, I think the kid intimidated her, because she sure as shit intimidated me. If you've ever had a little girl intimidate you and not punished her for it, I wouldn't mind knowing you.

Faven followed me that afternoon, and most afternoons that summer. Mariam worked out at the Purina plant, so it was either the library or at home with her father who slept days and worked nights. Faven seemed to greatly prefer the library, though she was always much quieter when she arrived than when she left. Books brought her out of her shell, opened her world. I remembered why I started working at a damn library in the first place. I actually didn't mind the helpful shadow who gave me regular crop reports.

Over the summer when she wasn't pestering me, Faven managed to grow a healthy swath of stalks. Mariam bent my ear about it for twenty minutes when the crop hit waist high. She said Faven would hide in the middle of the little patch for hours and read, even after it was dark—she'd go out after dinner, and get this, Mariam says, she even asked if she could sleep out there instead of in the house. Got downright mad about it one night, apparently. Started crying and pitching a bitch, which didn't sound like the kid at all.

I asked her about sleeping outside right before she went back to school. She shrugged and said she just liked it out there. I asked her if it was getting a little cool. She said yes and then asked me to be quiet so she could read. I respected the hell out of that and fucked off. Kept my eye on her, though, and she did give me a little grin and wave before Mariam picked her up. That was the last we spoke of her little *Children of the Corn* act and I wish to hell it hadn't been.

* * *

Like I said, I walk home through Platt Park in autumn. Sit under the falling leaves and have a Lucky. Sunny days the sharp, cool wind slips over your skin with a sweet little kiss. When it's cloudy and smells like Greeley, the wind is ominous. It's going to bring snow and cold, and dark. Some cloudy day in late October I'm doing my thing after work, thinking about what I'm going to put in the pan for dinner. Faven leaves the swing she's been sitting on just kicking dirt, walks over, and sits opposite me on the bench.

"Hey, Faven. How you doing today?"

"Miss Cheryl, I have to apologize to you." Faven doesn't look at me, she's looking at the ground and fidgeting with the hem of her dress over the top of blown-out knees in her jeans.

"What in the world for, sweetheart?"

"I promised to weave you a tree of life with the wheat I grew."

"And you haven't?"

"No."

"Honey, that's okay, but do you want to tell me why not?" Now don't think I'm an asshole, I wasn't asking to make it worse for her. Jesus—she seemed repentant enough. She still hadn't even looked at me. But she came over to talk, and when a girl like that gives you her time, it means something.

"Well," she replied, "I wanted to." More hem-fraying.

"Did you get busy with school?"

"No. I wanted to make it for you, but then I didn't want to anymore."

"Have I done something wrong, Faven?" You ever disappoint a kid? Shit, for your sake I hope not.

"No, ma'am."

"You just stopped wanting to make something for me, or make something at all?"

"I don't really want to make stuff anymore. At all." She pulled the string on the hem long enough to fly a kite. Didn't seem at all worried that her mom might not be thrilled about it. Didn't seem to care about much at all, as far as I could tell. The light had gone out. I'd seen that happen before to plenty of women, married women who stayed married because what was the alternative? Never thought I'd have to see it with a young girl, but who was I fucking kidding?

"Did someone else do something wrong?" I narrowed my eyes and stared hard at the top of her bent head. Four symmetrical poofs with twin blue balls on each of the ties held her sweet black hair tightly in place. Perfect for playground shenanigans, but bright colors were all wrong in the bite of the October wind as the clouds' mean gray raced overhead.

"I started to weave your tree. But then my father said it looked nice. And he asked if I would make one for him when I finished yours, and it would be a special gift."

"Ah." I took a big old hit on that Lucky and tried to talk myself out of the truth. But you can't talk yourself out of what men do to us. This girl sure as shit never would. "And so you didn't want to even finish the one you started for me."

Finally, I got a look. Christ, I wish I hadn't. I wish she'd never looked up at me that way, with those dull, dark eyes. But she did. Faven looked right at me for the last time. She and Mariam don't come to the library anymore. It's been almost eight months since I made that call to Colorado Human Services and I still haven't seen those dark bright eyes, except sometimes at night if I'm dumb enough to try to sleep sober. Suppose I ought to give up wanting to see that girl again, but I don't know if I can. God, I'm sick of this world.

A hundred and one out and it's a fifteen-minute walk to the

last night of the world for BJ's Carousel, all for this. "Get your BJ's now or never!" Corky shouts from the end of the bar for the fifth fucking time in the past hour.

He's shitfaced, but to be fair, so is everyone else. Ten sheets to the wind and the sun is just setting now on this great and glorious July night. Goddamn, I'll miss the place when it closes. Just goes to show, you can miss a headache if you have one long enough.

Known him thirty years and never had a problem with Corky. He's pocket-sized and harmless. Hell, to be honest, he's a good guy. I thought for sure AIDS would get him in the eighties, but for all the screwing he was doing, the little bastard was far too busy raising money to die. Spared by the gay gods for all his offerings to the drag alter. Shit, his Sophia Petrillo alone was enough to guarantee immortality if God even exists. Which He does, I'm sure, that sadistic patriarch.

Men, including God, are terrified you'll laugh at them. But bless those heathen queens, those boys sure aren't. They use laughter like a vaccine and use mean like a surgical knife and it's fucking good medicine for all of us. I laughed at Corky enough through the years to make up for a lot of the it's-just-a-joke white boys we choke down every day.

"Cheryl!" Corky's finally done staring at the boys. He gives a gay little wave and shouts over Martha Wash. Why are bars so fucking loud? Oh—right. So you can't hear yourself think. He sashays over, takes my hand, and does a little twirl. "You heard the lady! Everybody dance now!" He'd worshipped Wash since the Sylvester days and lost his goddamn mind when she came to Denver Pridefest. Pale little bitch even worked his way backstage at Civic Center Park for a picture. Don't know who he blew for that delight and I don't want to.

"Corky, you asshole." I wave my cigarette at him like a fly-swatter. I'll smoke if I damn well please. What are they going to do—shut down the place down? "You put on my song, we'll dance." Why the hell not? I'll dance with a nice boy any day and BJ's deserves a proper send-off.

"Why the hell not!" He sashays away. I don't know what he's going to have to do to the deejay, but again, I'd rather not know. Men have their own currency and shit am I glad to be fucking poor. Still, I'll miss this place. I will. Bob's owned it since day one, what, forty years ago? Through the good and the bad and the really bad, and he's done a lot for us. I respect that. I went to John's funeral with him in nineteen eighty-something when all the lovers were grieving. We all did, even Corky. It was Corky's last funeral, he couldn't take any more after that. AIDS was just hitting too many boys to keep up with, and I watched it kill even the ones who didn't die from it. I guess freedom comes at a price.

Well, fuck. Corky did it. ABBA starts up and four G-and-Ts in, I can't resist just one turn around the floor. The most action I've had in ten years at least. Jackie keeps promising to set me up, but God—I wouldn't be caught dead with most of the butches she messes around with. If I want to screw a man, I'll screw a man, thank you very much.

"You seeing anyone, Cheryl?" Corky looks up at me and winks. He knows I'm not, but he just loves to rub it in.

"Yeah, fucker—your mom."

I laugh, he laughs, and there we are—two dancing queens twirling on the deck of the *Titanic*.

"You and Jackie still on the outs?" he asks.

"In and out since nineteen ninety. But it's fine. Shit. She came around last night for dinner and had the gall to ask me if I'd made a will yet! I told her what she could do with my dead body. I don't give two fucks about any of the rest of it. She says she's done with me, but I don't believe it."

Jackie is too scared and too dumb to ever really leave me. And I don't have to tell you how that feels. ABBA stops and so does the fun. I shove through sweaty men to get back to my stool and of course some tanned, twinky otter has slipped onto it.

"Clear out, pretty boy." I reach over him to grab my drink and my Luckys and he smirks at me.

"Anything for you, beautiful." That smirk. That one the white boys use like a billboard advertising their fucking God-given right to make you eat shit.

"You goddamn asshole." I put my finger right in his face. "Just because your frat kicked you out for being a fag doesn't give you the right to talk to me that way. This is *my* bar. You think I'm going to let you talk to me that way in my bar?"

"It's nobody's bar anymore, bitch." He snickers and turns his shit-eating grin at his pretty friends to make sure they're all in on the joke.

"Now, honey." Corky flags the bartender and points at Goofus the pretty hairless boy wonder. "Let's just all be quiet and drink. Everyone gets a round on me. Same with you, Cheryl. Nobody's fighting tonight."

"Shit." I light a Lucky and sit on the warm stool. "Not enough gin in the world, Corky."

"No, there isn't. But we can pretend." His tiny blue eyes twinkle as he gazes over my shoulder around the bar. The man's been tossed into paddy wagons, watched half his friends die, fucked dozens of boys he doesn't love, become old and invisible to the community he's given everything to, and yet here he is, eyes twinkling. What an asshole.

"Just what did you tell Jackie she could do with your dead

body, Cheryl?" he asks, and there's that damn twinkle. What the fuck is so funny about death?

"Shove it up her ass. And just what's *your* plan, Corky?"

"I don't know what the good Lord's got in store for my body, but I know what I'm doing with my soul. Tonight. This is it."

"What?" I tilt my head.

He reaches into his shorts and holds up a small, clear bottle full of what could be vodka but certainly isn't. "Best shit you'll ever have. You want to come with me?"

"What? What the fuck are you talking about?" I set down my drink and take his out of his hand and set that down too. "Just what the fuck are you *talking* about?"

"This is it. Look around you, Cheryl." He waves a fey hand at the sea of silver-haired men milling around in tight leather and jeans, half of them bare-chested with man-tits starting to sag. Among them are peppered dark and blond heads trolling for free drinks or trading sex for the drug du jour. "This is the ghost of Christmas future showing us the way it's going to be, and honey, I'm not here for it. I have just loved this ride. Loved it even when I hated it. Loved it even when I got the clap from the love of my life. So tonight's my wake, baby. Could be yours too!" He shakes his drink at me and finishes it, flags for another.

"You selfish, cowardly son of a bitch."

He shrugs and pockets the vial. "Suit yourself. But I'm going out on a high."

Well, that fixes it for the night. How the hell am I supposed to properly send off BJ's when all I can think about is Corky's dead body—

"Hey, you little twit." I grab his arm before he can saunter off. "Where exactly are you going to carry out this ridiculous plan?"

"Center stage, baby, just like Ms. Wash. Civic Center Park. I'm leaving now and gracing every gay bar on Broadway with my presence on the way up. Last cocktail I'll ever have at eleven, a little more of this and that," he pats his pocket, "and I should be gone by the stroke of midnight. They say alcohol helps it along, so who knows. Sounds pretty good, doesn't it?" He winks at me again.

"Stop winking, asshole, and just let me think. Good God."

He doesn't wink, but he does grin. "You believe in God, Cheryl? I do. Haven't set foot in a Baptist church since nineteen seventy-five but Mama didn't raise me to blaspheme. I can't wait to meet my maker and party in heaven. Hell, I bet the drinks are free and the boys are clean!"

"You think your mama's waiting for you up there, just sitting on a damn cloud knitting a scarf? You're dumber than you look."

"I don't know about that. But don't you want to see Kathy again?"

"Now don't you dare bring her into this." Like I hadn't thought about Kathy the minute that man started talking about this nonsense. She'd been the only one I let stay with me, so she was the only woman who'd ever really left me, even if she didn't have a choice about it. Missing Kathy made me want to believe in Sky Daddy big time. I slapped my face before things got out of hand.

"That's just the thing though, isn't it?" he continues. "I miss them all, girl. I miss them all. But I miss who I used to be most of all."

Only a dumbass would argue with that. I thought about Kathy. Who she used to be, and the drunk khaki-coated Delta Tau Delta boy who ran her down, probably after he raped some girl. I thought about Jackie, whose husband beat her until she gave up men forever and stole part of her she's never gotten back.

Most of all, sitting on that barstool, I thought about Faven, who never even got a fucking chance to be who she really was in the first place. How she laughed and ran through the stacks all summer and then stopped in the autumn. I thought about all the broken women of the world and who I had been before I'd opened my eyes and given myself a front-row seat to their pain.

"Corky, I take it back. You're not a coward. You're an asshole and you're selfish, but you're sure as shit not a coward."

"Well, thank you, darlin'. It wasn't my place to ask you to do it too. I'm ready to go, just not alone. Hold an old man's hand one more time?"

He offers his limp wrist and what can I do. What can I do? I take it. Smash out my cig, finish my drink, and we sashay together through mourning revelers, out into the hot summer night just coming to life on Broadway.

JUNK FEED

BY MARK STEVENS

Glendale

Katy Cutler's neatly trimmed right eyebrow arched like the top curve on a question mark.

"When I imagine private investigators, I picture them on long stakeouts, sitting in their cars eating greasy sandwiches out of paper bags. So perhaps you never—"

"That's kind of a movie-type cliché." Wayne Furlong swallowed hard. He hoped she didn't press the question. "Trope, I guess. Never quite sure of the difference."

"The point is, we can't afford to let this linger," said Cutler. "The only ones who want to book a room in the hotel are the podcasters and amateur snoopers who treat murder cases like a ghoulish hobby. The wannabe investigators. The pseudo journalists. The sickos. Business is bad enough. The pandemic, of course, whipped our ass."

"And most restaurants."

Cutler, the general manager for the hotel and its embedded restaurant, shook her head in a sad combination of disgust and dismay. It had been two years since the pandemic put the economy on ice and one year since the return to "normal" began, albeit at a lethargic pace. "We started off even worse. Right before 2020, we got clobbered by a bad review. Vicious. And then all the others piled on too. Like jackals on a dead antelope."

"I'm more than willing to look into it, but—"

"But what?"

Cutler slumped against the leather of the high-backed booth inside Tang. The sensational murder had played out fourteen floors above, in the steel-and-glass obelisk hotel known as The Grange. Tang's brutal critique had been delivered by restaurant blogger Timothy Powers. For two decades, Powers had served as a scourge to fine dining establishments across Metro Denver, with the occasional whack at swank pompous eateries in mountain villages too. Powers was a nom de food. When the newspaper industry shrank like a boiled chicken, Powers agreed to a buyout and took up work as a PI with his given name, Wayne Furlong. But Timothy Powers never stopped writing restaurant reviews. It was his gift to the universe. One well-protected anonymous blog page. One Instagram account with 45,000 followers. To Furlong/Powers, saving the masses from overpriced and artless cuisine was as important as helping wives nail cheating husbands or, every now and then, assisting in a murder case.

In fact, Furlong/Powers at that moment was sitting in the same booth where he had dined during one of three visits he made to confirm the fact that Tang was tasteless.

"But I'm not terribly optimistic about finding something, given all the scrutiny to date." If Cutler had video surveillance of her austere dining room, as inviting as a Turkish prison, she could have spotted Furlong's sizable frame on repeat visits and noticed that he had sent main courses back on the first two occasions and quietly shoved the contents of meal number three into a paper bag for further postmortem of the crisis-level mélange back in his modest home kitchen. Except Cutler would have to see through a few disguises to spot the repeat customer. Thick glasses. A change of clothes. A hat. Etcetera.

"Glendale police," said Furlong. "They brought in Denver

police too. And the Colorado Bureau of Investigation. And all the reporters who—"

"Reporters." Cutler hissed it. She sat back up. "Leaches. Nosy fuckers."

"Well, I—"

"You can't really think a reporter can solve a crime like this, do you?"

"Not necessarily, but asking the right questions—"

"Oh, please," said Cutler. "That's like a mystery writer's wet dream."

At fifty-two, Katy Cutler was feisty. Furlong liked her edge. But, like the food at Tang, she was overly complex. Too many bracelets on one wrist, a tattoo of a fork on the other. Severely tweezed eyebrows. Chunky mascara. One thin gold necklace weighed down by a heart-shaped emerald stone that rested on her bony sternum and dared anyone to ponder the plunge in her neckline. When she had greeted him at first, the word *stork* popped into his head, given her height and angularity. She had a birdlike manner of shifting her head around, looking at him from different angles.

"Whether a reporter or a PI," said Furlong, "it seems to me that all the questions have been asked. Asked and answered, as the lawyers say. Someone is lying. Goes without saying, even though I just did."

Furlong caught a whiff of bleachy cleanser, not one of his favorite restaurant aromas. He glanced down at the white tablecloth and noticed a faint purple smear where a blueberry had once lost its life. Tang had just opened for lunch, yet an elderly couple in a booth across the way were turning to statues while waiting for a server to greet them. Not much had changed, despite the Powers savage review, which had been titled "Junk Feed: Tang Flat."

"Podcasts too," said Furlong. "One seven-part series already. I mean, going to the trouble of hiring actors."

"And another producer came sniffing around last week." Cutler shook her head, turned her mouth down in disgust, as if she had just had a bite of Tang's indigestible matelote, with its chewy eel. "We politely told them to take their microphone and go, well, interview themselves. Though *interview* might have been a different verb."

"Noted." Furlong smiled. "It's been seven or eight months of relative quiet in the media, especially once they got that first-year-anniversary story out of the way. Why now?"

"I want you to find the killer. That's all."

"What's your theory?"

"The only one that makes sense."

"The only one that makes sense," said Furlong, "except for the superb alibi?"

"That one," said Cutler. "Tyler Hyde. Golden boy. Ken Doll of the spreadsheets, I called him. Right? Nothing else makes sense, yet of course we are bound to look elsewhere. Right? If we want closure."

"Bit of an elusive concept," said Furlong. "Don't you think?"

Cutler gave it some thought. "Not so sure. This is a whole different animal."

This involved three facts that added juicy bits to the story. One, decapitation. Two, rugby. Three, that the murder happened in the enclave of Glendale—a hole the size of one M&M candy in the fat gooey donut of Denver. Glendale was home to 5,000 residents. Denver proper, 750,000. Metro Denver, an ever-burgeoning 2.8 million.

In the early 1950s, Glendale leaders had fought and won

the right to prevent being annexed by the expanding state capital. As a result, over the ensuing decades, Glendale ran with a special flair. Two strip clubs. When pot was legalized, they stayed open until midnight. Apartments galore. A singles-ish vibe. And self-proclaimed RugbyTown USA, given the fact that in the early 2000s, the city built a stadium and athletic facility devoted to the niche sport.

The city, more recently, had hired Billy Duncan as a marketing guru. His specialty was sponsorships, particularly naming rights for the stadium and corporate branding for athletic gear and stadium advertising. Duncan was murdered on his ninth extended stay at the fourteen-story Grange Hotel. He was in the process of moving from San Francisco but appeared to be in no rush to do so. Duncan's partying lifestyle seemed like a one-man campaign to keep the Glendale economy afloat. He was a frequent visitor at both strip clubs, had managed to bed several women from each of the two spots, spent piles of cash at restaurants all over the tiny burg, and developed a carousing lifestyle with a growing circle of male friends including a few rugby players who were also known for their partying ways, all of it well-documented on Instagram. Want to party? Find Billy Duncan. Bring money.

By day, however, he was a hard-nosed shark. He delivered professional and well-prepared reports in public and private meetings with the city. He did his job. City leadership was thrilled—and were equally entertained by his wild-side exploits.

Using software that searched for irregularities, Duncan found something fishy with city revenues. The stadium complex included an extensive event and conference center, with a variety of options for large and small occasions. It was also home to a sports center that drew hundreds of workout warriors every week to a gleaming gym and a smorgasbord of classes from Zumba to yoga to indoor cycling. Duncan, unsure of where the problem was located, or how high up the organizational chart, had quietly brought his evidence and suspicions to the district attorney for Arapahoe County, Glendale's governmental mother ship. Party boy by night, straight-arrow businessman by day.

The problems seemed to point to the person in charge of city finance, a man named Tyler Hyde. Single. Blond. Trim. And the opposite of Billy Duncan—a quiet bureaucrat. The allegations of financial irregularities, however, depended on an algorithm that analyzed actual income versus projected revenues. There were no hard facts. Then, Duncan's grisly demise. Yet on the night of the murder, Hyde was in a long meeting online and had the recording to prove it.

The upside of cracking the Billy Duncan case was obvious— helping solve a nasty murder and improving Wayne Furlong's reputation as a PI. The downside would mean giving Tang another chance to foist mediocre food on the masses. Sure, a murderer might go free. But how to balance one bloody night with years and years of overpriced, crummy grub?

"Katy Cutler thinks *what?*"

The head of hotel security for the Grange Hotel was Ed Bostrom, retired Glendale cop. Furlong found him in his inner sanctum of security camera monitors and a console of beeping electronics in a sweaty room behind the registration desk. Crew cut. Square head. Girth like salad wasn't a thing.

"Same case, same questions," said Furlong.

"So you want a guided tour?"

"I gather one needs an escort, so, yes."

Bostrom made a show out of studying the watch on his hairy wrist. "I guess I can spare eight minutes, and that includes riding the world's slowest elevator." He was right about that—the lethargic lift worked as if it were underpaid and underappreciated.

"This elevator?" said Furlong.

"Three shafts, three elevators," said Bostrom. "But he likely waited to be on this one—closest to the security camera in the hall on the penthouse level. Fourteenth floor. One step out and he whacks the camera with a heavy club or something and it spins around enough to give us a good steady shot of the wallpaper."

"And nothing useful from the brief second he steps out of the elevator."

"A hoodie and a neck gaiter took care of that," said Bostrom. "There's a nose you can see for point-three seconds in the video and they tried some facial recognition software, but really? One nose?"

"Nobody got on or off with him?"

"If they did, they don't remember. He can pull the gaiter up and the hoodie over at the last stop too, of course."

"Wasn't it unusual for Duncan to be in his hotel? At night?"

"No," said Bostrom. "His night of carousing had not yet begun."

"And man in hoodie is never seen again."

"No."

The Grange Hotel, a dark monolith on the east side of Colorado Boulevard, was built as a high-end joint. Rooms starting at $350. Suites starting at $850. Still, the space around the elevators was bland and generic.

Many of the newspaper stories had come with maps. And dotted lines. Elevator. Room. Stairs. Dumpster where head was found—three blocks away.

Furlong remained a step behind Bostrom. While Furlong had trimmed down from his top weight during the go-go foodie days at the newspaper, it was rare to feel outsized. Despite the plush hall carpeting, Bostrom plodded with a certain thunder.

"One bone saw?" said Furlong. "Not much to carry. Or hide."

"And something for a garrote," said Bostrom. "Coroner thinks garrote and then he cut right on that same line. Of course, the sawing eliminated evidence of the garrote. You know. Win-win, I suppose."

"Serious hatred," said Furlong.

Bostrom said nothing.

Unlocking the door to Duncan's suite, room 1400, required two of Bostrom's keys. The room was a sea of white. A wall of windows took in the panorama of the Colorado Front Range, all coated with a fresh blanket of white snow. At the forefront, Glendale looked like it had been dunked in crème anglaise.

"Jesus," said Furlong.

"Twelve-fifty a night," said Bostrom. "Cutler has talked about a remodel—turning this into three rooms or gutting it and putting in another restaurant."

The horror . . .

"She wanted to call this one Tin. Tin and Tang." Bostrom grimaced. "Get it?"

"Unfortunately." Furlong took in the sunken living room, a kitchen worthy of a modest mansion, and doors that opened to three separate bedrooms. "New?"

"New everything." Bostrom was making a circuit of the interior, as if to make sure nobody was hiding. "There was no passing the stains off as abstract designs." He stopped at the sound of muffled voices outside the door. "Jesus H."

Furlong shrugged a question.

Bostrom pulled the door open with a furious yank. In the hall, framed by the doorway, stood a small Asian woman wearing a giant set of black headphones. She held a thick fuzzy stick. The stick was pointed up at the mouth of a tallish slender man who, based on his pale pallor and nonfashion of chocolate corduroys and olive sweater, looked like he spent most of his time in a dark basement.

"Who the hell are you?" said Bostrom.

The Asian woman beamed. "You're Ed Bostrom—hi," she said. "Amy Ito with 'Criming America.'"

Furlong winced at the irresponsible verbification.

"The podcast?" said Ito. She shifted the microphone around so it practically tickled Bostrom's chin. "We tried to book an interview with you . . ."

Basement Boy looked wide-eyed, a bit terrified.

"Turn that fucking thing off," said Bostrom.

"I was interviewing Tim McAvoy here about his theory that the murder of Billy Duncan was a conspiracy," explained Ito. "That there had to be several people involved. Given, you know, all the things that had to go right to pull off such a messy murder, without someone seeing something. Up here."

"Get the fuck out—"

"We have probability experts who have analyzed the likelihood of a single individual being able to execute all the steps needed, and this is an individual who says—"

"If you don't head right back down to the elevators, I'm going to put my hands on both of you—"

"He said he saw one of them carrying a duffel bag and it appeared to be wet. Dripping."

Furlong smiled to himself. All the true crime podcasts had trained a national army of amateur murder investigators. On the one hand, it was a wonder that any crime went unsolved. On the other, the mushrooming breed of pseudo news promoted the idea that with every story there could be a cover-up, an alternate version of reality, or a secret cabal behind the scenes. In this world of dueling microphones, where every opinion was given equal weight, claims were treated like facts. Rumors were crossbred with gossip. Innuendo mated with supposition and produced an illegitimate baby of flapdoodle that only needed a few believers to keep it well fed and nourished until it could stand on its own two feet. And never die.

"And you're only coming forward now?" said Furlong to McAvoy.

"Well—I saw the article online about 'Criming America' recreating the whole investigation and—"

"And you thought you'd make some shit up to get famous." Bostrom grabbed the top of Ito's long gray sword of fake fourth estate. He squeezed the tip like a sponge. Ito's mouth dropped open in shock. Bostrom put his other hand on the bottom of the shaft and yanked. The microphone cord came free from the recorder that was strapped to Ito's chest like an explosive device.

"You will pay for any damages," said Ito.

Bostrom bent the microphone with two fists. "And you'll pay the fine for trespassing when I haul your nosy ass to court for coming up here where you fucking don't belong."

Outside, after escorting the still-complaining Ito to her Subaru, Bostrom lit a cigarette.

"She probably paid that shifty kid a few hundred bucks to make some shit up."

"The case of the dripping duffel," said Furlong, playing along.

* * *

One thing Furlong knew was to challenge every assumption, to come at it like a chef testing every ingredient, right down to the quality of the peppercorns. He treated himself to a roasted chicken banh mi at a hideaway joint on East Alameda. This was Furlong's third visit—a month between stops to verify consistent quality over time—and the Timothy Powers side of his brain started to stir at the first bite of the delectable sandwich. But something was off. The tender chunks of meat were slathered with a garlic sauce that nicely complemented the crunchy crisp cucumber and fresh blast of cilantro. Yet the pickled carrots and daikon, what should be the soulful center of flavor for each bite, was humdrum. There was no kick. No sparkle.

Furlong checked his notes, glanced at the pass-through serving hatch into the kitchen, and realized that a serene older Vietnamese chef from his last visit was missing. In his place, a young, roly-poly white guy who was studying his phone between orders. Furlong made his way to the restroom, always another point of information for Powers's reviews, and peeked in the kitchen.

"Where's Mai Pham?" he said.

The kid looked up. "Made him an offer he couldn't refuse." And laughed. On the counter stood a giant glass jar of pickled vegetables. The jar's label screamed its mass-produced provenance.

Furlong drove his Mini Cooper to Enterprise—his shared office space in the uber-hip RiNo neighborhood near downtown. The middling banh mi and the impostor ingredients had planted a seed.

Enterprise gave him a veneer of official status. Furlong was treated like a father figure by the start-up whiz-bang tattooed gang that came and went at all hours of the day and night. For this bunch, it was working on your future IPOs by day and guzzling IPAs by night. Furlong's age made him a quaint anachronism. His restaurant tips, however, were golden. He had suggestions for all taste buds and expense levels. He'd developed a few relationships with the tech-savvy youth, which had come in handy on more than one occasion.

"Gather is just like Zoom, right?" said Furlong.

"With a few differences—including the fact that the dashboard is a snap. Any grandma can figure it out. Zoom got complicated."

Brie Chambers was part of a team that was developing an app that had something to do with bitcoin. Furlong's head hurt just trying to understand the basic concept. Chambers had short blond hair streaked with bright tangerine. She had a generous sunbeam smile and a tall, athletic presence. Her graceful body was right at home in tight black jeans and a loose purple turtleneck. She sat next to Furlong on a bright-red couch in one of the many mini living rooms around Enterprise that were designed to encourage collaboration or relaxation or both. She sipped on steaming tea that smelled like already-smoked pipe tobacco and which she had explained was called Roy Boss, "but spelled r-o-o-i-b-o-s and is really good for bone health and digestion and comes from a South African bush." Furlong wondered about the power of marketing and storytelling to entice perfectly beautiful young people to ingest such odd products. Like grapefruit beer. Or marshmallow popcorn. And all such trends seemed to happen from coast to coast. Regionalism was dead. It was very possible Timothy Powers was working up a rant. Furlong squelched it—for now.

"What's going on?" she said.

"I've been asked to take another look at that case involving Billy Duncan—"

"What? Oh my god. Seriously? For real? My roommate is obsessed."

"Really?"

"She likes all those true crime podcasts, murder docs. Those network shows where they drag out a murder case for an hour. And—right—Gather was a thing in the Billy Duncan deal. What was his name?"

"Tyler Hyde."

"Yep," said Chambers. "Tyler Hyde. Always thought it sounded like trying to hide, but there he was, right in plain sight."

Furlong opened his vintage laptop. He pulled up the recording from Gather—seventeen men and women in a two-hour online meeting. He hit play.

"I remember I had just moved here from Bushwick and I thought, where the hell is Glendale, what the hell is Glendale?" said Chambers. "Also, where's the glen and where's the dale? Duncan's body—well, most of it—was found the day after I got here, so it was sort of a welcome-to-Colorado thing you don't easily forget."

"Some greeting," said Furlong.

"Creepy. So Tyler Hyde?"

"Was in this meeting when the murder happened," said Furlong, pointing to him. There were three rows of boxes—six frames in the top row, five in the middle, and another row of six. Hyde, head and shoulders only, sat in the middle of the group of five in the middle row. Dead center. He wore a plain green pullover and round brown horn-rimmed glasses. "The meeting started thirty minutes before the camera got whacked by the man in the hoodie when he stepped off the elevator."

"My roommate would probably say, *Are you sure it was a man?*"

"Agreed," said Furlong. "But the cases involving dismemberment by women are rare." He paused the recording.

"A proud talking point for your gender."

"So proud," said Furlong. "Anyway—"

"Tyler Hyde never left the meeting, right?"

"Right."

"He lived close enough, if I remember, but it was like he had the perfect alibi."

"Right."

"Remind me why Tyler Hyde was even a suspect, then?"

"Billy Duncan had brought Hyde's name to the DA. Duncan had spotted financial irregularities."

"Embezzlement?" said Chambers.

"It's unclear."

"And?"

"And Duncan's suspicions were never proven."

"Because Duncan was killed," said Chambers. "But Hyde could have been ticked off about the allegations."

"Sure."

Furlong hit play on the Gather recording again. A copy of the two-hour meeting had been sent to the DA's office the day after the murder. By email. Anonymously. It was as if the email provided instant inoculation for Hyde: *Don't bother coming after me.* Hyde was questioned by police. His entire demeanor was polite and cooperative, though he shunned any public statements. The recording of the snooze-a-thon meeting found its way onto YouTube for anyone to see.

"What was the meeting about again?"

"A nonprofit. Schools in Africa. He's on the board."

"Thief by day, do-gooder by night?" said Chambers.

"People are complicated," said Furlong.

"You watched the whole meeting?"

"Me? Yes. Had to. He's there for the duration. It was well-reported at the time."

"Well-reported?" said Chambers. "What exactly does that mean?"

"These days? I'm not so sure. Is there any way, you know, from a technical perspective, to rig this?"

"What do you mean, *rig?*"

"I'm looking for the simplest answer," said Furlong. "Maybe he's not really there?"

"He's participating," said Chambers. "I can see him."

"Yes, at the beginning he's in charge of the fundraising committee and he makes a big report."

"And it seems like real time?"

"I mean, he's taking questions. Yes."

"And then?"

"And then the meeting moves on to other business and he's—" He's what? Just sitting there? "Would it be possible to switch your Gather feed to a recorded video?"

Chambers thought about it. Shook her head like dawning realization. Said, "My roommate is gonna go nuts."

For three days, Furlong followed Tyler Hyde back and forth to work. It was a mere four blocks from his eight-story apartment building to the city offices, but Hyde drove his tiny Kia to work because at lunch he ran swift, efficient errands and grabbed a cheap bite. To go. He was usually back in his office within forty-five minutes. If anything, Hyde appeared to be upstanding. Purposeful. He walked with his shoulders up. He held doors for women. He drove with care. He kept to himself.

On the fourth morning, as Furlong began to think Hyde might not give him anything to work with, the man emerged from his office at ten thirty a.m. and drove to a bank just over the Glendale border in Denver. Hyde hustled from his car, stepping around puddles in the melting snow. At the bank entrance, he sprayed a glance around like a lawn sprinkler on crack. He rested his gaze for a second longer than necessary on Furlong's car. Furlong saw how Hyde's face might have looked during the crime. Sheer darkness. Furlong shuddered.

However Hyde reacted when he returned to his car, it didn't matter. Furlong could call the Arapahoe County DA and show them what he'd found. He could invite Katy Cutler to a restaurant—one with good food—and show her what he'd found. He could dial up Amy Ito and ask her if she'd like the truth—a dubious prospect—and show her what he'd found. He could drop Ed Bostrom an anonymous note and let him be the hero. But Furlong wanted this one. He wanted to watch Hyde sweat. Part of himself enjoyed watching false fronts fall. He shared that same trait with Timothy Powers.

Next, lunch at the second-fanciest hotel in Glendale. Hyde sat at the bar. He ordered a beer and a sandwich. Furlong watched from a table, letting a cup of coffee grow increasingly cold. On stakeout days, Furlong remained vigilant against liquids. Hyde ate quickly. He paid with cash from a wad of bills, and then walked across Cherry Creek Drive South, Cherry Creek North, and into Shotgun Willie's. Furlong gave Hyde a ten-minute head start and paid the thirty-dollar cover. Daylight outside, midnight inside. Furlong took a seat at a table, ordered a ten-dollar bottle of Coors Light from a seriously bored waitress.

Tyler Hyde had a ringside seat at one of the two six-sided dancing stages, each with its own 99.9 percent naked woman.

The club smelled like cotton candy and sweat. An invisible deejay cranked "You Shook Me All Night Long" as if the party was going full throttle. Furlong and Hyde were the only customers, but Hyde's attention was devoted to the dancer at his stage. She wasn't dancing. She squatted on her pink pearlized heels, and her arms were wrapped around her rubber-band knees. They were chatting. Hyde occasionally took bills from his wad and scattered them at the dancer's feet like confetti. She laughed. She listened. She smiled. She took off Hyde's glasses, cleaned them with the only tiny scrap of fabric she was wearing, and laughed some more. She gave him a quick kiss on the cheek. This wasn't about flesh. Or lust.

After Hyde's three-song conversation with the dancer, he stood up and left. Furlong waited two minutes, tossed a twenty-dollar bill on the stage for his dancer, and followed. Hyde walked back across Cherry Creek and returned to the office—a "lunch" of just under three hours. Furlong waited. At five thirty, full dark in late January, Hyde drove himself home.

Furlong went to the foyer holding an empty box wrapped in frilly red paper with a bouncy white bow—one of many such props in his trunk. When the first person arrived, a young woman, he said, "Surprise gift I'm supposed to leave at 802. Buzzer doesn't appear to be working." The woman punched in a code on a keypad. Studied him. Furlong shrugged. He followed her inside. He pressed the button on the elevator for the eighth floor and gave the woman the most reassuring smile in the world. The woman got off at the third floor. "Don't get me in trouble," she said.

The doors closed. Furlong opened his phone and pressed play on the voice recorder, put it in the outer pocket of his coat.

The third knock on Hyde's door finally brought a "Who is it?"

"Someone you want to talk to."

A long moment. "Answer the question."

"I have a proposition."

An even longer moment.

"I can call the cops."

"That would make my job easy."

The door opened. "Fuck," said Hyde, standing in the opening just big enough for his face. "You didn't sip your fuckin' beer one time."

Furlong barged his way in, let the heavy door slam behind him. He dropped his prop gift on a side table.

"What the fuck is that?" said Hyde.

"A ruse," replied Furlong. "I think you're familiar with the concept."

"Who the hell are you?"

Hyde backpedaled down a long hall to a small living room. On the far side, a nook kitchen. A sliding glass door led to a two-seater balcony. Hyde's drapes were open. A copy of the *Economist* lay facedown on an ottoman in front of a comfy brown leather chair. A cup of tea steamed on the side table. Something lemon, thank god, not rooibos.

"I've emailed the police." It was a lie. Furlong suddenly realized that it probably wouldn't have been a bad idea to bring an extra human along. In case Hyde panicked. "Copied your boss at City Hall. Top brass with the whole rugby team too. The newspaper too."

"About?"

Up close, Tyler Hyde was a portrait in perfection. He was old-school handsome. Good cheekbones, a perfect coif of thick blond hair. Blue eyes. A solid physique. There was

158 // Denver Noir

a model-level asymmetry to his face. He looked preppy and youthful.

"It was a slick little trick," said Furlong.

"What?"

"There was a moment on the feed when your image froze. What? Three seconds? And when you come back it looked so normal."

Hyde shook his head. "No."

"You appear to be taking notes. For what? Ninety more minutes? You appear to be engaged. It was kind of a gamble on your part, because what if you got asked a bunch of questions, right? Or even *one*? But you didn't. It was a big meeting."

"No," said Hyde. The word came out not like a denial of Furlong's assertions but as recognition that it was over. "I was right here."

Hyde moved to the kitchen, still backpedaling. Was there a bone saw hanging out with the knives? Something he might grab for a garrote?

"When your part is done, then comes that weird freeze thing and you come back on and it's a video of yourself. Pretending. I recognize the set." Furlong jerked a thumb at the brown leather chair. "That must have been hilarious to sit there and record. Ninety minutes of pretending? There you are. Sitting, listening, taking notes. Occasionally nodding your head."

"No." This time the word came out desperate.

"You probably had to record that at least a few days ahead of time. It couldn't be a last-minute thing, right? You needed a long evening meeting the same night Billy Duncan was in town. You needed to be ready."

"No," said Hyde.

"You could keep the look simple—you in a chair, right? Kind of a plain backdrop?"

Hyde looked confused. "What?"

"On the recording, your drapes are open. Sure, you re-corded at night to be careful. But there's enough of a reflec-tion from the apartment building across the way to see the lights in your glasses. It's not much, but it's there. In that first section? It's not there. No reflection. And if you're trying to tell me you used three seconds of your frozen image to open the drapes, well, that seems like a bit of coincidence and aw-fully hard to do in such little time."

"No," said Hyde.

"Was Billy Duncan right? About the money business? Some money was missing?"

"Nothing." Hyde slumped down on a white chair at a small side table off the kitchen. He looked defeated.

Maybe this would be easy.

"No? Nothing?"

"His algorithm." Hyde spat the word. "Was wrong. It wasn't about that." He shook his head. Stared through the table to the center of the earth. Steeled himself. "He thought I should be more social. He wanted to find me a girlfriend. He couldn't fucking believe." Air quotes. "That I didn't have Facebook, didn't have Twitter or Instagram. Wasn't on Tinder. That I chose to live quietly, that I did my job and went home. I am not some fucking piece of data."

"You killed him because—"

"He taunted me constantly at work. Whenever he was in town. I was like his fucking project. I reported it all to HR. It was harassment. I don't think they took it seriously. But he asked me out to dinner, said he wanted to apologize. Claimed he'd back off but only if I agreed to let loose for one night, do whatever he thought might be fun."

Hyde took a hard breath. He sat up straight. He gave Furlong that same glare from the bank door. That darkness. That flipped switch.

"He gets me in the strip club. We've had a couple of drinks. He's been taking photos all night—meals, cocktails. He's got an opinion about every single bite. Whatever. He's posting every freaking thing along the way. *Fabulous this* and *fantastic that*. I'm trying to play along, figuring it will be over soon. At the club, more drinks. He buys me a private dance in the back. Small room with one big red chair. We both go back there and he gets the dancer—"

"The one today?"

"Yeah."

"And he's taking pictures the whole time. Boobs in my face. He wants my tongue out. I'm being humiliated right and left. I want to crawl into a hole. I felt sick to my stomach."

"And?"

"And the taunting didn't stop. Now, he's got photos. Now, he says he can post them online to prove I'm party hearty." Air quotes. "His words."

"And you go back to see the dancer—"

"Marlena. Yes, once a month. To tell her that wasn't me that night. To tell her I'm a better person than—" Except Tyler Hyde spots the problem with trying to take the moral high ground about how he did or did not treat women when he'd put a garrote around Billy Duncan's neck and cut off his head. He put a hand to his eyes. Covered them. "Humiliated," he said. "Every bone in my body."

"So you took care of business."

Hyde stood. He nodded. He shrugged. He walked calmly to the sliding glass door. He gazed out. He tilted his head back. He opened the door and stepped onto the balcony.

Furlong felt the cool air rush in and wondered if Tyler

Hyde could let one whole day pass without thinking about what he had done, without wondering if he would ever get caught.

Furlong reached for his phone to turn off the recorder and dial Glendale PD. He watched, helpless, as Tyler Hyde climbed over the railing and dropped out of sight into the dark, dark night.

"Sort of right there in plain sight," said Katy Cutler. Same booth as the first meeting. She slid an envelope across the table.

"Sort of."

"That's what I call closure."

"In a way," said Furlong, thinking of the fresh terror for those who heard Hyde's body slam into the cold hard ground. Who went to investigate. Who saw what eight floors of free fall will do to flesh. And bone.

"And now all the chittering, blathering types can move on down the road. Find another case to muck around with."

"But maybe if there had been no endless stirring of the pot, you might not have called me." Furlong had given it all some thought. "And Tyler Hyde would have lived to be an old man."

"So you're saying these leeches . . . did some good?"

A server arrived with a small plate.

Furlong studied the morsel. A red goo, flecked with shards of pink, sat atop one slice of cucumber. The substance reminded him much too much of what he'd found when Hyde splattered. Furlong's appetite withered.

"Amuse-bouche," said Cutler. "Avocado and chili sauce aioli with roasted black tiger shrimp."

Out of politeness, taking one for the team, Furlong put

the tidbit in his mouth. The shrimp were afterthoughts in the sea of garlic. The cucumber failed to crunch. The spice was lost.

"Interesting," said Furlong. The remnants of sauce left a weird texture in his mouth. "Believe me when I say I'm no expert. Now I'm the amateur lobbing in unsolicited opinions. But something's not quite right. I'd look at everything. Every element. You know, ingredient. You might think something is there—but really, it's not."

NORTHSIDE NOCTURNE

BY MANUEL RAMOS

Northside

I didn't give it a second thought when the young white man was shot outside Gaetano's at Tejon and Thirty-eighth. Way I saw it, that wasn't news. People been shot in the Northside for years, didn't matter that the Chicano barrio was quickly turning into something else, something whiter, something with more money.

I figured the dead guy was new to the neighborhood, part of what Petey, my cousin who went to college, said was gentrification, and that he'd crossed the wrong homeboy. Most of the time I didn't understand Petey and this was one of those times. All I knew was that the Northside was changing, and white people were buying up houses, tearing them down, and building two or three ugly boxes on lots where gente like my Aunt Julia had lived in one house for fifty years and more, and where she'd raised five children, four cats, and about a dozen parakeets.

Some of us natives stayed, we weren't totally gone, but no denying it was different. For years, brown had outnumbered white on the Northside, but now raza was back to being a minority. I didn't recognize the old hood, and I felt like a stranger in my hometown.

Change ain't never easy, conflict and drama and that kind of bullshit, and even I'd tangled with a couple of the newcomers stepping out of one of the remodeled breweries after last call over on Thirty-second. The drunks were loud and rude and belligerent, and it looked like it was chingasos time until Petey stepped in, risking his pretty face, and calmed down me and the two bearded jerks.

The guy who crashed through Gaetano's plate-glass window must've tried too hard to win the argument, and without Petey's negotiation skills in play, it wasn't hard to imagine that the situation spiraled out of control until someone said, *Hell with it*, and concluded that only a bullet through the throat could end the conversation.

Like I mentioned, I didn't give it much thought. I'd learned long ago to mind my own fucking business. Not that I wanted to intrude. Not my style. Not anything I needed. I didn't mingle with young white boys or old-school bangers with guns. But when a second young white guy was shot a week later, this time coming out of Chubby's with a beef-and-bean special in his hand, I admit it gave me pause. It looked like someone had declared war on gentrification, and odds were that I knew that someone. I'd probably gone to Horace Mann Middle School with the dude, and if he hadn't dropped out or checked into juvie or knocked up some shorty and was hiding out from her old man, we might've sat in the same row of desks in Mrs. Calabrese's history class at North High.

The second shooting caught everyone's attention. "The Denver Shooter" became the hot topic at family dinners or when we watched the Broncos games. Old friends I ran into had wild opinions and speculations about the killer, and radio talk show hosts spewed even wilder conspiracy theories meant to explain the shooter. I never brought up any of my own ideas. My thinking got as far as a crazy dude with a gun, which, in my experience, was all anyone really needed to know.

TV news reporters flocked to the area, where they waited

to interview people coming out of bars and restaurants in what they called the Highlands and LoHi—what we called the Northside. I heard one of the reporters talk about rising tensions, community town halls, and city council debates, and then ask a smiling couple pushing a baby carriage if they felt safe walking the streets of their new hometown. They kind of giggled and shuffled their feet and then they said, "Of course"—what else could they say, right? No way they wanted their mama and papa back in Chicago or their friends in Boston to think they'd made a mistake moving to a million-dollar house in Denver. So, hell no, they weren't afraid.

They were lying, obviously. Shit, there'd been plenty of nights in the past when I felt anything but safe on the Northside streets, and I was born here. Downright vulnerable, truth be told. Looking over my shoulder, checking out everyone cruising. And that was way before any so-called gentrification. On the other hand, I wasn't all that uptight about what was going down. After all, I didn't fit the victim profile, right? Know what I'm saying?

I asked Petey about the shootings one Saturday afternoon when we were stretched out at his house, drinking beer, snacking on Taco Bell nachos and conchas from Panadería Rosales.

"It's crazy, no doubt," he said. "Could develop into a mini race war if one of the hipsters returns fire, or just shoots the first Mexican he runs into, because he's lost his cool, his mindfulness, like they say. Everyone thinks the shooter must be a Latino."

"Always that way. That's what I think, truth be told."

Petey smiled in that way he had that made me nervous. "And you got no real reason for thinking that, right?"

I squirmed in my seat. Sometimes talking with Petey was complicated. I hadn't learned how to outargue him, and he'd been in debate mode since the second grade. "I'm just saying that odds are that the shooter's someone you and I probably know. That's all."

"Yeah, I get it," he said. "Nothing changes. But what's worse is that it's stirred up the cops." Petey talked between mouthfuls of beer and soggy tortilla chips. "That always means trouble for everyone but the troublemakers."

"That can't be good. There's more patrols around here, for sure."

Petey nodded. "Two skinny white boys get pegged and the blue army invades. Used to be that a Mexican kid was getting shot every other day and there wasn't a cop anywhere within five miles of the Northside."

"Yeah, like when the Inca Boys and the Northside Mafia were gunning for each other. Shit, I was in La Raza Park the night they lit it up with automatics and shotguns. I hid under a park bench like a punk. Not a cop in sight until the shooting stopped and Dogface had cashed out."

"And Pony Boy ended up in a wheelchair." Petey paused. Pony Boy had been his best friend when they were kids. He hadn't seen him in years.

"Ah, the good old days," I said, like a wiseass.

"Shit. You crazy, man."

The third shooting went down in the Locavore market parking lot. Weird to say, but that guy was lucky. He lived. He was carrying a bag of organic groceries and Colorado wine to his Subaru when a bullet opened up a stream of blood from his hip and he dropped to the asphalt like a brick tossed off a roof. Wine and bread and apples and cheese scattered around the bleeding man. No one saw the shooter, but the rep for the cops told the ten o'clock news that the bullet must've come from a passing car. Strictly a guess, since no one saw nothing. Or maybe the cops knew something they weren't revealing. As usual.

The Northside got a little tense after that.

Two days after the third shooting, Petey and I sat on the cracked steps of the porch of my mother's house, enjoying the view of four demolished or almost-demolished homes that were surrounded by orange construction net fences and massive dumpsters overloaded with junk and probably asbestos. My mother had so far resisted the tidal wave of offers for the old house, and when I asked her why she didn't take the money and move, she looked at me with her one good eye, shook her head, and simply said, "Where the hell we gonna go, mi'jo?" I didn't have an answer. Still, the money sounded good to me.

I asked Petey what he thought about the drive-by theory. "That make sense to you?"

"Maybe," he said. "But that means there's at least two people involved."

"The driver and the shooter."

"Yeah. Which could happen. But these types of shooters usually act alone. They don't trust other people, obviously. But it might be a pair of locos. There's always exceptions to rules."

"How can it be that no one's seen anything? It's like ghosts are taking pot shots at anyone foolish enough to go out on the street. Nobody sees nothing."

"Damn good question," Petey said, but he didn't have a clue.

I didn't see Petey for a few days. I had to take care of a bunch of stuff for my mom—pay bills, pick up prescriptions, clean up the storage shed—and Petey was kept busy at work. He had a good job with a printing company downtown, but occasionally he'd work late into the night because of a big order or a rush job. He was trying to save money. He'd decided he should finally marry Christina, so he was putting in as many hours as he could.

I was between gigs myself, and I couldn't earn a little extra cash making deliveries for my Uncle Orly anymore, but that's another story. He wouldn't be back on the streets for at least three years, with good behavior.

When I handed Mom her high blood pressure pills, she just kind of sighed. She stuck the bottles on the shelf over the kitchen sink and sighed again.

"What's wrong, Ma?" Something was bothering her, and I knew she would never simply tell me. I always had to dig it out of her.

"Oh, Eddie. Nothing. Nothing for you to worry about. No te preocupes. No es nada."

Shit. Speaking Spanish was another bad sign. "Come on. Don't be that way. What's wrong?"

"Nothing new. Same as always. These damn drugs and the electricity, and now we're gonna have to fix the car. And the house taxes. How are we paying the taxes? They're twice as much as last year. It's always something."

"Money. You're talking about money and how we don't have much."

"We never have." She took in a deep breath, and then she tried to smile. "But we always seem to make it through, don't we? It'll be okay. Just feeling sorry for myself."

Well, that made me feel like crap. "I'll go talk to Jake and ask him to put me back on his crew. That was a good job, while it lasted. Outdoors, exercise. He's getting busy again now that winter's almost over. He told me to look him up when landscaping season came back. I can do that. Jake paid good, remember?"

She nodded. "And you almost killed yourself. Your asthma acted up, that's what I remember. I had to take you to the clinic. That's what I remember. We're still paying on that bill. You can't do that kind of work. You could've died. That's what I remember."

"It was just allergies, Ma. I'll get something for that. I'll be okay. Don't worry. I got this." Not really, but I had to step up.

She picked up a card from the counter.

"I'm going to call this guy who says he buys ugly houses. What do we want to stay here for anyways? I've been thinking. You're right, the money is good. That one guy said he'd pay three hundred thousand for the house, as is. We could be out of here by the end of the month."

That shocked me. She had to be very worried to consider selling. "You don't want to do that. You should get another bid. And like you always say, where we gonna go? Whatever money you get will just go for another house, a more expensive house, with more bills and expenses."

I realized I was contradicting everything I'd been telling my mother for more than a year, but I knew selling the house would break her heart. She got married in that house, took care of my dying father in that house. I had to get a job. It was as simple as that.

"And anyhow, it's not a good time to sell," I said.

"How can that be? Look around here. Everyone's selling, moving out. Even Maggie's gone." I knew how much Mom missed Maggie, who'd sold her house last year after living across the street for decades.

"Petey told me the market took a hit because of the shootings. All the developers have reduced the prices they're willing to pay for houses on the Northside. Petey said people should wait until the shooter gets caught, then the higher prices will come back."

"Petey don't know everything, mi'jo."

I let it go. I had to give her time and space. I doubted she would follow through on her threat to sell. At least, not right away. She had a habit of getting down whenever the bills were due. That's the American way. Riding high in April, shot down in May. Or so went the song.

When I hooked up with Petey again, and I told him what my mother said, he shook his head and tried to explain how selling was a bad idea. "The developers like to say that the Northside is a neighborhood in transition. Which means there's still a few Mexicans left, like you and my tía. And *in transition* means smaller offers, especially when you add the shootings and killings. If your mother can wait, eventually she'll get a lot more for the house."

"She don't want to wait. She got it in her head that three hundred Gs is like the magic solution to our money problems, and that's all she's seeing."

"It will be twice that in another few months. I wouldn't be surprised if the shooter is a real estate agent trying to drive down prices so he can buy cheap and then sell high after the shootings stop." He laughed to himself the way he always did when he told what he thought was a joke, but I often didn't think he was funny. This was one of those times.

"This is serious, Petey."

"Patience, man."

"Not something my mother is famous for. And I gotta say, I'm getting tired of dealing with the same old shit every month. It's been like this ever since Dad died. A move might do us some good. Or it might be a big mistake. Who the hell knows?"

My outlook had turned dark, and I felt tired and useless. Maybe it was the shootings, maybe it was dealing with my sorry-ass situation. I wasn't much use to anyone, particularly my mother.

That's when the signs began to show up. They were cheap-looking notices that were probably made on a home printer and then copied like a hundred times. I saw them all over the Northside on dumpsters, utility poles, fences, buildings. Each one said the same thing: *WARNING—DANGER! White people are being shot in the Highlands! Protect yourself! If you see something, say something!*

The signs didn't specifically say, *Watch out for Mexicans, they're shooting white people*, but they came close.

When I showed my mother one of the signs, she almost cried. She slumped in her chair and shook her head.

"I'm calling that agent. We're moving, Eddie. The Northside is gone, and I don't want to live here anymore."

We talked for an hour about selling the house and moving, and the bills that seemed to get bigger each month, and how her medicines didn't work as well as they used to, and about a dozen other things that worried her and made me more anxious and uptight. We talked about the problems, but we didn't have any solutions.

I left the house that evening not sure what I should do. I wanted to help my mother. Real help required money, and I didn't have any. I walked to the park to clear my head, but everywhere I went I saw those goddamn signs. I ripped one off the side of a liquor store, threw it away, and saw a dozen more plastered on the walls. I ripped off as many of those that

I could reach, then I ran to the corner and tore up another half dozen that were taped to the bus bench and the traffic light pole.

All along Thirty-eighth, the signs mocked me. I stood on the corner and stared up and down the street. I thought there were hundreds of those things, maybe thousands, stuck on trees, buildings, whatever. I started to shake, and my throat felt dry, brittle.

"What the hell?" I whispered to myself.

I decided I needed a drink. I turned in the direction of the Black Bear Brewery, the closest bar I could think of. Not my usual place but I was in no condition to be choosy.

A lonely jazz riff from a sad guitar floated above the street.

I kept walking at a fast pace and tried to ignore the signs that surrounded me on the street. I thought about bills, medicines, taxes, car repair, my mother's tear-stained face. I replayed what Petey said about change and selling houses. I tried to convince myself that I could work for Jake again, fuck the asthma. The more I thought about all the shit, the darker my mood tumbled.

I caressed the pistol I'd jammed into the pocket of my coat before I left the house. It was my father's. I'd lifted it from the kitchen drawer where my mother kept it, loaded, "just in case," she would say when I'd point out the danger of a loaded gun. I couldn't explain why I took the gun. I just knew I had to have it with me. Maybe it had something to do with the shootings.

I walked past a small shop where a light glowed from the back. The light shined on someone sitting in front of a computer screen. The sign over the doorway said, *Magnificent Properties, LLC—Donald Bunton, Licensed Realtor.* Several photographs of homes and condos were taped to the plate-glass window. There was also one of the damn signs in the window, although it was twice as big as the signs stuck around the neighborhood, and in better shape. I guessed that it was the original.

I hurried to the alley and looked for the back of the agent's shop. I didn't have a clear-cut plan. I moved without thinking. I finally knew what I had to do, and that was enough. I pulled out the gun and walked in the semidarkness of the alley. I was about to look in the back window of the shop when I heard someone behind me. I twisted around and pointed the gun.

Petey jumped and put up his hands. "Whoa, buddy. It's me, Petey. Take it easy, Eddie."

"What the fuck? I could've shot your fucking head off. Jesus!"

"Your mother called me. She's worried because you took the gun. I've been looking for you. I followed your trail of ripped-up signs, then I saw you turn into the alley. I was across the street. What the fuck are you doing?"

"Never mind about that. You better get out of here. I got business to take care of. Go on! Beat it!"

Petey slowly walked up to me, his hands still raised. "I'm not going anywhere, not until you give me that gun. You know that."

Petey's face was lit up from a streetlight, like he was the star of the show. I always thought that he looked like my mother, which wasn't weird since his mother, Aunt Julia, was my mother's sister. My aunt and my cousin were pretty, even beautiful. Petey and Christina were a good-looking couple. They'd have beautiful children. I saw that and more in Petey's face, and I knew I had to give him the gun.

"Here, keep the damn thing. I doubt it even works."

He took it from my shaking hands. "Let's go home, Eddie," he said, almost whispering. "We'll figure something out. I can help. Your mom's gonna wait to sell. She said to tell you, so you wouldn't worry."

"I—"

Headlights blinded me before I could finish. A car roared into the alley, and like a creature of habit, I backed away, my hands raised to the sky. The patrol car screeched to a stop only a few feet from Petey and me. Red, white, and blue lights flashed, and a pair of cops jumped out of the car.

"Drop to the ground! Show your hands, now!"

Petey turned to the cops. I knew what he was doing. He had to explain everything, ease the situation, calm everyone down.

"Don't—" I started to say.

"Gun! He's got a gun!"

The cops fired their weapons and I fell against a wall. Petey spun around once, twice, dropped to his knees, then to his back. Blood started to flow as soon as he collapsed. I crawled on my hands and knees to Petey but one of the cops jumped me and held me down and all I could see was the starless night sky and a thin sliver of yellow moon. The only sounds I heard were the guitar music and Petey's hard, heavy breathing.

After that night, the night Petey died, the shootings stopped. The story on the Northside was that Petey had been the Denver Shooter. I knew that was wrong, but I never corrected anyone who told that story. Some things never change.

PART III

Things to Do in Denver When You're Young

WAYS OF ESCAPE

BY Barbara Nickless

Union Station

The dogs heard me coming before I could see them in the dark. Rex and Terror, my dad's hunting dogs, a pair of black Labs. He'd raised them from pups, loved them like children; they were the only creatures around here he never hit.

The Labs roused themselves in the dog run and shook off the night's chill—the sound of their feet padding on concrete guided me as I edged my way forward. I was moving from memory so I wouldn't need a light. Fifteen steps from my window to the dog run with a slight angle west to reach the gate.

My fingers clasped the latch and lifted it. My heart was thunder in my chest, banging out, *Run, run, run!* But I eased through the gate and patted the dogs' rough fur, felt their noses warm and moist in my cupped hands. I fed them from the bag in the shed and knelt to whisper into their ears how much I'd miss them.

I'd thought about taking Terror with me. He was younger than Rex. Tougher. But if I took my dad's dog, then he'd sure as hell come after me.

When I let myself out of the run, the dogs crowded after me, whining as I closed the gate. I wondered if they would miss me. I wondered if I'd see them again.

Seventeen steps to the side of the house. I was halfway there when the world turned a velvety gray, the stars morphing from diamonds to pearls. The house and the fence and the trees took form like a fade-in on a movie screen.

I picked up my pace. But as I cut around the side of the house and jogged past the porch, Mom called out softly, "Persephone."

My name in her mouth was as soft as the rustle of silk. But it might as well have been a fist.

I stopped.

"Mom." I hung my head so that my hair covered my face. I hadn't wanted her to know I was leaving until I was long gone. So that *he* couldn't ask her about it. So that she wouldn't have to lie.

More than anything, I was afraid she'd ask me to stay. Because if she asked, I would. Which meant I'd never get either of us away from here. I'd disappear into the chaos of our home like wood surrendering to flame.

But Mom said, "I'm glad you're going, Seph. Truly."

I raised my head. She was on her feet on the porch, a white blanket around her shoulders. She hadn't turned on any lights; all I could see in the spreading dawn was the swollen left side of her face, the mark of his hand still on her cheek. Last night, Dad's rage had been a cyclone.

My eyes burned. "It's not for long, Mom. Six months tops. I'll have enough money saved by then. I'll come back for you and we'll—"

"Stop." Her gait had a sideways hitch as she hobbled to the top of the stairs. "Just promise me you'll take care."

"I will." The knife's leather sheath pressed hard against my ankle.

"You know how much I love you, right?"

"I know."

"Don't forget it. Now go. I'm just going to stand here and watch my last child walk away."

"Six months," I said again. Then I turned my back on the house and her and once I was walking, I walked fast, staying in the weeds and out of the gravel on the long lane that led to the road, avoiding even that small sound. I turned back once, but though the world was brighter, the ranch house was nothing but angled darkness.

Mom was a mere patch of white.

My plan was to catch a westbound freight across the Colorado plains to Denver's Union Station. Dad might tear apart our town looking for me. He might talk to the sheriff, get him to issue an APB.

But he'd never think to look for me on a freight train.

Union Station was my lodestar.

I walked for an hour in the warmth of the climbing sun. When I reached the rail yard fence, I turned back to take a last look at the faded homes, the broken asphalt, the row of businesses with their empty storefronts and dusty windows, the derelict slaughterhouse. I breathed in sunbaked earth and animal dung and a flat, fetid scent Mom called the reek of despair.

I gave the town the finger then slipped through the hole in the fence that I'd found two weeks earlier. The gap was hidden behind an old cottonwood tree and the boards all around were bright with graffiti. I wondered how many kids had used this opening to slip into the yard and catch out on their dreams, most likely headed to Denver, same as I was.

Two trains sat idle in the yard, just as I'd expected. I'd done my research—I'd memorized schedules and numbers. Not for nothing was I known as a nerd. I hunkered down next to a shed until I was sure the coast was clear. It would have been better to go at night when I couldn't be spotted. But Dad didn't let me sleep anywhere except my own bed. He would have known right away that I'd run.

When I was sure the coast was clear, I hurried along the westbound coal train, looking for an empty boxcar—the five-star hotel of rail riding. But I had to make do with a coal hopper. I clambered up the ladder and settled on the metal platform. It was spacious. The overhang of the car would give me some shelter and, as long as I lay flat, the steel skirting provided cover from any railway police.

My biggest fear was that once Dad realized I'd run, he'd hire Mark Endcott. The first time my dad hit my mom hard enough to break something, it was Endcott who showed up at our door after I called 911. My mom told him she'd tripped, and he'd told her she should be more careful.

He'd known damn well what had happened. No doubt he'd had a good laugh with my dad about it later. *Can't let 'em get uppity*, he'd probably said.

Endcott left the sheriff's office a few years back and opened a private practice. He spied on cheating spouses and roughed up anyone who bounced a check or couldn't pay their tab at the Dirty Saddle. He also hunted down runaways. A lot of kids took a good hard look at their parents' lives—the debts, the violence, the alcohol—and decided they weren't sticking around to see how things turned out. After hanging out his shingle, Endcott found nine of those kids and hauled them back. When he dropped them off with their parents, they were all sporting bruises.

The coal hopper gave a hard jerk. The floor of the platform vibrated. Metal shrieked up and down the line.

I broke into a sudden, terrified sweat. For a moment I was so scared that I almost jumped clear of the train with the thought that I could get home before Dad even knew I'd been gone.

"Stronger every day," I whispered to myself. It had been my mantra since I was thirteen.

Surely some of it had stuck.

I crawled to the edge and watched as the train picked up speed, the floor humming beneath my hands and knees. Minutes later, we were out of the yard and rolling past yellow-gold grassland. Hereford cattle grazed in the distance. Clouds swept over the sun and the sky turned gray, heavy with the hope of rain. I unlashed my tarp from the frame of my backpack and used the pack to hold it down until I needed it.

Then I leaned out. The wind slapped my face and made a flag of my long hair.

"You can go to hell, Dad!" I screamed. "I'm free!"

A few hours into the day, the clouds began to spit rain. I'd unrolled my sleeping bag as far as possible from the deadly gap between the cars, and now I crawled inside and drew the tarp over. I pulled out the only postcard my brother Russ had sent after he'd run away; he'd mailed it to a friend with orders to pass it along in secret. It was a photograph of Union Station. On the back he'd written, *Made it! Job hunting. I'll be back for you both!!! Much love, Russ.*

He never came back.

I tucked the postcard away and propped my chin on my folded arms.

I knew that when I got to Union Station, I'd feel like I was walking into Nirvana. Already I had soaked up every available fact about the place. It was located in Denver's historic LoDo district; it was supposed to be one of the most beautiful stations in the country; it had been around since 1858 and was listed in the National Register of Historic Places; it was the only station in the country that provided bus, light rail, and passenger train service. The immense neon sign, *Travel by Train*, that hung over the entrance was both a recommendation and an homage to a bygone era.

I rolled onto my back, stared at the dull light filtering through the tarp. The rain carried the sharp-edged stink of coal, which was a thousand times better than the stench of manure.

As soon as I got to the station, I'd take a self-guided tour. Visit all the shops. Eat at the Cooper Lounge on the mezzanine overlooking the Great Hall. Buy a book at the Tattered Cover bookstore. Soak it all in before I made use of the monthly bus pass I'd purchased online long ago, when I'd first decided to run. I'd use the pass to get to the apartment of a friend of a friend where I was going to couch surf, then use it to get around Denver while I looked for work. I'd be seventeen in another two days. Maybe I'd find a job in one of the fancy restaurants in LoDo. Maybe I'd get really lucky and nail a position at the Tattered Cover.

Most importantly, I'd stand where my brother had once stood. And my mother before him.

I pulled out my journal and made a sketch of Russ standing under the *Travel by Train* sign. My pen skittered across the page with the jittery motion of the train.

I wondered what the kids at school would think if they could see me. Persephone the nerd. The bookworm. A literary dork making her own Huck Finn journey on a river of steel.

I knew what else they called me. The dweeb with T&A. After I turned thirteen, my body betrayed me by taking on the hourglass curves of my mother. Boys who'd been my friends started to look at me with a hunger I didn't understand. I don't think they understood, either. They were stumbling blind, driven by an instinct that told them I was something they should own. By high school they'd learned what their hunger was about. And I'd learned to wear loose clothes and walk with my arms crossed over my chest. And to never drink at parties.

Dad had begun giving me the evil eye every time I left the house. He never laid a finger on me. Not in that way. But sometimes I caught the same hunger in his eyes.

After a time I set aside my journal and lay down, using my sweatshirt as a pillow. I fell asleep to the iron lullaby of the train, a long, slow song punctuated by a concussive wind slapping the plastic tarp.

My mother was a classical pianist, and years ago she played at a lot of venues in Denver. Twice she toured in Chicago. If you look up her name on YouTube, you'll find clips of her performances. She fell in love with my dad when he was a violinist with the Colorado Symphony. That was before he lost three fingers clearing debris from a lawn mower. Long before he decided they should move to eastern Colorado and try ranching. Three months after they moved, Mom had Russ. A year after that I came along. Dad got himself elected city manager and—the way he told it—got back some of his self-respect.

Disappointment turns some men mean, and by the time Russ was in middle school, Dad was a tyrant. Mom said that a man who'd played Vivaldi the way he once had still owned his soul. But Russ and I knew the truth. Dad must have dug down deep to find the kind of cruel he carried. He wasn't coming back from that.

After I was born, Dad said Mom shouldn't travel and leave her family. And besides, a city manager's wife needed to be visible in the community. She stopped touring and took up the church organ. Everyone agreed that she was the best organist they'd ever had at First Faith.

Throughout my childhood and early teens, my brother Russ was my best friend. He looked after me, teased me, shared his cigarettes and books. Took our dad's punishment for both of us. Then, when he turned sixteen, he left town. Dad notified the National Center for Missing and Exploited Children. He had Russ's name posted in all the places you post those things.

But after that postcard I figured he was probably dead. If he was alive, he would have come back for us, like he'd promised.

After Russ left, Mom sold her piano. She stopped playing the organ as much. And after Dad broke her hand last year in some weird echo of his own loss, she didn't play at all, not even when the cast came off. Now and again I'd come home from school and surprise her listening to Bach or Schubert on the classical music station. But whenever she saw me, she'd snap off the radio.

One time I asked her why she'd stopped playing. She sat down at the table and said, "Sometimes we start off with the wrong dream, that's all."

"Your dream wasn't wrong," I told her.

But she just shrugged and lit a cigarette. "Your dad won't stay like this."

"Mom." I dropped my backpack and put my arms around her. "We should leave."

Her eyes darted to the door and she dropped her voice to a whisper. "There's no escape, Seph. Not from a man like your father."

Dimitria Argos used to be beautiful. Lush and earthy, the kind of woman who would have caught Zeus's attention if the myths were real.

Dad was no Zeus, but he'd changed her life forever.

* * *

I woke to the shriek of metal as the train slowed and slack rippled down the line, jerking each car like a terrier shaking a rat. I braced myself as the ripple reached my car and rocked it violently before continuing on down the line.

A short time later, the train stopped.

It was late in the day. I rose to my knees and fumbled in the twilight for my flashlight. I tucked it into a side pocket of my backpack so that the beam shone upward, bouncing off the metal sides of the car, then dug for the cheese and crackers and grapes I'd brought. I made up a plate for myself and perched on my knees so that I could see over the skirting.

It was near dark; the horizon glowed red, as if volcanoes were erupting just beyond the curve of the earth. Darkened farmland stretched like wall-to-wall carpet, with hills rising in shadowy humps in the distance. Beyond them, the Rocky Mountains rose blackly, stars mere pinpricks in the gloaming.

The mountains meant we were close to Denver. That frontier city turned millennial haven, with the most beautiful sunsets in the world, according to my mom.

I leaned out. Nothing but train in either direction.

And, a short way down the line, a small light that bobbed and weaved along the tracks.

I ducked back and switched off the flashlight. My heart took off at a gallop that made my stomach heave. I pressed myself to the floor of the platform.

Was it possible? Had someone spotted me getting on the train and called the sheriff? Could my dad have ordered the train to stop?

I cried out when, from the east, there came a roar and another train shot past. An intermodal with right of way.

"Hey!" called a man, after the noise of the passing train subsided. "I saw your light."

I clenched my fists and hunkered down, squeezing my eyes shut like a child. Anyone will tell you, I'm timid. Like a mouse. Keep your head down, get good grades, don't do anything stupid—my refrain of survival.

Beneath me, the platform shuddered as feet hit the ladder.

"Hey!" the guy shouted again.

The intermodal was now far in the distance, carrying its voice with it. The night fell silent. Then footsteps rang out on the platform.

"Why, hello," said the man.

I unscrewed my eyes and looked up.

He was a silhouette cut out of fire. I couldn't make out any detail—not his age nor the color of his clothes. He was just a man-shaped hole against the sunset.

But I could smell him. Grease and smoke and rusted iron.

He crouched next to me and held up his light. I studied him while he looked me over. He had blond dreads and eyes the color of topaz. He wore a pair of jeans and heavy boots and an old rain jacket. He eased back the hood. He was actually kind of cute, and maybe not too much older than me.

He grinned. "I saw your light. Thought you'd want company."

"I don't," I said stiffly. Relieved he wasn't my dad. Terrified as to who he might be instead, cute or not.

The grin got wider. His teeth were perfect. "I've been waiting two days for a train to stop. And here comes one with a beautiful woman on board. You going to kick me off?"

"There are lots of cars. Pick any one but this one."

He settled onto his haunches. "You haven't been on the road very long, have you? Don't see too many girls out here. Mostly dudes."

I said nothing.

"That's okay. You'll get to know what lonely feels like soon enough. Are you hungry?"

"Please go."

Instead, he slung off his immense pack and settled in next to me. He rummaged through the pack and came out with a camp stove, a can of butane and another of beans.

"I got plenty to share," he said. He thrust out a hand. "Scrape's my road name. But the name my parents gave me back when they thought they'd make good parents is Hayden."

I responded automatically, shaking his hand. His knuckles were rough with scars.

"You have a road name?" he asked.

"No."

"Then with those curls of yours, I'll call you Ebony Locks. Or maybe Brains, since you look smart with those glasses. And I do like smart women."

"Really?" I couldn't keep the sarcasm out of my voice. That's what boys said to me before they tried to get my pants down.

But he laughed. "It's true. Smart women and smooth whiskey." He pulled out a large bottle of Old Crow, uncapped it, and took a long swallow before passing the bottle to me. "Finest dinner you can have on the road. Beans and bourbon."

Surprised at myself, I took a swig.

While we waited for the beans to heat up, he turned on a battery-powered lantern and shared a handful of photos he kept in a pocket. A brother. A younger sister.

I found myself showing him pictures of Russ and my mom. "She studied at Juilliard," I told him. "Her dream was to play at Carnegie Hall. She would have made it."

188 // Denver Noir

"What happened?"

"My dad."

I showed him my favorite picture—the one of my mom standing inside Union Station. Dimitria stood on the stairs that led from the Great Hall up to the elegant mezzanine. It was impossible to tell whether she was ascending or descending. Either way, she was radiant in her green gown with her throat and shoulders bare, her curls swept into an updo.

"You look like her," Hayden said.

But I shook my head.

After we ate, we curled up in our sleeping bags on opposite sides of the platform and watched a storm ignite over the mountains. It was headed our way, shimmers of lightning illuminating a bruised sky.

Not long after, the train started up again.

I woke in the pitch black. The rain sheeted down. I snuggled down into my sleeping bag, and that's when I realized Hayden was next to me.

"You were screaming," he said into my ear.

I'd been having a dream that Endcott hunted for me. He walked along the train, shining his mega-beam flashlight into every car, tilting his head back to sniff the air like a hunting dog. He was muscle and claws and teeth. When he found me, I saw myself through his eyes: a mouse in a trap.

The wind turned, and rain came in sideways, sluicing across the platform. It felt hard enough to sweep us right off the train.

"You're shivering," Hayden said. He propped himself up and turned on the lamp, so our little space glowed beneath the tarp.

I huddled against him and his arm around me was hard

with muscle. He braced himself to keep us from sliding on the slick floor as the train rocked.

"You smell good." His voice was slurred.

We were both at least a little drunk.

I considered turning toward him to offer my lips to his. Then his hand found my breast.

"Stop!" I kicked back against him.

But he just shifted and moved back in. "I can keep you warm."

What I smelled on him now was a carnivore reek of adrenaline and wildness. I'd smelled it often enough on my dad, right before he drew back a fist.

"No, Hayden. No." I talked to him like he was one of my dad's dogs. Firm. No room for argument.

"Come on," he said. "I fed you. Gave you bourbon."

We swayed as the train rounded a bend, helpless against the tidal force of the rails. We were helpless against almost everything. Whether we were smart or stupid, weak or bold. Whether we were coddled as children or scorned. Birth strands us on uncertain ground and it's up to us to find our footing. Many of us never do.

He rolled me onto my back. Water dripped from his dreadlocks into my eyes. I hadn't been this cold since the time my dad took me hunting and couldn't get a fire started.

Men, I realized, were like trains. Single-minded, relentless, chewing through whatever got in their way.

As Hayden groped, my terror built—a known and familiar thing. This was violence wound into what should be sacred. Ownership where there should be gifts given and received.

An image rose of my mom's broken hand. Her voice saying, *I was going to play at Carnegie Hall.*

Fury lifted in me like a black, viscous liquid. I was filled with it, as if my blood had turned to pitch and then caught fire and now boiled beneath my skin.

I pulled up my knee and stretched my hand toward my ankle. My fingers found the knife hilt and I yanked the blade free.

"I'll cut you!" I yelled.

He lifted his head, looked at me in surprise.

I didn't mean for it to happen. The threat was meant to be enough. But the train jerked, and he rolled forward, and the handle slipped in my rain-slick hand. Without resistance, the blade popped through his flesh and bit deep.

He yelped and fell back. Blood filled his cupped hand. "What did you do?"

"I'm sorry!" I cried. "Oh my god, I'm sorry." I yanked off my sweatshirt, wanting to stop the flow of blood.

He stared at me with wild eyes, then scooted away. I heard him scrabbling across the platform. The wind caught the tarp and sent it sailing into the dark. The lantern fell over.

"Let me help," I called to him. "Please."

The train curled into another bend. He struggled for purchase, and as the train righted again, he slid along the platform toward the crushing gap between the cars.

"Hayden!" I screamed.

For a second, as he teetered on the edge, I saw the boy as his parents must have seen him. Back when they still thought it was a good idea to be parents.

Eyes the color of a pine forest, hair like wheat.

There came another jerk of the train.

Then his cry as he plunged into the gap, followed by a sound like a wet slap.

Then nothing but the grinding of the wheels.

* * *

In the morning, I hopped off that freight and walked across the Denver Millennium Bridge and into Union Station. The place was everything I'd hoped it would be. Beautiful and polished and filled with light and the bustle of people who had places to go, things to see. But for me, all the shiny and new, all the tantalizing smells and the gorgeous things in the gorgeous shops, all of it was just hollow glitter now.

Now I had to keep moving.

Whenever I sat still for too long, I became a bomb ready to explode.

Maybe that was what I'd always been. Maybe that was the definition of a murderer—a person not too much different from everyone else. Until someone finds their detonator.

Like a moth to a light, I went into the Tattered Cover bookstore. The main store was only a few blocks away. But this tiny space still caught the flavor. I searched through a rack of postcards and found the one Russ had sent me.

"May I help you?" a woman asked.

I turned. A woman not much older than me, with gold curls instead of black. Glasses not too different from mine. I could have been her, in a different life.

I wanted to ask her how long she'd worked there. If she'd ever seen a boy who looked like me. Instead I said, "Do you have any postcards that show Union Station before it was renovated?"

"You mean historical ones?"

"Not that long ago. The late 1990s or so. My mom came here back then."

Her brow furrowed. "There aren't any on the rack. But if you give me a second, I'll look in the back room. We keep a lot of stuff related to Union Station there."

She called out to someone named Josh to watch the register and disappeared through a door. When she returned, she carried a slim stack of cards.

"Like these?" she asked.

I flipped through them. One showed the Great Hall with its immense wooden benches, where my mom would have waited for her train. A different one flaunted the mezzanine; its enormous windows revealed a sky the color of a Colorado pinyon jay. And a third showed the wooden stairs leading from the hall up to the gallery, the stairs where my mother had posed long ago, back when she could still make music.

I bought them all.

I gave myself an hour to take in the rest of the station and to think about what might have been. I found two of the original wooden benches. I studied the white rosettes around the sconces—symbols of the columbine, the Colorado state flower. I spotted the original ticket window, now incorporated into the Terminal Bar. I paused beneath the hall's sixty-five-foot ceiling and imagined walking up the stairs to the Crawford Hotel and staying in one of its specialty rooms—one styled like a luxurious nineteenth-century Pullman train car.

Then I went back outside under a gloriously blue sky and breathed in the air I'd planned on breathing for months, maybe years. I walked through the glass doors of the Union Station Pavilion, which housed the underground bus termi-nals, and descended the staircase. I checked the departure times and gates. I'd crash at the friend's house for a couple of days while I decided on my next move—my next city, my next state, whatever took me away and away and away.

The tunnel seemed to go on for miles. Three football fields, I remembered reading. I located my gate and sank onto a bench.

A transit cop came strolling by. Bile rose hot and sharp in

my throat. In the tunnel's soft light, it was like all the metal on the officer glowed. Like he *radiated*. Like he was shedding sheets of electricity in curtains that snapped and sparked.

He drew closer.

Tell him, said a voice. *It was an accident. Tell him.*

I buried my face in my arms.

Tell him. Before it's too late.

A familiar voice said, "Seph."

I lifted my head before I could stop myself. Not three feet away from me stood PI Endcott.

The transit cop walked on by without a glance.

"Well, well," Endcott said. "I'd've thought you were smarter than that, Seph. Purchasing a Denver bus pass with your debit card. Guess you thought we wouldn't look back that far. Wouldn't put two and two together. You're the smartest kid in school, the teachers tell me. But here you are."

He sat next to me, put a hand on my knee.

"It's time to go home. Your dad's got a few words he'd like to say to you." He smirked and leaned in, took a sniff. "You *smell,* girl."

He stood. I noticed for the first time how soft he'd gone since leaving the sheriff's office. His belly poked at his shirt. His face carried rolls of fat around the neck, like linked sausages.

"Come on, girl." When I stood, he gave me a push. "I'm right behind you."

I dragged my feet all the way back out, feeling acceptance of my fate suck like mud at my heels. I heard Mom's voice saying, *Sometimes we start off with the wrong dream, that's all.*

Sometimes, I wanted to tell her, *someone steals our dream.*

Outside, the sun was still a blaze of glory in a sky like the vault of a chapel. People hurried by, gulping down sandwiches and lattes, checking their phones, chatting with friends.

I walked over to the light-rail tracks and watched a train approach.

"What are you doing?" Endcott gripped my elbow.

I had choices. Even with a blackened soul, I had choices.

There were a lot of different ways to live your life. When you'd done something you never thought you were capable of, it opened doors into a dark place filled with infinite possibility.

There was power to be had, once you found your detonator.

I thought hard about it as the train pulled into the station, only feet away. A stumble. A nudge.

But that would be letting a short-term goal get in the way of something far more important.

The train pulled to a stop.

Maybe I no longer deserved a shot. But my mom did.

Carnegie Hall, here we come.

I pulled free of Endcott's grip and gave him a smile that made his eyes narrow. I turned on my heel, heading away from the vast station with its terminals and train tracks, its historical building and pavilions.

He hurried after me. "Seph? Persephone! Young lady, slow down."

"Why don't you walk faster?" I tossed the words over my shoulder. "I know my dad is dying to see me."

SANGRE

BY D.L. CORDERO

Auraria

"Gota."

Rogelio heard the whisper from his threadbare blue recliner, drowsy brown eyes opening to the feel of goose bumps creeping up his legs. The bedroom he shared with his second-youngest brother was vacant, save himself, as the whole two-story brick house should've been despite the rustling in the hall. He leaned forward, straining to listen, looking at his watch.

Only five minutes past nine.

His trim black eyebrows knit together. His mother, father, sister, brothers, aunt, uncle, and cousins should all be at Mass, praying with the rest of the parish that continued to gather. He couldn't bring himself to go with them, a hesitance that boiled into heated arguments with his mother. No matter how much she guilted him, he couldn't be persuaded into stepping foot inside another católica after Archbishop Casey had every priest in Denver tell its people to vote for the bond that robbed Rogelio of his home.

La alma de la comunidad, that's what St. Cajetan's was. And still those pillos used her to undercut their fight. The city would've torn the church down too if his people hadn't managed to save it, something they couldn't do for their own homes and businesses. He could still hear Father Garcia reading the archbishop's letter. His chest burned, words cutting, mind reeling through confirmations, weddings, funerals, Easters, Christmases, all the life lived in and around that church.

"Gota." Footfalls followed the voice that he couldn't believe was speaking. Hot sunlight made the back of Rogelio's head and neck itch, sweat. He tried to steady his breath, heart knocking against teeth, nails tearing into armrests.

"Dame una gota."

He didn't understand what the whistling voice was asking for. A drop? A drop of what? His eyes widened when a shadow darkened the lip of his door.

Light, insistent knocking. "Río."

"¿Qu-quién es?" Stupid question. Only one person shortened his name like that.

The bookcase by the door, dressers, bunk beds, the coffee table by his feet, they all rattled. A ringing in his head grew unbearably loud. When tunnel vision set in, he squeezed his eyes shut.

Loose black hair and braids cascading over shoulders, red lips curved up, brown skin creasing around dark, friendly eyes. He saw her standing outside his door, wearing la falda roja he loved to climb into so he could play with silver necklaces that dipped under the collar of white peasant blouses. Bangles on her wrist chimed as she reached forward.

The doorknob turned. The bedroom door creaked. His eyelids peeled back, and Río stared, chest heaving, sweat pouring down his temples. At the threshold of the hallway, past his now open door, lay scattered pictures, a smattering of white feathers trailing from them, across his floor and into his lap.

He shot up, walked into the hall.

Every photograph at his feet was of her and him, his gaze landing on one with his younger, little body balanced on her hip outside the family home that had stood two blocks west of St.

Cajetan's. The Auraria home was now broken beams and rubble, lost two months after they lowered her body into the ground.

Tears beaded at the corners of his eyes. Heat in his face, down his throat, into his belly. "I'm angry about it too." He wiped his cheeks. "No se que hacer."

"Dame una gota."

The sound of running followed the whisper this time, chills rushing down his spine. He grabbed the picture, chased after the footsteps until he rounded a corner. The chain was swinging from the ceiling. He took a deep breath and pulled, stairs to the attic lowering with one smooth yank. His feet clattered up worn, hollow steps and pattered across the gray planks he swept once his family moved out of public housing and into this place by Lincoln Park. They somehow managed to buy it after scrimping and saving when the city underpaid them for their former home.

A breeze swept past his face, rustling the hem of the white tablecloth he'd laid over the wooden table he'd waxed himself. The altar was coming together, albeit slowly, with Río decorating it privately during the days leading up to Día de los Muertos. She was the one who'd taught him how to prepare, how to honor and to celebrate. A woman standing in and out of time, she chose to reclaim traditions lost to their family. She was proud of what others said she should let go, held her head high when they saw her difference. He loved how she commanded respect, even if people scorned her for what she held sacred.

In the end, who did they seek when they were sick? La bruja. La curandera.

Her red lips curved into a knowing grin when they returned to her and their people's wisdom.

Río dug into his pockets, found a lighter and a plastic-wrapped disc of marzipan candy. His heart slowed when he peeled the powdery round free and set la ofrenda on her favorite porcelain dish. His fingers traced the raised, painted roses and green stems running the dish's rim, his other hand lighting the tallest of the white candles on the table. Rogelio set down the photo he'd brought from the hall, propped it against the candle as it burned. His feet backpedaled until they hit the legs of the fold-out chair he'd taken from Casa Mayan after it closed. The metal creaked under his weight.

He already had her picture centered on the second level of the altar; he had painted the frame gold two nights ago. The metallic sheen glistened in the flame and in the speckled sunlight peeking through the attic's shuttered, round window. Resting over the purple, red, pinks, and blues of el papel picado he'd crafted, the tissue paper created a colorful skirt under her face.

He was missing several things. His anger toward the church made it difficult to place the saints and crucifixes on the top level. He would wait until the night before Día de los Muertos to put them up, leaving those supplies covered and stacked beside his chair. Her small plot of marigolds lay wasted under the rubble of the neighborhood. Río wasn't sure if he would be able to buy any, with how tight money was. Same with copal.

But as he sat there in the dim light, it didn't feel like she minded.

He wrapped anxious hands around knees. How the days dragged on without her. His father always kidded about how much he was like her, not understanding how true that really was.

"Tía Paloma," Río's soft voice floated onto the altar, stroked her picture, held up el dulce de cacahuate.

The house creaked and moaned.

"I'm listening, Tía."

The white tablecloth billowed. He felt the cool breeze cutting through space like a knife, whirling around the tall white candle, red-orange flame dancing, Río feeling a heat spread across his cheeks as the fire brightened. Footsteps creaked toward him, slow, deliberate, heavy. The candlelight changed direction, spotlighting the house in the picture of Río and Tía Paloma until it felt like the fire was burning inside the windows.

And then he felt it, someone in front of him, the air dense and unmoving. Cold swept over his body like a hug, pushed him deeper into the metal of the fold-out chair. His vision blurred.

Blood in the streets. Blood in the ground.

He stood amid the rubble of the Auraria neighborhood dressed in a red skirt, huipil, and shawl, holding her hand, staring at the shape of the house they still saw silhouetted against moonlight.

She whispered in his ear and let go.

Río opened his eyes when he heard the front door open, not realizing hours had passed since he sat down. His family poured inside, bodies filling the two floors below him. Laughing, singsong voices swam into brick walls and ceilings. Bedroom doors swung open. Closets peeled back to receive dress shirts, pants, and skirts. Pans and cutting boards clattered in the kitchen, and soon he heard his mother calling for help with Sunday's meal.

The candles on the altar had gone out. He sat in the dark, watching speckled sunlight fall on the photograph of his little smiling self in front of his home.

"Rogelio," his father called from the base of the attic stairs.

He stood up, body heavy and relaxed.

"Rogelio, will you come?"

He strode across the floor. Before taking a step down, he glanced over his shoulder, eyes peering at the dark shape of Tía Paloma's framed photo. "I'll be right there," Río said with a smile. "I'm coming."

"What does he want it for?" his mother asked his father, in reference to the sewing kit Río wanted to borrow.

"Does it matter, Esther?"

He felt it best not to ask for it himself, since Mom huffed around the house past sundown. Throwing dishes into the sink louder than needed, groaning without prompting, and providing one-word answers. Queen of guilt trips, her quiet anger could seethe for days after being defied. He hoped to get used to it one day, but he cringed as he listened to his parents' sniping from outside the closed bedroom door.

"But David, if he needs to patch something up, he can ask me to do it," she kept on.

"Honey, just give me the bag."

This would go on for a while. Río decided to head down into the kitchen, grab a cup of water, and wait for his kind-hearted dad. The scent of onions, garlic, oregano, guajillo, and ancho chilies hung thick in the air, remnants of el pozole he'd helped his mother and Aunt Rosa make. He hoped the aroma would bake into the walls and floors, stamp this house theirs, cover everything in cultura.

Drawing water from the tap, he sat at the dining table, not meaning to choose the wobbly chair, but in the dark he was still getting used to where everything was. He listened. His parents' muted voices dropped like pebbles down the stairs, tinny laughter from sitcoms spilled from his aunt and uncle's room, giggles from his younger brothers and cousins skipped across the living room ceiling. They always played under the covers past bedtime, parents turning deaf ears to the noise as long as the boys didn't get too rowdy. He wondered what game it was tonight. Disco dancing or playing Dirty Harry. He hoped they weren't pretending war like he found them doing last time. That always set their uncle off. Río's ears sought out his six-year-old sister, but she fell asleep fast and hard at seven p.m. When he listened for outside, he found nothing but a few distant shouts and hushed rancheras. With the national fuel crisis, the streets were empty.

He stood, returned to the sink. Water rushed into his glass. His mind ran back to the box in his closet. He'd kept as many of Tía Paloma's things as his family let him, whatever wouldn't sell. He often held the cotton, polyesters, and rayons of her dresses to his chest, cried into them when he didn't want anyone to hear. How many nights had he stared at his closet door, wishing his brother wasn't in the bunk below him so he could try something on? He was roughly her size, slender and not much over five five. He worried about his shoulders, broader than hers, opposite of his hips, straighter than hers. And his feet, too big. He couldn't imagine fitting into her sandals.

Río turned off the faucet, stepped back, and panicked. He whirled around after bumping into someone. Tall, looming over him, musk thick and heavy. Río shook, his glass shattering, water spilling across the floor. His bare feet cut and bled as he stumbled back, Río yelping at the dark figure there so close behind.

"You scare too easy," Uncle Ernesto said, Río's shoulders tightening at the raspy voice. "If you're like that, pay more attention."

Río gripped the sink, felt his knees knock when he

smelled alcohol on his uncle's breath. Didn't take much beer for Ernesto to start calling him the names Río's father forbade. Whenever Ernesto drank, Río worried he wouldn't stop at names. He was getting bolder, scarier.

The refrigerator door opened, blue light casting shadows across the heavy bags under bloodshot eyes. Ernesto cracked open a Coors, his glare hot on Río's face. Feet hurried down the stairs. Río's father flicked on the living room light, then the kitchen's when he saw blood on the floor.

"¿Qué pasa aquí?"

Ernesto gave his cuñado a sidelong glance. "What you mean, what's going on?" He took a swig from the bottle, brown bubbles fizzing. "What's it look like?"

"I don't know what it looks like." David stood in front of his child. "That's why I'm asking."

Ernesto's cheeks pinched once his gaze drifted to what David gripped in his hand. Esther's pink sewing bag. "I'm doing your boy a favor, hermano. Teaching him some damn situational awareness."

David's nails dug into the pink canvas. "Don't you *teach* Rogelio anything. Go the fuck to bed."

Ernesto cocked his head back. A dark, static laugh popped in his throat. He lingered there under the white kitchen lights, seconds stretching. The cuts on Río's feet stung but he didn't dare move, trying to shrink into his father's back. Uncle Ernesto hadn't been like this before getting drafted. They didn't have the dough to keep him from going, so everyone cried because they thought he'd come back from Vietnam dead. He came back weird and angry instead.

"Ernesto, I told you to go back to bed."

"You're too soft on that boy, David."

"I swear to God, if you don't get out this kitchen."

"What? You finally gonna show Rogelio what a real man's like?"

"Carajo cabrón, I'll make you get your sorry ass upstairs." David stepped toward him with a swiftness that made Río's hair stand. Must've had the same effect on Ernesto because he was retreating, though not without hate-filled jabs.

"That damn hippie's gonna ruin your business."

Río slid to the floor, his father chasing his uncle upstairs. Turning the sole of his foot inward, he picked at glass slivers.

"Quit being stupid about that job, it's good money!" Ernesto yelled. "So what if the sissy doesn't fucking like it?"

Río startled when it finally happened, the explosion months of tension built up to. Hard bangs against hallway walls, dull thuds of flesh on flesh. A shout and grunted moan when someone fell against the floor. Río froze. A bedroom door slammed shut. He waited, wiping his face as footsteps came back down the stairs. His shoulders dropped from his ears when he saw his father step into the kitchen.

David still held the pink canvas sewing bag. He set it on the counter, crouched, and reached.

"I'm okay. It was an accident." Río pushed him back, looking him over but finding no damage. In the scenarios played out in Río's head before falling asleep, his father usually won. Having trained as a boxer, David knew how to take and land a punch.

Río tended to his foot, wincing as he dug out glass shards from the arch and heel. He hated the way the corners of his dad's lips drooped, the furrowed brow and narrowed eyes, would do anything to stop it. "It's okay. Don't worry." Río chuckled, his voice high.

David grabbed a clean dish towel. Despite Río's protests, he wiped the blood from Río's hands and feet. "His disability will come in soon and Rosa's up for a secretary job with El Molino. Just a few more days. I'll watch him the whole time."

"Papi, I'm fine." Tight lips, eyes closing in a feigned smile. "Maybe he's right. I can cut my hair." He'd only started growing it out after graduating high school in May. "It's shaggy and gets in my eyes."

"Mijo," David said firmly, but with a tenderness that held Río close, "no le hagas caso." He tied the towel tight around Río's foot, his rough carpenter hands tucking back loose strands of Río's straight black hair. "It looks good on you."

His eyes welled up. He fidgeted with his hands. "Thank you."

The TV upstairs went off. No laughter in the house. Everyone was listening from unseen places. He stood, his father making him lean on him for support as he tested out the pain. Río held his face in a tight grimace when David insisted on helping him walk up to bed.

They mounted the steps, the creaking underscoring everyone's quiet. Río couldn't stand it. "What job was Tío talking about?"

His father paused. "Don't worry about it, mijito."

"'Course I'm gonna worry about it." He frowned. "Work slows down going into fall. We need the money so what's this job you don't wanna take?" He leaned against his bedroom door, stared into his dad's coffee eyes. Crow's feet on weathered, light skin.

"They need supports put into St. Catejan's and some of the houses on Ninth Street while they restore 'em." David crossed his arms.

Río understood the hesitance, which wasn't only about sparing his own feelings. After decades upon decades of his people living and growing in Auraria, the nice folks of Denver felt threatened by the largely Chicano neighborhood. Mayor McNichols went so far as to call it *blighted*. The tight-knit community didn't even know that the Urban Renewal Authority had moved to build a college over their homes until the notices went out about having to move. His dad had been a part of ARO, the group of Aurarian residents that opposed the displacement. Now that the hammer had firmly driven the nail into the coffin, David probably didn't want to set foot on the land he'd fought to keep.

"When did they ask you?"

David's lips tightened. "This morning."

"At church?" Heat boiled in Río's chest. He sucked in a breath and let it out slowly, thinking about the box in his closet and Paloma's picture on the altar. "Take it." This was the opening he needed. "I'll help."

Río helped load the dinged blue Chevy pickup truck in the morning, sky gray with early dawn, late October air cold and dry. With their house on the corner of Lipan and Twelfth, he could see both the Lincoln Park Homes and the park itself, a scrappy piece of land with wide, bare cottonwoods and a swimming pool. The housing project he liked less, rows and rows of identical brick buildings. Square, no character, just darker brick for trim, chain-link fences to mark off brown yards, clotheslines that got so heavy they bowed out.

They took Mariposa Street up through Westside, crossed Colfax, and met the fenced-off stretch of land they once called home. After some waiting, cross-referencing with foremen, and finagling around chawed-up streets, they met with the white man who'd recruited Río's father over the weekend.

It wasn't too surprising that his dad got tapped for this. Wasn't that what they always did? Take, and then have the people they'd taken from build? His father was a decently well-known carpenter, his business having branched into restoration jobs around Denver. With his light skin, straight hair, and first name, he was white-passing enough to be accepted into spaces other Chicanos weren't. The last name De Santos sometimes confused people, but often, those who didn't speak Spanish pronounced it DiSantis, which lead to conclusions about David being Italian.

Río didn't have that kind of advantage. He stayed in the Chevy while his dad took a jaunt beyond the fenced-off section that protected stolen homes from the rest of the construction. Gates within gates.

He looked through the truck's back window, heart clenching. They'd taken down the businesses and houses in sections, but now he could see all of the neighborhood was flush with the ground, piles of bricks and rubble scattered for miles. His eyes landed on what the vultures considered historic enough to reuse. St. Cajetan's and its rounded Spanish façade, stained glass peeking over screened-in fence. He read the name *Tivoli* lettered on the smokestack of the brewery, followed St. Elizabeth's tall spire to her gleaming gold cross. Immanuel Episcopal paled in comparison, Río barely able to see the peak of its roof past the frames for the new campus buildings. He hadn't spent much time around that church, but now he longed to see its rough pink and gray stone face.

These four buildings would become shells, guts ripped out for revitalization. Again, Río thought about the word Mayor McNichols used to describe his neighborhood. Blighted. How was this repurposing of scavenged parts better?

David patted the hood of the Chevy, Río swiveling back to see the white man in his early forties wander off in the direction of the building frames, blue hard hat bobbing, cream-colored button-up tucked into khakis. Río opened the car door as his father pulled on his tool belt. Río's feet hit rocky ground with battered brown work boots.

"We're gonna measure." David pointed at the pad of paper tucked under the passenger dashboard. Río grabbed it and slipped a ballpoint pen behind his ear. He followed his dad past the fence blocking off the Ninth Street houses. Thirteen Victorians on either side of a dug-up street, including Casa Mayan where he'd washed dishes during high school. Groussman Grocery stood on the corner, white stone balusters intact. Río still didn't understand exactly how this part of the neighborhood got saved. Something about an anonymous donation to an organization calling itself Historic Denver. Fundraising, negotiations with the city, he'd kept up with the effort only in passing. Every time he heard about it, all he could picture were blue eyes seeing value in the homes of his neighborhood once everyone who loved them was gone.

David waved him over from the porch of number 1015. In the gray morning light its squared, hipped green roof and yellow brick walls looked sickly.

The rest of the day whirled by. A flurry of measurements, trips to the lumber mill, sawing, drilling, and hammering. Having stayed up most of the night patching a skirt and blouse in the attic, by the time his father ended their workday, Río was going cross-eyed. The only things he continued to pay close attention to were the entry and exit points to the construction site, the paths leading to the Ninth Street and St. Cajetan fences, and the width of the chains that looped them closed. For how contested the displacement had been, there was barely any security during the day. Come evening, he didn't see anyone guarding the site after one of the workers rolled back the gate and padlocked it shut.

"Gotta make one more stop." David rolled down his visor, blocking the lowering sun from his face as he drove.

Río closed his eyes, trying to rest. He planned to be up all night. He nodded off at the first stoplight heading back into the Westside, barely registering the truck being placed into park and his dad stepping out.

Maybe it took ten minutes, maybe thirty, but when David hopped back into the truck, Río felt something was different. He blinked, rubbed his brow, realized they were on Santa Fe outside Flores by Torres. Up and down the street, kids in costumes were already making their rounds, little vaqueros, ballerinas, and skeletons trying to get the best Halloween candy before the sun blinked out.

And in his dad's lap sat trimmed marigolds wrapped in brown paper, one red rose amid the gold pom-pom blooms.

"I talked the foreman into paying me up front." David pulled the rose free. Taking his pocketknife to the thorns, he shed them one by one, his face soft as he worked. "I knew you were missing these for tomorrow." He slid the cempasuchitl into Río's lap, small plastic bag of copal caught between the flowers.

Río's voice caught. He'd always known his dad wasn't like everyone else, that he was his own kind of family man.

"You can wear your hair however long you want, wear any clothes you want, see anybody you want." He pulled Río's face into his large, rough hand, undid the tight knot of hair at the nape of Río's neck. "I've known a long time. Paloma helped me understand." He tucked the rose behind Río's ear, let heavy hair hide the stem. "There is nothing you can do that will make me turn my back on you."

Río's whole body sank into David, spilled sobs into his chest.

"What do you want me to call you? Dime quien eres."

* * *

Río told her father about her plan on the drive home. David listened, hands at ten and two, nodding as he thought things over once he parked the Chevy outside the house. She was surprised when he offered himself as lookout, that he believed her without flinching. Her dad and Paloma were close, but it wasn't until this moment that Río understood how deep their bond was.

He helped her string the marigolds like beads, insisting they work on the garland in the living room while her mom, sister, and brothers prepared tamales at the dining table, stack of corn husks toppling over. Vicente Fernández and Lola Beltrán warbled through the radio while arroz rojo steamed on the stove, replenishing the household aroma of garlic, onion and chilies. David explained that Esther had wanted to make this food after last night's fight. That she and the children spent all day moving Aunt Rosa and Río's cousins into their other sister's house on the Northside.

"Esther," David called from the living room, tying off a finishing knot. "¿Y Ernesto?"

She answered after a pause. "Rosa didn't want him with them. I'm not sure where he went, but I made sure he knew better than to come back here."

Río's brothers snickered. Her sister chimed in: "Mommy played tag with Tío using a two-by-four."

David asked Río to wait until the rest of the family went to sleep before slipping into Tía Paloma's clothes. Mom still needed time before she felt comfortable explaining things to the kids, and it was best that no one else knew what they were going to do. At midnight, Río and her father slipped into the attic, David lighting the incense and placing arroz y tamales on the altar while she changed.

La falda roja plumed when Río let it fall from her hips to her ankles, the cotton soft and twirling as it moved. The black huipil had large red roses and marigolds woven into la tela, smaller ones embroidered in shining thread front and back, leaves decorated in three colors of green. Paloma's rebozo matched the skirt, deep crimson, black hem and fringe. Río wrapped it around her shoulders, put the rose her father had given her back behind her ear, and smoothed down her black hair.

She turned toward her father. Her cheeks burned. Gaze trained on the floor, she took an anxious step forward, stopped when he looked over his shoulder and rose. His hand covered his mouth. Río clenched her shawl.

She gave a broken chuckle. "I bet it looks—"

David wrapped Río up into his arms and pulled her in tight.

Wordless minutes later, they pushed the truck half a block down the street before cranking the engine. They drove dark, empty streets for ten minutes, David turning off his headlights when they rolled beside the fence. Río hopped out before he came to a stop. She pulled the heavy-duty bolt cutters from her waistband and bore down on the padlock, forearms flexing, shoulders straining. She heard it snap and tore the chain away, pulled back the gate and rolled it into place the second her father backed the truck onto the construction site.

Under the clouded moon, David stepped onto the land. He took the chain from Río's hands and wrapped it around the fence posts, pulling his own lock from his pocket. "Go." He tossed her a flashlight. "Ten cuidado."

"Are you sure you don't want to come see her?" She ground gravel as she pivoted toward him.

"You didn't see me there when she showed you she wanted

you to come." He snapped the lock into place, patted her head. "Besides, I'll see Paloma anytime I look at you."

Río's heart swelled.

"Watch for my headlights. One flash."

She nodded and ran.

Her work boots pounded the dusty ground of the torn-up streets, the hem of her skirt in her hand, flashlight beam swinging in front of her. She darted toward the rounded curves of St. Cajetan's, able to see them dark against the sky despite the black of the night.

"Gota."

Gales carried Paloma's voice to Río, gusts growing stronger the closer she drew near. She wheezed, the air cold and hard, but she kept dropping one foot in front of the other, even when she stumbled over rubble, even when sweat dripped into her eyes and stung.

She passed St. Cajetan's, the church feeling too tall, walls pulling in and out, inhale and exhale. Río drove forward, thought the ground started to feel like membrane, soft and springy. Wind whistled high and low. Maybe the land was singing.

"Dame una gota."

She skidded onto the dirt road that led up to the Ninth Street houses, veered right at their fence, knew where her home would've stood even though the streets were missing. Tripping her way down a rocky path, she scrabbled over rubble that jutted from piles, splintered wood beams biting into her forearms, shattered glass tearing at her palms.

She got caught on a broken wall a few feet off the ground, her thick locks grabbed by fractured rafters. She pulled but couldn't break free, seeing stars in front of her eyes. Something translucent reached past her face, wind whipping into the wood and knocking it back.

She fell. The air knocked out of her lungs when she hit the ground.

Then she realized she was there. Río staggered to her feet, spun in place. "¡Tía!"

"Dame una gota de nuestra sangre."

The clouds over the moon parted. Río turned off her flashlight and saw Paloma in wispy translucence, standing in front of the wreckage that was their home. Her intangible form wavered in the night, but Río could tell Paloma's hand stretched toward her, palm upturned, fingers cupped. Río reached, her hand cut open from the glass of the ruins.

"Our blood is in the streets." Paloma's body became as solid and bright as the moon when Río's droplets fell into her hand. "Our blood is in the ground." Thick red pools grew under Paloma's feet, spread into the wreckage. Wind gusting, earth shaking, broken bricks and girders rose from their open graves and stitched themselves back together. Paloma stepped toward Río as glass crashed into wholeness. Mortar slapping against brick, nails hammering into wood, shutters cracking open, and doors slamming shut. Paloma flashed so bright Río had to cover her eyes.

"We are the land," Paloma whispered. Her hands wrapped around Río's face. She pressed her cold forehead against Río's, closed her eyes, and as she lingered, she grew warm.

Lights flickered on in the homes that stood tall again, gabled roofs cutting into the dark sky, colors deepening under the moonlight. Blue curving trims, red arches over windows, white brick shimmering with rainbows while pines and cottonwoods sprung from the ground.

Children chased barking dogs through swept dirt yards. Mothers gathered on porches, lips red, heads tossed back. Men smoked together on corners, shoving each other and smirking. Battered trucks puttered down paved streets, dandelions lining the sidewalks. Work clothes fluttered in the breeze, strung from crisscrossing lines. Aroma of baking bread, stewed tomatoes, simmered garlic, onion, and oregano. Milk bottles knocking by the dairy. Hops and yeast marrying in the brewery.

Paloma opened her eyes. St. Cajetan's doors flung back with a scream, candles burning in the stained-glass windows. Hymns poured from the walls. Organs spun melodies. A torrent of blood rushed down the church steps, spattered into the street, joining the scarlet rivers seeping from the Ninth Street houses.

"Never let them forget," Paloma's voice echoed across the neighborhood. The ground pulsed. Río saw people she did and didn't know rise from the earth to stand across Auraria. Skins of brown, bronze, and black, dark eyes turning toward the moon.

"Make them remember us." Paloma spread her arms wide. "Walk tall and speak for those who have fallen."

Four years later, Río stood beside her father, mother, sister, and brothers at the back of a crowd that gathered for a ribbon cutting at Metropolitan State College. Her thick black hair swept her waist as the wind rustled the red skirt she wore, silver bangles on her wrist shining in the sun. It was bright, the concrete hot. Río stared at the large brown square the city built over razed homes. Much of Denver was turning into the shape of building blocks. Río wanted to knock them all over.

A blue ribbon hung between hand railings placed on either side of the building's glass door. Mayor McNichols stood in front of it, at a mobile podium with a speaker that made his crackling voice bounce across sidewalks.

"Today is a step forward for our city . . ."

David nodded at Río as he handed her his pocketknife. Lowering the rebozo from her shoulders, Río pricked one of her fingers while hiding her hands within the folds of the shawl. She passed the knife back and, after a few moments, lowered her hand to the earth.

She felt the heartbeat under her sandals.

The masses of brown, bronze, and black bodies rose from the earth as Río's gaze returned to the blue ribbon before the doors. Thousands of her people surrounded the building, stood among the living, gathered beside, before, and behind the mayor.

Río held David's hand. She asked him what he saw.

His eyes watered. "We're closing in." His breath caught. "We're all closing in."

The mayor's grin flashed. ". . . we celebrate progress . . ."

Río ground her teeth, raised her bloody fist, and the ancestors opened their mouths when she opened hers.

DREAMING OF ELLA

BY FRANCELIA BELTON

Five Points

Ll he wanted to play was jazz, and to one day play trumpet to the First Lady of Song's voice. So when *the* Miss Ella Fitzgerald walked into the Silver Sax one chilly November night in 1956, Morgan could hardly believe his dream might come true.

It was half past midnight, and the night was still young. Morgan swayed on stage, blowing a hypnotic tune on his trumpet and swinging with the rest of the fellows in the Sax's house band. Along with his brass, piano and drums, alto and bass, jamming and jiving, thumping and thriving, just another weekend night down in The Points. The Harlem of the West. Welton Street in Denver was your last stop for jazz between St. Louis and California. And Morgan felt electric.

In between songs, Morgan pulled the yellow silk handkerchief from his tan cotton jacket, the best thing about his Sunday suit, and wiped the sweat from his face. Despite the cold outside, the room was sultry and thick with heat and tribal jubilations. Smoke and the aroma of beer hung in the air like fog after a snowstorm.

A smattering of couples sat at the round tables before the bandstand. Men in snazzy suits with carefully knotted ties, ladies in lovely dresses with strings of pearls, talking, laughing, taking sips from glasses of fancy cocktails or bottles of beer. Cigarettes perched on the edge of ashtrays or clasped between fingers, periodic drags producing tendrils of blue haze past parted lips.

A commotion broke out at the entrance, and people craned their necks to see what was happening. One of the bar girls hurried over to where the club's owner, Charles, spoke with the bartender. He lowered his head so she could put a hand to his ear. Charles's head snapped up, an incredulous look on his face. He peered over her shoulder as a statuesque woman walked in wearing her quintessential Edwards-Lowell sable coat. Charles rushed over to take it off her shoulders. They exchanged an enthusiastic greeting and hug. The buzz of voices in the club rose in pitch and volume, and Morgan knew what folks were saying without hearing their words.

That was the First Lady, and she had honored the Silver Sax with her presence.

Morgan's ring finger paused midkey and his horn drifted from his lips. The note he blew hung in the air for the briefest of moments before vanishing from the ether. One by one his bandmates ceased playing.

Any of the greats could have walked into the joint, Duke Ellington, Dizzy Gillespie, Billie Holiday, but tonight it was Lady Ella herself. The woman who took her vocal cues from the horns and made them her own. The woman who Morgan had listened to all his life and dreamed of meeting. The woman who now elicited a silence in the Silver Sax so deep, it commanded spiritual deference.

After an eternal moment, Miss Fitzgerald said, "Don't stop on my behalf, boys. Keep playing." Her voice irresistible and smooth. Her smile irrepressible and kind.

Morgan brought his trumpet back to his lips and picked up the notes he'd dropped off. The rest of the fellows followed his lead. There was a new energy flowing in and out of the club until the place burst at the seams with all the people suddenly pouring in.

Word was getting around . . . Lady Ella was in the Silver Sax.

In all likelihood, she had performed at one of the fancier venues downtown. As famous and revered as she was, however, even she was not allowed to stay in the hotels there. Denver was as segregated as any city down south. Tonight, she would be staying at the Rossonian here in The Points, where all the jazz royalty were welcomed with open arms.

Charles escorted Ella to the high-back cushioned booth seating running the length of the south wall. He instructed the staff to block off the seats around them so Ella wouldn't be disturbed.

Morgan blew into his horn and his fingers trembled as he pressed down, up, down along the valves. Goose bumps took over his body, knowing Ella was listening to him, and he tried not to stare.

Charles and Ella chatted intently; their heads bowed together. At one point, Charles pointed to the stage, and Ella nodded with a discerning gaze. Her glossy, high-wave bouffant shimmered in the glow from the wall sconce above her head.

When Morgan and the band finished their last song before taking their fifteen-minute break, Charles rose from the table and approached the stage. To Morgan, he said, "Ella likes your chops. I told her you're Milton's boy. Me and your father played a couple of times with Ella back in Harlem."

Morgan knew this. Charles had told him stories on more than one occasion about the jazz greats he and Morgan's dad had jammed with. It was one of the reasons he wanted to be good as—no, better than—his dad. Morgan not only wanted to play a song with the Queen of Jazz, he wanted to be first trumpet in her band.

Charles beamed as if he were Morgan's father. "Ella is going to grace us with a song tonight." He leaned in so that only Morgan could hear. "I also heard she *might* be in the market for a new trumpet player, so show her what you're really made of, son." Charles winked.

Morgan's knees almost buckled, and he gripped his brass for emotional support. He couldn't believe it.

"Okay, boys, let's do this." Charles clapped his hands and bustled back to the table.

Morgan's pulse raced through his veins, and he reached under his jacket to pull away the sweaty shirt from his skin.

Tommy grinned from ear to ear. He played multiple instruments, but the saxophone was his baby. "Man, what a night this is turning out to be."

Ray, on bass, intoned as only an old man could, "Did I ever tell you about the time I got to play with Billie Holiday and she—"

"Yes!" they all chimed together, hooting with laughter.

Ray grumbled, ". . . young think they know everything." He chomped on his cigar.

Heart thrumming, Morgan took a deep breath, brought his horn to his lips, but then lowered it. He needed to be smokin' tonight, because he had only one shot to impress the Lady and be invited to play in her band. One clunker and he was finished. There were too many other cats out there who would swoop in and snatch the prize.

Someone brought the microphone and set it out front.

Larry, the bartender, made his way over to Charles and spoke in his ear. Another whispered conversation, but this time the expression on Charles's face changed from anticipation and pride to shock. He looked right at Morgan. He took a deep breath and marched forward. The solemnity on his face a frozen mask.

Morgan's heart sped up to a staccato beat. Was Charles going to pull him from the set to put someone in with more experience? Nothing doing! He was going to play his trumpet for Miss Fitzgerald if it was the last thing he did.

"Morgan, I've got something to tell you."

Morgan shook his head. "No, you're not taking my chance. I have been waiting for something like this all my life."

"Your Aunt Beatrice called. You're needed at the hospital."

Morgan furrowed his brow and shook his head. "I don't believe you." He turned away from Charles.

But Charles jumped onto the bandstand and grabbed Morgan's shoulder. "Son, your mother had a heart attack. She's dying."

For a second, a horrible-terrible-Lord-please-forgive-me second, Morgan didn't care. He looked around the stage and out at the full house. All those people waiting to hear Lady Ella, and he, Morgan Marshall, was going to play his trumpet with her. A once-in-a-lifetime opportunity to distinguish himself, not live under the shadow of his father, and possibly his only chance to join the Great Lady's band. He ran a calloused finger over the initials MM etched around the mouthpiece on his trumpet. The engraving originally stood for Milton Marshall, but now it was for Morgan.

He gritted his teeth and pressed, released, and pressed his fingers along the trumpet keys. His throat constricted, and he willed frustrated tears not to appear.

"You going to be all right, son?" Charles gripped Morgan's shoulder tighter, his eyes shining with sympathy and pity. If anyone knew what Morgan felt right now, it would be Charles. He was the one who'd brought the trumpet to Denver ten years ago, after Morgan's dad died in Harlem—shot on stage when a fight broke out in the audience. Milton Marshall had been gaining notoriety with his brass in New York and sending money to Rose, Morgan's mother, every week—until one day, it stopped. Instead, a Mr. Charles Xavier Lewis, saxophonist and best friend to Milton, showed up on their doorstep. He gave Rose the trumpet, but she threw it away, saying, "I always told Milton that he was playing the devil's horn and one day the devil would collect his due."

Morgan had fished the horn out of the trash and taught himself to play it. He was ten years old then and had been playing ever since. After all these years, he was finally going to be heard and acknowledged in his own right, and not only as Milton's boy. People would know *him*, Morgan Marshall, the best damn jazz trumpeter coming out of Five Points.

A hard freeze of deep, unabiding shame iced his veins. *Jesus, what's wrong with me?* All he could think about was himself. His big break, while his mom lay dying, could have already passed away, for all he knew. What kind of selfish son was he?

And yet . . . was his mom right? Had he been playing the devil's horn and now the devil was coming to collect his due? But instead of coming for Morgan, the devil was going to take Rose?

No. Morgan wouldn't allow himself to believe that ridiculous claptrap.

He looked out at the crowd one more time, absorbing the energy. He brought his gaze back to the stage. Miss Fitzgerald conversed with Henry at the piano. A soul-crushing envy squeezed his heart. "Yes, yes, of course, I need to go."

He jumped down from the stage and shoved his way through the crowd. He glanced back over his shoulder. Miss Fitzgerald had taken hold of the mike and the crowd cheered. The opening rendition of "Dream a Little Dream of Me" filled the room, another trumpet taking the lead. Morgan clenched his jaw. Tommy.

Miss Fitzgerald crooned out the first few lines and her voice followed Morgan onto the street. A bustle of people loitered outside and still, he could hear that voice, and worst of all, the trumpet accompaniment. His fingers played along the keys on the horn in his hand. He closed his eyes for a moment and imagined he was on the stage right now. Right there beside Miss Fitzgerald, and she'd turn her head, giving him an encouraging smile as she sang her words.

The chill wind bit him. He shivered and opened his eyes. He'd forgotten his coat and trumpet case. But he refused to retrieve them. He didn't want to see the Lady on stage and know he was *that* close to being up there with her. Instead, he headed south down Welton Street. The snowfall increased, and strands of Miss Fitzgerald's haunting voice faded behind him.

He strode past the multitude of shops and businesses on Welton, most of them shuttered because the night belonged to the bars, nightclubs, and after-hours joints. Pedestrians flowed around Morgan, bundled up for the cold Colorado weather. Men sported camel coats and overcoats, women were clad in furs and tweed swing coats, and all wore hats from fancy to plain. Nobody paid attention to the forlorn, coatless young man clutching a trumpet.

Morgan reached the corner of Twenty-sixth and Welton. Across the street, a crowd of people stood in line at the entrance to the Rossonian Hotel. Mostly white folks, a lot of them venturing into the area to hear jazz and rub shoulders with the greats. They could afford the cover charge and were let in first. Louis Armstrong, a Five Points favorite, stayed there a few weeks back, and people couldn't get enough. Morgan didn't understand what the fuss was about him anyway.

Morgan vowed he was going to be even bigger than Armstrong. And he could, if he joined Miss Fitzgerald's band and made a name for himself.

A Ritz cab drove past, and Morgan let out a loud whistle, flagging it with his free hand. The cab slammed the brakes, sliding in the slush. Morgan jogged over, opened the back door, and jumped inside. To the cabbie, he said, "Denver General." The vehicle continued south and took him to the hospital, where his mother lay waiting.

Morgan's aunt pounced on him when he stormed through the hospital doors. She was dressed to the nines in a clingy satin dress. A mink stole from one of her many suitors dangled from her arm. Her makeup immaculate, her hair done up right, but the scowl on her face would have any of those men retreating right back out the door. "What took you so long?"

Morgan's heart paused midtempo. Was he too late? "Did she—?"

"No." Her annoyance softened. "They stabilized her, but it doesn't look good." She took his hand and led him to the ward where his mother rested.

An almost grayish hue tainted Rose's light-skinned complexion. In the overbleached sheets and gray woolen blanket, she looked so tiny.

The hard soles of Morgan's shoes made a dull echo on the disinfected linoleum floor. He took his mother's hand in his. It looked washed out against his own darker skin. "Mom, I'm sorry. I'm here now."

Footsteps approached. A doctor walked over and retrieved the clipboard hanging from Rose's bed frame. He consulted the pages, then addressed Morgan and his aunt: "I'm Doctor Alwin, the physician in charge."

"What happened to my mom?"

"She had a stroke, which led to temporary heart failure. The good news is, she's going to make it."

Relief crescendoed over Morgan like the triumphant end to an otherwise sad melody, while a cold bitterness roiled beneath. He could've played a song with Ella! The heat of reprehensible shame burned his face and neck.

The doctor continued: "But it's going to be a painstaking recovery. She's going to need long-term care."

"What do you mean by long-term?"

"It all depends. It could be months, but sometimes it can take a year or more."

"Years?" Morgan stood aghast.

"Not necessarily, but she will need to be moved to a nursing home so she can have around-the-clock care. We can recommend one that takes colored folks."

A hard pit formed in Morgan's stomach. He wouldn't be able to afford that. But he needed to do something, otherwise his dream of traveling and playing jazz would disappear.

After the doctor left, Morgan turned to his aunt. "What are we going to do?"

She wrinkled her immaculate brows. "We?"

Stunned, Morgan stammered, "Well, yeah. We're family. She's your sister."

"Now, you know I love your mom, but I've got my own life to live. I can't be spending the rest of my days playing nursemaid to her."

Indignation spiked. "Mom took care of you while you were little girls, after your own mother died."

"That may be true, but I got a beauty shop to run and bills to pay." She looked him up and down. "You're a grown man. You can take care of your mama now."

Morgan glanced around to see if anyone was listening. There was a nurse at the other end of the room, fluffing the pillows under another patient's head. Morgan pitched his voice down a level. "I can't afford to put Mom in a home. It's going to cost hundreds, if not thousands of dollars." He brought his voice even lower. "But the good news is, I'm about to make it big."

His aunt laughed, sharp and loud. "You realize how many jazz players I know who swear they're going to make it big?"

"I'm different. Miss Ella Fitzgerald asked me to join her band." His lie held an overwhelming urgency. "I'll have more than enough money to take care of Mom, and . . ." It was his turn to look her over. ". . . you, for that matter."

"Boy, are you hearing yourself? You almost lost your mom tonight. You think you're just going to run off and play your trumpet and leave me here to take care of everything?"

"I didn't lose her, and now I gotta be able to make sure she's taken care of. That takes money. Look, how else am I going to pay for it? I don't make enough sweeping floors at Mallard's Grocery. And I only make three dollars a night at Charles's, which is the most any music joint pays in Five Points. But if I were in Ella Fitzgerald's band, I'd have enough to pay for everything." Not to mention, he'd be able to do the very thing he loved most . . . play jazz all day and night.

Beatrice harrumphed. "All right, say I help you out, but I can only do a few days, tops. I have a little bit tucked away, and Marlene can run the shop for me. You still need to get things set up with that home. And you're going to have to pay me back."

Morgan wrapped the woman in a bear hug. "Thank you, Aunt Bea. You'll see. It'll all work out."

"You better hope so." She draped her stole around her

neck, then paused before turning to leave. "If I were you, I'd pray for a miracle."

His aunt's words played over in his mind. He *did* need a miracle, because there was no gig with Miss Fitzgerald. It could have happened though. He was sure as the shine gleaming off his brass. One time, Dizzy Gillespie heard B.C. Hobbs laying down chords on his sax, and the next thing you knew, B.C. had a train ticket to New York.

All Morgan needed was to get his opportunity back.

Folks would probably say he was being naïve, that he had plenty of time to do his thing. But life was short. His father's early death and his mom's stroke proved that. And when it came to making it in the music biz, you got one shot. Lose it and, well, the public would move on to the next cat who could blow. If he didn't seize this now, he'd be stuck playing dives in Five Points for the rest of his life.

Morgan spent an unrestful, fretful night at his mother's bedside. He left the hospital the next morning without bothering to go home. Instead, wearing the same but now wrinkled suit, he stood in front of the Revival Church on Stout Street. His mother's church. Not the more popular Shorter AME Church, where according to his mother the women were snooty.

Trumpet still in hand, Morgan stared at the tall-steepled, white clapboard building he hadn't stepped in since he was a teenager. For years, his mother harped on him about how he needed to have the Lord Jesus in his life. And if there was any time Morgan needed the ear of God, it was now. He went inside and took a seat in the back row.

Recognizing Morgan, Deacon Bennett, an elder of the church, slowly shuffled over. "Young man, we heard about your mother. So sorry."

Morgan shook his hand. "Thank you, sir. I appreciate it."

A few other members approached Morgan with their well wishes and prayers for Sister Marshall.

Morgan remembered how when he first pulled the trumpet from the trash, he would practice behind Rose's back, while she was at work at the Deep Rock water facility, until one day she came home early and caught him. She beat his ass something good, though she conceded he was his daddy's son and trumpet playing was in his blood. She said, "But you need to be careful and be willing to pay the price."

Morgan was willing, all right, but the price would *not* be his mom. He had to make sure she got better. And because he didn't subscribe to her superstitious nonsense, he would prove to her that he wasn't playing the devil's horn.

Pastor Green droned on with his sermon, but said one thing that caught Morgan's attention: ". . . and let us remember what it says in James, chapter four, verse ten: *Humble yourself before the Lord, and He will lift you up.*"

Soon, the choir sang in joyful praise of the gospel, the congregation clapped with fervor, and the collection baskets made their way up and down the pews.

Pastor Green intoned, "Open your hearts and your wallets for the church's fundraiser for a new roof. Come thee and help the Lord as the Lord has helped all of thee. Amen."

The plate reached Morgan, and he rifled through his pockets, dropping in a dollar. The basket overflowed with coins and bills. Three more baskets circulated, then at the end, Deacon Bennett and another man poured them all into one large basket.

The church, Morgan thought, was not unlike a nightclub. Money coming in hand over fist.

That's right! Charles wore tailored suits and lived in an expensive house. Cash flowed into the Silver Sax like the South Platte River into the Missouri River. Why didn't he think of it before? Charles had helped their family from time to time, when Rose would accept it. Milton had been Charles's best friend, and Charles said he felt a duty to look after Milton's family.

Charles would help, of course he would.

And after Morgan hit the big time, he would pay Charles back . . . with interest.

Morgan staggered out of the church in desperate need of food and sleep. But he didn't stop for either. He made a beeline to Charles's. When he turned the corner at the end of California Street, the tension left him. Charles's car was parked in front of his house. Morgan hurried up the walk and let himself in. Nobody locked their doors in the neighborhood.

Charles was sitting at his kitchen table, going over some paperwork. When he saw Morgan, he stood, putting a hand on Morgan's shoulder. "You look like you haven't been home. I'm mighty sorry for your loss, son."

"Well, there's good news. The doctors were able to save her." Morgan set his horn on the table, bell down, and took a seat. He grabbed an apple from the fruit bowl and took a bite.

Charles returned to his seat. "That's wonderful. I'm happy to hear it."

"But the doctor isn't sure if she's going to fully recover."

"Damn. I'm sorry. She's a good woman."

"But that's not the worst of it. She's going to need long-term care, and I can't afford it right now."

Charles shook his head, letting out a heavy sigh. "I want to help you, Morgan, but money is tight these days."

Morgan leaned forward in his chair, the apple forgotten

in his hand. "But what about the nightclub?" He hurried on: "And I'm not asking for charity. It'll be a loan until I'm able to pay you back."

"It's not that, son. I know you would. But the Silver Sax has been losing money for months. I'm barely staying afloat." He indicated the piles of papers on his table. "I've been trying to figure out how to keep paying the staff and keep the lights on."

"How can that be? Music is booming in Five Points!"

"It was easier when I first opened the club. Now . . ." He shook his head, spreading his hands open. "I'm one of four dozen music joints here in The Points. The Rossonian is right at the center of it all. Can't get in? Well, the 715 or Casino or Lil's are only steps away. Famous and local jazz musicians all have their choice. Who wants to venture this far north on Welton to get to my place?"

"Miss Fitzgerald did."

"She's the exception. She likes to find the jewel in unexpected places. And bless her for it. Her agreeing to do a show tonight is going to help."

Morgan rocked back in his chair. "She's still here?"

Charles nodded, a weary but grateful grin on his face. "She's going to put in a special performance before she leaves tomorrow."

Adrenaline surged through Morgan. He sprang from his seat and began to pace. This was it. God was giving him a second chance.

Charles eyed him. "What is it?"

Morgan crouched by Charles. "Last night, you told me to show Miss Fitzgerald what I was made of, right?"

"Yeah, and she was sorry to hear about your mother."

"And . . . if she's using the house band again . . ." Morgan grabbed Charles by his upper arms. "Could I get another shot with her tonight?"

"You're the house band's trumpet player," Charles responded uneasily.

Not for much longer! Morgan stopped in his tracks. He wouldn't be able to leave with Miss Fitzgerald, even if she asked, though he was confident she would after she heard him play. First, he had to make sure his mom got the care she needed. The hospital wouldn't throw her in the streets, but the nursing home would expect their money up front. Rose would need to be moved soon, much sooner than Morgan would be ready to pay, playing in Miss Fitzgerald's band or not.

Money pouring into that basket at the Revival rose in his mind, and a smile spread across his face. What did they do with the collection money until the bank opened the next day? Hid it in the church until morning.

His aunt had said he needed a miracle, and his mom always told him that God helped those who helped themselves. Okay, she didn't mean it like this, but he would pay it back. He would send a large anonymous donation, ten times what he took.

Morgan let go of Charles's arms. He picked up his horn and strode to the front door, proclaiming over his shoulder, "Great, I'm going to be there tonight to play that song!"

Morgan went home to shower and shave. He had the perfect plan. He'd wait until dark, "borrow" the money from the church, and give it Charles for Rose's care. Then he'd impress the hell out of Miss Fitzgerald and be on his way to fame and fortune.

Easy-peasy.

Getting in the Revival's back office was simple enough.

Prying open the metal filing cabinet with the fireplace poker sitting beside the tiny room's stone hearth wasn't difficult. Using a screwdriver he'd stuffed in his pocket to snap off the flimsy lock on the heavy, ornate wooden box? Piece of cake.

As Morgan opened the lid, an exalted breath escaped his lips. Dozens of bills in stacked bundles lined the box.

"Morgan? Is that you, son?" Deacon Bennett stood in the open doorway, a flashlight in one hand. "What are you doing?"

Morgan slammed down the lid and held the box possessively to his chest.

Deacon Bennett shook his head. "You don't need to do this, the Lord—"

What did the deacon know about what Morgan needed?

Morgan moved, intending to pass the old man, but Deacon Bennett had set his flashlight down. He tried to grab the box from Morgan's tight grip. They struggled until Morgan wrenched the box away, swinging it at the deacon. The box hit the side of the man's head, the money spilling out. Deacon Bennett stumbled back four jerky steps before going down. The back of his head slammed into the edge of the stone hearth like an accent note in a discordant harmony.

Morgan's heart paused for several painful beats, then became a sustained, steady vibration against his rib cage. Helpless in his terror and unsure what to do, he knelt beside Deacon Bennett and took his wrist, feeling a faint pulse.

He should get help. But he needed this money.

His vision blurred as he saw blood seep toward the scattered dollar bills. His fingers trembled when he reached over the deacon's motionless body to collect them. Only when a single tear dripped from his cheek did he realize he was crying.

Sitting back on his haunches, Morgan wept as if exhausted

from a burden he'd been carrying since he was ten years old. He wept the tears that he couldn't when his father died—his mother admonishing, "Your daddy paid the price by playing that damn horn." He wept the tears that he should've when he thought his mother was dying. Full of resentment and rage for missing his moment with Ella Fitzgerald.

Morgan pulled out his yellow silk handkerchief, this time to wipe his tears. He stuffed the bills in his pockets. He knew he should try to do something for Deacon Bennett, but he couldn't. If Morgan went to jail, how would that help anyone?

He took the old man's wrist again—and this time, he felt nothing.

Morgan rose on unsteady legs. All he could do now was make it big and use the money he earned to pay back all his misdeeds. He'd send donations to the church, as well as to Deacon Bennett's wife. He'd also send money to Charles to ensure Rose got her proper care.

Praying no one saw him, he snuck out the back of the church and took the long way down to the music district. Using side streets and avoiding people. He needed to pull himself together so Charles wouldn't suspect anything.

Morgan walked through the back door of the Silver Sax. It would be another thirty minutes before the place officially opened. He found Charles in the back office and hoped he'd erased the horror of what he'd done from his face. Hoped that Charles would think the red eyes and haggard expression were from grief and lack of sleep.

He emptied his pockets, dumping the money on the desk. It was close to five hundred dollars. Morgan had stopped to count it in a deserted alley. "Can you make sure my mom is taken care of while I'm gone? I'll send more."

Charles looked at the crumpled bills piled on his desk. "Where are you going, and where did you get the money?"

Morgan decided to not answer the first question and went to the one he'd prepared a lie for: "Playing the dogs at the Mile High. It was my lucky day."

Charles raised an eyebrow.

"Look, I played everything I had and won. God is looking out for me. He knows I want to play jazz and travel, and He put that opportunity in front of me two times. What else could it be but destiny? And . . . well, I . . ." Deacon Bennett lying on that cold church floor appeared in his mind. "Well, God helped me out and let me score that money."

The skepticism left Charles's face, replaced by a broad grin. "It sure does seem like God is looking out for you. Ella is definitely in need of a new trumpeter."

Anxiety seared Morgan where exultation should have resided. Everything he did led him to this moment, this victory. Instead, nausea threatened him, and he shuddered to keep it at bay.

Charles studied him, brow furrowed. No doubt he expected Morgan to be ecstatic about the news, so Morgan obliged. He slapped the palms of his hands together. "Hot damn! You see what I'm saying. It's destiny, baby!"

Charles laughed. "That it is." He gathered up the money and locked it in his office safe. "I'll make sure your mother gets the care she needs. The club is going to be in the black after tonight."

And it was true. The Silver Sax had a full house. The fullest Morgan had ever seen it. This was the night dreams were made of.

The First Lady of Song arrived in all her elegance and

splendor, wearing a blue metallic brocade gown. She expressed joy about his mother's expected recovery. Morgan, subdued and contrite, expressed his gratitude for her compassion and generosity.

Ray and the rest of the fellows waited on stage. All wearing their best suits and ties, and all clean-shaven and shoes spit shined. When Morgan joined them, they each gave him their solemn well wishes for his mom's recovery. But the occasion was too momentous to keep their excitement in check for long. Morgan couldn't blame them. If it were under any other circumstance, he would be crowing the loudest right now.

Charles walked on stage so he could introduce the Sax's special guest himself. All the fellows grinned as they took their places. Morgan moved beside Ray, who said, "You okay, kid?"

Morgan nodded. His finger rubbed the initials on his horn.

Charles finished his intro for Miss Fitzgerald and she took the stage. The crowd erupted in a cacophony of applause. Morgan wondered if it was like this for her every night, and if one ever got used to it.

As the crowd's adoration started to fade, Ella turned to Morgan and smiled an invitation for him to begin. He inhaled deeply and pressed his lips, buzzing into the trumpet the opening notes to "Dream a Little Dream of Me."

The fellows joined in. Ella did her trademark scat, then sung those lovely words. Her soothing voice made Morgan forget about the wretched things he'd done, all in the name of chasing a dream *and* being a dutiful son. The music was a balm to his troubled soul.

To play the sweet, sweet music was all he ever wanted.

Morgan closed his eyes. Ella's voice and his horn were the only things that mattered. Not Deacon Bennett, not Charles, not his mother, and possibly not even his father.

As they reached the song's final chords, he opened his eyes.

Two uniformed officers moved through the crowd. No one seemed to notice, so fixated were they on Ella. The cops' attention never wavered from the stage, but it wasn't the Queen of Jazz they were interested in. They only had eyes for Morgan, would-be legendary jazz trumpeter straight out of Five Points.

The song ended, and the crowd was on its feet. Ella's smile was radiant, and she bowed, then turned to present Morgan.

Yes, he probably would have gotten that coveted invitation. But he wouldn't be leaving Denver tomorrow. And it wasn't his destiny to play in the great Miss Ella Fitzgerald's band.

He had it all wrong.

God didn't put the idea of stealing the church money in front of him. It was the devil, and like his mom told him, the devil always collected his due.

ON GRASMERE LAKE

BY MATHANGI SUBRAMANIAN
Washington Park

The day they found her father's body, Nithi's feet moved on their own, carrying her out of her front door and down Louisiana Avenue, toward Washington Park. It was winter, and pale, leafless maple and oak trees twisted toward the sky like bleached bones. Renovated homes alternated with cleared plots of land, the houseless dirt turned up like freshly dug graves.

It's over, Nithi told herself, *it's all over now.* She waited to feel relief, but all she felt was the wind, cold and fierce and lifeless, beating against her cheeks.

Nithi lived with her mother, Priya, in a bungalow on Clayton Street that Priya inherited from her parents. Priya's mother had died of breast cancer when Priya was in elementary school. Her father had died of a heart attack when Priya was nineteen, just days after she told him she was pregnant with Nithi.

"I dream about him," Priya told Nithi. "He sits on my bed, we talk. He still smells piney, like his favorite aftershave. It's so . . . comforting. So real."

Nithi's dead father, Jason, visited her dreams too, though his presence was anything but comforting. His form shifted and blinked, as though what was left of his body couldn't get a proper grip on the atmosphere. Waves of fury radiated off him, shimmering hotly. He never spoke to Nithi. He just watched her, his pinprick pupils inky black, his irises blue as broken glass.

Were his eyes blue when he was alive? Nithi couldn't remember. All she remembered was the way hatred spewed out of him like lava, the way his fists cratered the walls of their home, turning it into a foreign planet, a landscape unable to sustain human life.

At Grasmere Lake, Nithi collapsed onto her favorite bench by the dirt path that led to the lawn bowling club, and faced the frozen water. A flock of Canada geese slid across the frozen surface of the lake. A few of them broke away from the group and rose, honking, beating their long, sharp wings against the frigid air. Their choked voices cut a silver path through the corpse-gray sky.

Nithi tucked her down jacket tightly around her legs. Not that it made a difference: on the walk over, her body had grown too numb to feel anything, even the frosty air. Her phone buzzed in her pocket.

"Are you okay?" Priya asked.

"Yes," Nithi lied. How many times in her life had her mother asked if she was okay? How many times had Nithi said yes, when she really meant no?

"Don't worry, kanna," Priya said. "Farah Aunty's the detective on the case."

Farah Aunty was Priya's mother's best friend. They had gone to South High together. *This is good*, Nithi told herself. *Farah Aunty's smart. She'll take care of this.*

Nithi clutched the phone to her ear and whispered, "Amma, I can't lose you."

"No one's losing anyone," Priya said steadily.

Nithi wanted to believe her. But after everything that had happened, it was hard to remember what hope felt like.

In high school, Nithi would study her reflection in the mirror, searching for traces of her father. Jason was white, his hair blond and thinning. There was something wan and discolored about him, as though he were already half-dead. Nithi's skin, on the other hand, was dark brown, her hair thick and black, like her Tamil American mother's. When Nithi found no evidence of Jason in her high cheekbones, her snub nose—all inherited from Priya—her shoulders would sag with relief.

Her first year at Community College of Denver, Nithi took a course called "Human Services for Families." In one unit, they discussed domestic violence. The required reading felt like a time line of Nithi's parents' lives. Survivors of abuse, the text said, tended to start dating their spouses young (Priya and Jason met in high school), to have little family support (Jason was in and out of foster care; after her father's death, Priya was an orphan), and to have a limited social network (as far as Nithi knew, Farah Aunty was Priya's only friend).

Abusers, the text said, often had histories of trauma. Jason never talked to Nithi much about his childhood—he never talked to Nithi much at all—so she couldn't confirm this. But when she read about abusers' lack of employment, their heavy alcohol and drug use, their history of depression, she thought of her father coming home at the end of the day, his time unaccounted for, his collar reeking of smoke and cheap beer, his eyes bloodshot and bagged.

Nithi shuddered, remembering those evenings. She would do her homework, Priya would return from her nursing shift at Rose Medical. The two of them would make dinner together, cheerfully gossiping about Priya's colleagues and Nithi's classmates, amiably arguing about how much was too much salt. Then Jason would arrive, and the air around them would congeal. In her nervousness, Nithi would grow clumsy, dropping vegetable peels on the floor or nicking herself with a knife. Jason would swoop down on her like a raptor, berating her for making a mess, for not being able to do anything right. The pressure cooker would shriek and he would yell about the noise, tell Priya to learn to cook something besides her damn foreign food. The women crept around him, trying to erase themselves, or, if they stayed visible, to be Jason's idea of perfect. But it was no use. Whatever they did, it was never enough. He was always angry. They were always wrong.

"We can't keep living like this, Amma," Nithi would say. "We have to leave."

"We will," Priya promised. But the years passed, and they stayed, and they stayed, and they stayed.

Despite the cold, the park was crowded. A pack of blond women in athleisure gear circled the lake, clutching coffee cups in their leather-gloved hands. A young Latinx couple walked their Pomeranian down the hill from South Franklin Street. The tiny creature darted, startling a family of ducks. Nithi breathed deeply, trying to leash her spasming heart.

Nithi heard footsteps on the dead grass. In a minute, she saw that they belonged to a brown-skinned woman wearing a long green peacoat. The stranger stopped to watch the sunshine bounce off the lake, and then settled on the bench next to Nithi. Nithi turned away from her, hoping she would understand Nithi was not in the mood to talk. But if the woman saw the gesture, she ignored it.

"It's not so bad in the sun, is it?" the stranger asked. She smelled like mothballs and talcum powder, like an antique store. "I love this lake, but the lake at the north end of the park, Smith Lake, is my favorite. You know it used to be a beach? In my mother's time, people swam there. Well, *she* didn't. Black people weren't allowed. People like my mother. People like you and me."

Nithi raised an eyebrow, wondering if she should correct her. Nithi's skin was dark enough that she was often mistaken for Black, especially in Denver, where every person of color was assumed to be either Black or Latinx.

The woman continued, "My mother and her friends protested here once. The police came, and they beat them." Nithi stared into the woman's eyes. They were lighter than Nithi's, almost golden. "That's what men do, isn't it? They hurt us. Especially when we fight back."

Nithi thought of the sound of her father's fist in her mother's stomach, his open palm on her mother's face. For the first time all morning, she shivered.

In her dreams, Nithi spoke to her father, but he never replied.

"I'm not afraid of you anymore," she said, wondering if the dead believed the lies of the living.

Other nights, she asked, "Why did you hate us so much?" What she really wanted to ask was, "Why did you hate *me* so much?"

Still other nights, she chanted, "You can't hurt us now, you can't hurt us now, you can't hurt us now." Repeated it like a mantra, her body rocking back and forth until she exhausted herself, falling out of the dream and into a viscous, colorless sleep. Nothingness covered her like a weighted blanket, heavy and black and impenetrable.

It wasn't pleasant, dreaming of her dad, but it was an improvement over her usual nightmares. Before Jason died,

Nithi's nights were plagued by nightmares of escaping her home with her mother, only to find her father following, hunting them like prey.

"He didn't used to be like this," Priya said sometimes. "For our second wedding anniversary, he surprised me with a home-cooked meal—baked macaroni and a salad. We ate it after you fell asleep. Some nights, he brought home flowers for no reason. In the fall he brought black-eyed Susans, my favorite. In the spring he'd bring home lilacs. His favorite."

Nithi tried to imagine this man who pulled casseroles out of ovens, who knew the name of a flower whose blossoms felt like crushed velvet. She remembered nothing gentle about her father, nothing redeemable. Any kindness he had shown Nithi or her mother belonged to a history only Priya had known.

The ice on Grasmere Lake was lined with frost. Slowly, the sun's strengthening heat bore down on it, fissuring its weakest parts. When it finally cracked, it sounded like breaking bones.

Nithi studied the woman on the bench. A pattern of bruises bloomed across her cheekbones, circled her neck. A raised scar mountained her face from her temple to her jaw. It reminded Nithi of the way Priya looked in the mornings, before she put on her makeup, her dupattas, her infinity scarves.

"Are you okay?" Nithi asked the woman.

"Oh, all this?" she asked, waving at her face with a gloved hand. "I'll be fine."

"Do you need help?" Nithi asked. "I could help."

But could she? When Nithi graduated from high school, she got into Grinnell, her dream school. Instead of leaving the state, she registered for Community College of Denver. She said it was to save money, but really, it was because she was afraid that if she left Priya at home alone with her father, Jason would eventually kill her.

Instead of protecting Priya, Nithi's decision made things worse. Her father cursed Nithi for staying home, for not getting a real job, even though, as far as she knew, Jason didn't have one either. To appease him, Nithi took an early morning shift at the Whole Foods off the highway. Jason blamed Nithi's lack of ambition on Priya's parenting, her bad genes, her inability to be a role model. The beatings started earlier, and they lasted longer. Until he died.

Or, more accurately, until he was murdered.

This was why Nithi still feared her father. Why, when he came to her in dreams, insubstantial, furious, she shrank from him. Because she knew that the circumstances of her father's death could destroy her. That his violence was larger than the grave.

"Are *you* okay?" the stranger asked. She pulled out a handkerchief and handed it to Nithi. It was only then that Nithi felt tears sliding down her face, freezing on her chin.

"No," Nithi whispered, taking the handkerchief and wiping her eyes. It smelled fresh, like it had been dried in the sun. "I did something terrible, and now someone else is going to pay for it."

"Oh, now," the woman said kindly, "you seem like a nice girl. How bad could it really be?"

"Bad," Nithi said, her body heaving with panic. "Really bad."

"Huh," the woman said. All around them, dead cattails rustled, their bodies stiff and broken. "Why'd you do it?"

"I don't know," Nithi said. "I was just so angry, you know? So mad."

"There, there," the woman said, patting the sleeve of Nithi's down coat. Her hand felt insubstantial, like a gust of wind. "It'll be okay. You'll see."

Nithi nodded dumbly, avoiding the stranger's incandescent eyes.

Three months ago, Nithi took an evening shift at Whole Foods. Their family needed the money—Rose Medical had cut down Priya's hours, and although Nithi's father claimed he had a job in construction, whatever he made, he didn't share. The extra shift meant Nithi wouldn't be home until after dinner, when her father's violence was always at its worst.

"I'll be fine," Priya had said. "Don't worry."

Nithi had told herself all kinds of lies about the consequences of her absence. *It's not like being there stops him*, she reasoned. In the past, Nithi had tried prying Jason off of Priya, but her father was strong, and he would send Nithi ricocheting across the room. Once Nithi had called the police, but they took forever to respond. By the time they got there, the fight was over, and her father had driven away. The police hadn't believed Nithi and Priya's story, and even if they had, they said that there was nothing they could do. One of the officers—a woman—handed Priya a business card.

"In case you want to see about a restraining order," the woman said.

As they walked away, the male officer asked, "Why'd you do that? You know they never call."

The female officer shrugged and said, "One day one of them might."

In her human services course, Nithi read that survivors of domestic abuse are most vulnerable when they leave. Leaving, Nithi read, sent abusers into the blindest, most murderous rages, rages that got victims killed. It was, in short, next to impossible. The only choice was to stay where you were and to try to survive.

"Here, take this," the stranger said, reaching into her coat pocket. She pulled out a heart-shaped locket, the kind Nithi sometimes saw in old movies, or in the vintage stores on Colfax. When the stranger held it up, the silvery metal caught the sun and tossed the light around the park, glittering on the lake's petaled ice, the lawn's melting snow.

"It's beautiful," Nithi said. She reached for the necklace and clutched it into her palm. The metal was so cold that she could feel it through her gloves. "But I can't take this. It's too nice."

"It's good luck," the woman said. "You need it more than I do."

Before Nithi could protest, the stranger stood up and walked away.

The night her father died, Nithi drove home from Whole Foods, her neck tingling, her arms riddled with goose bumps. She tore through the empty streets, far above the speed limit, some force she couldn't describe pulling her to her mother, churning her stomach with dread.

She was right to be afraid. When she walked through the door, her father had her mother up against the wall, his hands clutching her throat. Priya's skin was tinged with blue, her eyes popping from her head. It was, Nithi was sure, the last moments of her mother's life.

The locket caught Nithi's reflection, stretched it into a distorted version of her face. It was like staring at a stranger. Her phone buzzed, breaking the spell.

244 // <small>Denver Noir</small>

"Mom?" Nithi said. "Are you okay? What's going on?"

"So you remember that robbery gone bad? The one on Elizabeth Street?" Priya asked.

"Yeah," Nithi replied cautiously. A man had broken into a house and tried to steal some antique jewelry, some electronics. He'd been caught in the act: the owner came home halfway through. The thief ended up killing her—a woman, Nithi thought, although she wasn't sure why she remembered that. Farah Aunty was investigating the case. She had told them about it one night over dinner, a few days before Jason died.

"Well, Farah says that your father was responsible for it." Priya's voice was heavy with—something. Was it exhaustion or relief? *Maybe both*, Nithi thought.

"So what does that mean?" Nithi asked.

"It means they're not going to look into who murdered your father," Priya said. "At least, not right away. See, the DNA match means that Farah just closed a case—and a really prominent one too—so there's no pressure on her to open a new one. Not until they do the paperwork and trial and everything—which, Farah says, could take awhile. So long that they probably won't be able to do a thorough investigation of your father's death. When you wait that long, apparently, the leads go cold."

"Did he do it, though?" Nithi whispered. "Did he kill that woman?"

"He's charged with a crime, kanna," Priya said. "Does it matter which one?"

Nithi watched the ducks dip their heads into the lake, their tails pointing toward the sky, their bright orange legs pedaling frantically, keeping them afloat. She slumped on the bench, spent. Memories warmed her icy blood.

The night her father died, the night she'd seen her mother up against the wall, seconds from death, Nithi felt herself rise out of her body, as though she were watching the scene from the ceiling. She watched herself snatch the cast-iron frying pan, the one they used to make dosas. She watched herself charge her father. And then she watched herself pummel him, over and over, on his head, his neck, his face. She watched herself smash his skull, his nose, his rib cage. Long after he lay on the ground, bloody and lifeless, she kept beating him, beating him, beating him. Her vision was clouded with a red fog, and her bones clattered with a clotting, crimson rage.

When it was over, she returned to her body, her senses sharp as a wild animal's. She felt the heft of the skillet in her hand. Smelled the coppery tang of bloodied metal. Heard her mother gasping, her damaged windpipe desperate for oxygen.

Nithi rushed to her mother's side. "Are you okay?" She wept. And then she repeated, "I'm sorry, I'm so sorry, I'm so, so sorry."

Her mother, broken and near death, stroked Nithi's hair, kissed the top of her head, and croaked, "Call Farah."

And then, when Nithi fished her cell phone out of her pocket, Priya said, "Tell her I killed him."

"What?" Nithi said, the phone already pressed against her ear.

"You heard me. Tell her it was me."

Farah must've been the one to take the body to the empty old house on Josephine Street. The one that, when they demolished it, turned up Jason's corpse. In the crime scene pictures, the bulldozer was still there, its steel jaw poised above the pile of bricks, its neck stretched like a viper. Nithi's father's broken hand stuck up through the dirt, stiff and ghostly and still.

No investigation, Nithi thought. No opportunity for her mother to turn herself in. No reason for Nithi to hate herself, first for being a murderer, and then for letting her mother take the blame. *It's all okay now*, Nithi told herself. *It's all okay.*

She held the necklace up to the sun. It twisted like a pendulum on its chain. The stranger was right—it really was good luck. Nithi saw now that the locket was encrusted with jewels—red, green, blue. She watched them glimmer against the surging clouds, spiral in the sudden wind.

"Oh my god!"

A woman ran toward Nithi, eyes bloodshot, face bare. She looked so much like Nithi—the same coloring, the same curly dark hair. But also the same look of desperation, of sleeplessness. Of being haunted.

"You found it!" the woman said.

"This?" Nithi asked.

"Yes!" Gently, the woman removed the locket from Nithi's hand and opened it. On one side was a picture of the stranger Nithi had spoken to a few minutes earlier. And on the other was the face of this woman, the one who was talking to her now.

"It's yours?" Nithi asked, bewildered.

"It was my grandmother's. I thought we lost it," the woman said, her voice breaking. She cradled the necklace. "Of course it was here. This was her favorite bench. She must have dropped it the last time she came here."

"*Was* her favorite bench?"

"She passed away. Three months ago," the woman said. Her pupils reflected the geese and the ducks, the lake and the trees, the snow and the ice. The whole park was trapped, there, in the rings of her eyes. "There was a robbery. You probably heard about it? The guy took a bunch of my grandmother's jewelry. I thought they'd taken this too. Really, it means so much to me that you found it. And to think it happened just as I was passing by! What luck."

"What luck," Nithi repeated.

"Thank you," the woman said, clutching Nithi's arms through her coat. "Really, thank you."

"Where did you say your grandmother lived?" Nithi asked.

"Elizabeth Street," the woman said. When she walked away, it looked like she was being swallowed up by the sky.

EL ARMERO

BY MARIO ACEVEDO

Globeville

I exit the number 12 bus at the corner of Forty-fifth Avenue and Camino de Frida Kahlo. Traffic rumbles above me. I'm under the Mousetrap, an immense concrete confusion straddling Globeville, where Interstates 25 and 70 intersect north of downtown Denver. I take a moment to catch my breath. The air carries a metallic tang and tastes of grit filtering from the rush of trucks and cars on the overpass.

My path is blocked by yellow tape and a battered metal placard: *Detour Desvío*. Tire marks from construction equipment crisscross the sidewalk. To my left extends an immense pit where the highway will be broadened. Es el año de Nuestro Señor 2027, and time for the politicians to pay back favors by diverting public money into more "infrastructure."

I take note of the arrangement of square holes beneath the overpass where the footings for a new foundation will be poured. My gaze continues to the existing interchange. Street legend has it a lot of problems were solved when that part of the highway was built. Snitches and witnesses disappeared, buried beneath thick layers of concrete.

I shrug. Not my concern what happened. Nor what might happen.

In that mysterious way that rumors circulate through the barrio, I got word that Toro needs me, which is why I'm here. I want to hope I know why he summons me, but I know I'm wrong.

I amble north, taking it easy. If I walk too fast, the left side of my chest hitches, constricting my breath.

I pass the parking lot where bolillos queue up to take advantage of today's specials at Sweet Buds Cannabis. Round the corner, cars, pickups, bums on bicycles wait their turn at the take-out window of Pato's Liquor Drive-Thru. While the weed store looks as neat and slick as a Starbucks, Pato's is a cinder-block shack flanked by walls of particle board, the surfaces coated by flaking house paint and tattered posters advertising cheap beer and whiskey. There's little in my surroundings that isn't tagged with graffiti. The posts of streetlamps litter the sidewalk like fallen timbers, mowed down by bad drivers.

Across the street stands the city's latest attempt at solving the area's crime problem. An electronic billboard cycles through a red X canceling a pistol, bullets transforming into doves, and the message: *Stop the shooting! Love one another!* The mayor says this billboard is a peace memorial to the victims of gun violence. She calls it "a compelling symbol of hope triumphing over despair, of virtue over lawlessness."

But ask me and I'll tell you we have enough symbols.

Every time it rains, this stretch of real estate, from here to Elyria-Swansea, floods like a motherfucker, the way it's done for years, but the government never gets around to fixing that mess. Dolores Huerta Vocational closed due to lack of funding, which cut short both my GED studies and my chance for a certificate in applied electronics. Drug abatement and rehab counseling also got axed. Fiscal restraint and all that. Yet City Hall managed to cough up two and a half million dollars to shower on the media relations firm that designed this "symbol."

If you want more irony, here's some: The local gangster

wannabes use the billboard for target practice, and the more brazen they are about it, the better to gain street cred. One chica—all preggers—was strolling past when she got clipped by a ricochet. She not only lost the baby, she wears a colostomy bag for life. Talk about bad luck, ese. So the word around here is, don't get close to the Peace Memorial or you might get popped by a stray bala.

So why stick around?

Because you can run away to another town but as long as you live among raza, you'll end up in yet another barrio. Go a thousand miles, it's really just like you only got up on the other side of bed. The view is a little different but your situation hasn't changed.

For sure, one way out is the military. Because of the war against terror, which never ends, and a lack of volunteers, the army dropped its recruitment standards so low even someone as rasquache as me is eligible (that is, prestabbing). Uncle Sam dangles all the bennies: steady pay, enlistment bonuses, job training, mierda, mierda, mierda. Of the eight vatos I know personally who signed up, four never returned—meaning they found new lives somewhere else; two did come back in coffins, and one came back covered in burn scars and missing most of the top of his head. That's Tomas Sada—we used to call him Guapo. You'll see him out shambling about in his walker, drooling and pissing all over himself.

Then there's Marco Paz, a drone technician who came back from the Air Force strung out on Modafinix (weapons-grade Adderall that jazzed his brain to work at computer speed) until the morning he stretched his neck across the track of the J-Line light rail. When the cops showed up, they had to chase away the raccoons playing tug-of-war with his severed head. That's the image I think about every Veterans Day.

This afternoon I keep walking past St. Joseph Polish Catholic Church. Hard to believe the neighborhood was once home to Poles, Russians, and Slavs. Then the Italians came, followed by us gente. Actually, we were always here, but back then we didn't count.

Funny name for a place, *Globeville*. This misshapen plot of land abuts the South Platte River (what Mark Twain once called a "yellow trickle") and was named after a smelter. I wipe my nose, mindful of all the crap the government keeps finding in the soil. Cadmium, zinc, arsenic, lead. *Don't eat from vegetable gardens. If the air smells bad, don't go outside. Don't play in standing water.*

Arriving at Reies López Tijerina Acres (aka subsidized housing), I climb the outside stairs, slowly, to the third floor. The punteros on lookout give me the nod.

Toro answers his door on the second knock. His craggy face looms over me, and he glances to the tool bag in my hand. "Éntrale, Rafael."

Thick kohl sets off Toro's eyes, the color of rusted steel. The electro-ink on his thick neck dances like snakes on fire. A tank top drapes his broad chest and shows off biceps each as big and square as the business ends of sledgehammers. Gym shorts ride up on hairy thighs so muscular they seem powerful enough to bulldoze through a police roadblock. His massive, scarred hands are matching résumés of every beat-down he's given. Toro couldn't be more intimidating if he had horns growing out of his head.

But he's got his charms. I should know, me and him had a thing going for a while. Sometimes my vieja at the time, Delia, would join us. She and I used to watch Toro snooze after we'd worn him out, the tats on his wide back writhing and smoldering as they faded from neon yellow to a cool aqua color. Delia totally freaked out in a good way and she got herself inked up too. But then she overdid it like she does everything else, so balling her became like fucking one of those anime sex robots you can rent on Colfax.

Domestic Intervention Services peed their polyester pants in happiness when Toro came out about being bi (who isn't these days?), thinking that would put him in touch with his feminine side. They also loved that he bleached his hair and dyed it bright pink.

Toro lays a big paw on my shoulder and the old feelings soak through me. My knees threaten to give and as I think about falling, I want to drag him on top of me. I pretend to believe that I'm wrong about how he feels about me. I pretend to believe that things between him and me can go back to the way they used to be.

"Un cafecito, hermano?" He steps back to let me pass. "Pan dulce?"

Hermano. Sigh. I used to be his pan dulce.

The disappointment stings, but I hide the pain behind a smile. "Gracias. Después." A snack can wait, as I don't want to dribble coffee and crumbs all over my work.

Toro leads me through the cramped living room to the kitchen table. I pause once to catch my breath. The stairs about wore me out. Last year I got stabbed by Levon Spencer. No reason to carry a grudge though, Levon mistook me for Antonio Lopez—all us greasers look alike. I get it. Besides, Levon OD'd a couple of weeks later, so according to the school counselor, it's best to forgive and forget.

Always look for the blessing, right, ese? The blessing here is that stabbing, the collapsed lung, and the resulting breathing problems downgraded my health mobility profile to a 2B, meaning no hard physical labor, and so my name is automatically deleted from lists when jales for roofer and warehouse technician circulate through Community Force Placement. Thanks to the injury, the toughest gigs I used to get were as a flagman at construction cone zones, but the robots have taken those jobs like they have most everything else. Though they've yet to make a robot that can do what I'm here to do for Toro.

In the living room, throw pillows decorated with la Virgen and copies of noir movie posters are scattered over a sofa cocooned in clear plastic. A cumbia murmurs from a speaker alongside unlit votive candles on a spice rack. A calendar for Jimenez Tortillas hangs on the wall. Through the sliding glass door I scope out the narrow balcony where an ashtray sits in the center of a small patio table. Toro seems alone.

"¿Y tu tía?" I ask.

"Comprando sus frajos en el 7-Eleven." He opens the kitchen blinds to let in more light. I set my tool bag on the table and hang my backpack on a chair. I pull out the chair and sit. After I zip open my satchel of tools, I arrange what I'll need on a square of repurposed yoga mat.

As I do this, Toro digs into my backpack, curious, suspicious as ever. He stacks the books I carried onto the table: *Remains of the Day. Paisaje de otoño. Zen and the Art of Motorcycle Maintenance.* He fingers the book spines. "These any good?"

"I like them."

He grunts in approval. "Me cae que estudias. No como esos grifos que caminan en nuestras calles. We need more bookworms and fewer junkies."

From under the table, Toro retrieves a large canvas tote that he places in front of me. It's an RF-blocking bag. Inside I count five heaters—three 9mms, a .380, and a .38 Super. The bag smothers any tracking signals from the "smart" guns inside.

Toro makes his bones in this neighborhood as *el sicario
número uno*. You need to settle a score or send a message, *who
you gonna call?* Since violence is his stock in trade, he makes
extra cash fencing guns and ammo.

Returning to the bag, with a signal detector (that I stole
from my last day at Huerta) I check for an active GPS trans-
mitter. I figure the guns have been in the bag some time, as the
batteries are all run down.

"Can you do this one?" Toro handles a really nice PW-Pro
9mm stamped *SFPD*. "But I don't want you to fuck it up."

"Time me," I boast.

He sets the stopwatch on his phone.

I steady the PW-Pro in my left hand. "Go." With a portable
drill I bore a small hole in the back of the frame to puncture
the embedded microprocessor, which lobotomizes the gun.

Smart guns are designed to lock up without the necessary
permission code—supplied by a special ring, or a matching
smart watch, a fingerprint reader, some caca like that. But
there's gotta be a way to disassemble the gun in case things
need fixing. I center a brass punch over the take-down pin in
the slide, give a couple of taps with my plastic mallet, the pin
falls out, and the slide . . . well, it slides off.

I disable the locking solenoid with liquid weld. In another
minute, the grip panels are off and the frame lies bare on the
yoga mat. More taps with the brass punch and mallet, some
twisting with needle-nose pliers, the electronic interface
between the firing mechanism and the trigger falls loose,
and this PW-Pro is as high-tech as my abuelita's cast-iron
comal.

After fitting a small length of coat-hanger wire to replace
the interface linkage, I reinstall the grip panels. I put the slide
back on and rack it. *Clack.* Pull the trigger. *Click.* I repeatedly

work the slide and pull the trigger—*clack, click, clack, click*—and every time, the trigger snaps crisp as it should.

"Listo," I blurt out.

Toro announces, "Four minutes, thirty-three seconds." He grabs the PW-Pro from me. As he examines the pistol, I take a workman's pride in my craft, regardless of what consequences it brings to the community. I, a high school dropout, in less than five minutes, have outsmarted a gaggle of white-bread Silicon Valley engineers and their million-dollar solution to the epidemic of gun violence. It's a misdemeanor to alter a smart gun and a felony to show anyone how to do it. But just go to the dark web and you can find all kinds of tutorials for things you shouldn't do.

"Algo más." I pick up a nail file. "I have to alter the firing pin."

Toro lifts an eyebrow.

I explain: "The end of the firing pin is engraved with a code to trace the gun by imprinting the ammo it shoots. A quick swipe with the file and no more code."

Toro squints down the sights. "Maybe I want the code. Let the world know que una arma de los marranos fue que mordió un soplón."

It's not my concern what he does with the gun, but in this case, a snitch is gonna learn what happens when you cozy up to the law.

Toro loads the magazine with a couple of 9mm rounds he fishes from a pocket in his shorts, fits the magazine into the PW-Pro, and racks the slide. An icy chill freezes my nerves. What the hell is he doing?

He steps to the audio player and turns up the volume till it rattles the windows. Aiming the pistol at some books on a shelf, he fires lengthwise through the stack. Despite the loud music, the blast spanks my ears. The empty casing whirls toward me, bounces off the table, and rolls to the floor. The gun worked flawlessly.

He lowers the volume and, on the PW-Pro, thumbs the magazine release. The empty mag falls into his left hand. He cycles the pistol slide, catching the remaining cartridge as it flings out the ejection port. For a moment he bounces the pistol in his hand, appreciating its heft, smiling, smirking; it's not just a firearm but a fiendish weapon, something evil, a talisman of bad tidings. *Armed and dangerous.*

I want him to acknowledge what I've done for him. That I'm special. *His* special.

Instead he says, "Te aventaste, güey," then picks the spent cartridge off the floor and fits it like a hat on a nearby plastic Jesus.

Güey, like we're big buddies instead of ex-lovers.

Toro lays the gun on the table. He disappears down the hall, a door closes, I hear a shower run. I imagine the water spattering off his muscular body and recall when it was me soaping his smooth contours and the crevices between them.

I fumble my screwdriver and almost let it fall. The act of catching the screwdriver brings my mind back to task. During the next minutes, I take care of the other two smart guns. The last pair in the bag are ghost-gun knockoffs of Serbian Zastavas, which I inspect and deem okay.

He's left his phone on the table, and it vibrates with incoming messages.

The shower squeaks off. After a moment, he returns to the kitchen. His pink hair is slicked back so it looks like an old-fashioned bathing cap. He's changed into designer jeans, alligator cowboy boots. A nice shirt hangs unbuttoned over his chest, a fresh wife-beater plastered to his still-wet, hairy pectorals. Lingering at the hall mirror, he reapplies kohl around his eyes. He pulls a gold chain from his pants pocket and strings it around his neck. Stepping close to retrieve his phone, he smells of soap and cologne, and the fragrance makes my heart ache for things that will never return.

He thumbs through his messages. Furrows his brow. Nods. Grins. I don't know what he's up to; it's not my place to ask.

Regardless, my imagination starts to gallop, dragging behind it jealous thoughts. Who's Toro going to see? Melissa Chacon? Or Enrico "el Perico" Tellez? That diseased marica. Better wear two condoms when you fuck him.

I really want to ask, but asking means I care, and I don't want Toro to think that I do. I can't. It's long over between us. Tears pluck at my eyes, and I focus on putting my tools away.

Just as I zip my tool bag, Toro brings coffee and a campechana. While I finish the pastry, I watch him tuck the PW-Pro into his pants and fluff the shirt over it. He poses in front of the mirror, turning this way and that, like a ruca checking her ass for panty lines.

Since he's packing this particular gun, I figure he's heading out to work and not play, and the jealousy fades.

My business done, I slip my books into the backpack and grab my tool bag. Standing, I gasp for breath, then square my shoulders and face Toro.

Unexpectedly, he drops a hand on my shoulder. "Change in plans, vato. Espérame."

He walks out the front door and the dead bolt clicks. When will he return? How long am I supposed to stay here? I don't leave, because he owes me money, and besides, when Toro tells you to stay, you better stay.

I busy myself with my phone until I toss it aside, bored. I hope for his aunt to arrive and keep me company but she never makes an appearance. Maybe she smells trouble. I click on the television and when the screen asks for the password, I click it off and drop the remote on an end table.

I pick up my books and read for a while. I daydream about being a famous author like Leonardo Padura. As he did, I'll chronicle my life through a series of novels, make it a majestic tale. I know crime. I know survival. Hell, I even have the scars. Me, Rafael Muñoz, the *bard of the barrio*. Maybe that's my ticket out of here.

Afterward, I explore the cramped living room, analyzing the various trinkets Toro has collected since I was last here. My longing for him swirls in my head. I fantasize letting myself into his bedroom, crawling onto the mattress to luxuriate in his masculine scent clinging to the bed linen. I relive every delicious minute that we'd spent here, me taking each visit for granted, thinking there would always be a next time. And then, there were no more next times.

Twilight darkens the windows. I'm hungry and rummage the kitchen. I microwave a couple of tamales and help myself to a beer.

As the evening drags on, I stretch out on the sofa. The front door bangs open and I'm suddenly alert. I expect Toro's aunt but it's Ysidro Bustos, one of his gamberros. "Rafael, nos vamos."

My mind scrambles to catch up. I gather my bags.

"Leave those." He scowls. "Where's your phone?"

I slip it from my pocket.

"Leave it in your backpack."

After I comply, he nods toward the door. I follow him out. He shuts the door behind us, locks it with a key, and hustles toward the stairs. While he bounds down like a goat, I clasp the handrail and ease my way, step by step. Though the night is cool, each breath burns as it wheezes through my lungs.

Ysidro yells over his shoulder, "¡Apúrate, güey!"

I do my best to match his frantic pace. My chest tightens around the knot of my scar. In the pool of amber light beneath a corner streetlamp, a black SUV waits, its tinted windows sheets of obsidian. Ysidro hustles through the rear passenger door, leaving it ajar for me.

"¿Listos?" It's Toro, in the front passenger seat, Pacho Ortiz driving. Toro gazes through his visor mirror. "Rafael, glad you could make it, ese."

As if I had a choice.

We drive north, circle through Thornton, buy whiskey, stop someplace else for smokes, then turn back to Globeville. We halt by the Polish church and everyone but Pacho gets out. We're not too far from where I'd arrived on the bus. Pacho continues south on Camino. I figure the runaround is Toro leaving a false trail in the SUV's GPS.

The church looms dark and silent like a mausoleum. Small houses clutter the neighborhood, each a compact fortress. Porch lights outline wire fences and reflect the eyes of watchdogs. The Mousetrap blots out a swath of the night sky.

Toro explains nothing about why we're here, only walks into the construction site. Ysidro keeps at his heels, whispering. I trudge along, trying to eavesdrop, but their words are smothered by the whoosh of highway traffic.

We make our way through a gap in the temporary chain-link fence and proceed to a dirt ramp that leads into the pit. Headlamps spilling from the overpass sweep the area, backlit by construction work in the distance, creating a panorama of bizarre sculptures. Toro and Ysidro trot down the ramp but for me it's a grueling stop and go.

Our destination is one of the holes for a footing. Another vato emerges from the gloom, Chuy. Toro's most trusted matón.

The reason why we're here blooms.

The hole. Me.

My heart starts to race and my breath gets thick as glue.

Why me? It doesn't matter. Maybe Toro is simply cleaning house.

Lightheaded, I want to turn and run, but I wouldn't get far. A pressure builds against my temples. My mind somersaults, spinning with regrets and abandoned dreams. The scar in my chest feels like Death is clawing me with a bony finger.

Feet dragging, docile as a cow on the way to the slaughterhouse, I reach the plywood formers that circumscribe the square dimensions of the hole, about three feet square. Dizzy, nauseous, I force myself to gaze into the abyss, my grave.

I expect Toro, Ysidro, and Chuy to seize me and finish this business. Toro glances to acknowledge that I'm here, then goes back to chatting with the other two. His tats shimmer blue, then green.

Bastard! What's he waiting for? It feels as though a rope tightens around my neck and I'm about to swing.

A pair of headlamps approach. It's a small van, a 4x4 Prowler the construction crews use to haul whatever. The Prowler hums to a halt. The headlamps click off. The darkness swallows us again. Ysidro and Chuy open the back and drag free what appears to be a rolled-up carpet. But it's not. It's a man wrapped in a canvas tarp.

He's dumped on the ground as the Prowler circles and leaves. Ysidro and Chuy yank on the tarp until the man emerges, rolling like a hot dog. He flops onto his belly, hands behind his back, wrists and ankles bound with duct tape. He squirms, still alive. Ysidro uses his foot to push the man over but keeps him on the tarp.

Tape also covers his mouth. His ruddy face is flushed red

and his eyes radiate terror. Sweat trickles from his hairline. He's wearing jeans, a golf jacket, trainers.

Toro crouches and searches the man's pockets, withdraws an ID badge and a gold shield. He peruses the badge, then flips it into the hole. The shield is passed around. It's heavy, quality stuff, and reads, *Bureau of Alcohol, Tobacco, Firearms, and Explosives*. The dreaded ATF. Feds.

"Este cabrón estaba en la pista de mis negocios."

This doomed gabacho is about to pay the price for getting too close to Toro.

Toro dumps the shield into the hole, then reaches under his shirt and pulls out the PW-Pro that I'd earlier fixed for him.

The ATF agent's eyes latch onto the gun.

"Rafael," Toro says.

I look at him confused.

"Dame tu mano."

I present my hand.

He slaps the PW-Pro into my palm. Instantly, I know why I'm here.

"Eres más que tus pinchi libros," Toro says. "Ya es tiempo que crezcas. Que dejas la niñez y te mantienes de pie con nosotros como hombre."

He's thrown everything noble about me back into my face. From this point, there's only one way forward. At his side. As one of him. With this thought, the scar in my chest cracks open, becoming a drain that funnels every malignant thing in the world into my body.

The ATF agent shifts his gaze to me. His expression screams, pleading, begging for mercy.

But his fate is as sealed as mine.

The pistol, this instrument of death, feels heavy as though

it were carved from a tombstone. I grip it with both hands, shaking. I try to rise above myself, to float in an altered state above this putrid catastrophe, but I can't. Every detail remains in sharp focus, needles that etch this bleak moment into my conscience.

Toro snorts impatiently. His tattoos flare electric yellow. He cups the back of my neck and forces me to a knee beside the condemned man. Toro clutches my wrist and slews me forward until the pistol's muzzle presses against the agent's forehead.

The agent and I stare at each other—eyes misted with mutual fear and helplessness.

"¡Ya!" Toro barks.

I jerk the trigger, a loud bang cleaves my hearing, the gun bucks in my hand. Acrid smoke wisps, then vanishes. Ears ringing, trembling, I stagger to my feet.

Blood weeps from a puckered hole along the ridge of the man's left eyebrow. The eyeball below is distended, clouded, and turning gray, black. I recoil, gagging, convinced the eyeball is about pop out. The other eye glistens like polished glass. More blood fans across the tarp, behind his left ear where the bullet exited. The agent quivers in a palsy of agony. Snot bubbles from his nostrils.

Toro clamps onto my upper arm, steadying me. "De este momento, estamos siempre empatados, tu y yo, el y tu. No hay salida."

The dying gringo. Toro. Me. Our fates are locked together. Forever.

Toro takes the PW-Pro from my hands. Ysidro and Chuy bundle the agent in the tarp, then lift and upend him headfirst into the footing hole. He slides in and thuds against the bottom. I hear the rustling of fabric and a muted groan.

Toro picks up the spent cartridge shell and throws it in the hole. His fellow thugs grab nearby shovels and spend time tossing in dirt. Two minutes? Five? I don't know. All I recognize is that my already broken life is now a pile of useless shards.

On Toro's cue, we start back to the dirt ramp. A tractor rumbles from the adjacent construction area and parks close to the hole to angle a pneumatic rammer into the void. A percussive noise carries toward us as the tractor tamps the bottom of the hole. *Thumpa-thumpa-thumpa.*

I imagine the ATF agent, limbs contorted painfully, blood squeezed from the pulp of his mangled face, suffocating as the earth packs around him. By midmorning, he'll be buried under a pillar of cement and rebar. By the end of the week, the rest of the overpass will have been poured, entombing him beneath thousands of tons of concrete.

Is the agent forever disappeared? How long is the Mousetrap expected to last? A century? Longer? Perhaps it will outlive our government, our civilization, and our descendants will regard this structure as a historic relic, as inviolate as the aqueducts of Ancient Rome.

I struggle up the incline, so lost in my fugue that it isn't until I'm confronted by the electronic babble from the Peace Memorial that I realize we're back at street level.

On the sidewalk, we trek north. Toro lights a smoke. Chuy and Ysidro share a joint. Cars pass. No one sees nothin'. No one knows nothin'. Just another night in Globeville.

We arrive at the stop for the southbound number 12. The black SUV waits by the curb. Toro reaches into the rear seat and retrieves my backpack and tool bag. Up the street, a rectangular outline of yellow lamps heralds the approach of the bus.

Toro taps his phone. My backpack buzzes. It's my phone. When I check it, the text reads: *New deposit*.

Toro says, "Lo que te debo, mil quinientos," and then flashes a welfare debit card that he slides into my shirt pocket. "Un poco de propina. Loaded to the max, carnal. You and your mom are set for the month."

With both hands, he cups my face. Our macho jefe leans close and kisses me gently on the lips. He pulls back but keeps his big taurine eyes on me.

I wait for him to say something, to reassure me that I mean something, that I'm more than a tool, more than his chew toy.

Wordlessly, Toro and crew hop into the SUV and motor away. The bus eases forward, sighs to a halt. I climb aboard, show my pass, and slide onto a vacant seat. Through the window, I read the message cycling on the Peace Memorial: *Stop the shooting! Love one another!*

ABOUT THE CONTRIBUTORS

Alex Acevedo

MARIO ACEVEDO is the author of the national best-selling Felix Gomez detective-vampire series and coauthored the Western novel *Luther, Wyoming*. His work has won an International Latino Book Award, a Colorado Book Award, and has appeared in numerous anthologies including *A Fistful of Dinosaurs, Straight Outta Deadwood, Psi-Wars,* and *It Came from the Multiplex*. Acevedo serves on the faculty of Regis University's MFA program and the Lighthouse Writers Workshop.

Anthony Briscoe

FRANCELIA BELTON's love of short stories came from watching old *Twilight Zone* and *Alfred Hitchcock Presents* television shows in her youth. Her fiction has appeared in various publications and she was a finalist in the 2021 ScreenCraft Cinematic Short Story Writing Competition. Now, she is on a quest to write 1,001 stories before she dies—an audacious goal for a slow writer; she is documenting her journey at Francel.Be/Writing-Stories.

Joe Rogers

R. ALAN BROOKS teaches writing for Regis University's MFA program and is the author of the graphic novels *The Burning Metronome* and *Anguish Garden*, as well as his award-winning weekly comic for the *Colorado Sun*, "What'd I Miss?" His TED Talk on the importance of art reached one million views in two months. He hosts the *MotherF**ker in a Cape* comics podcast and has written comic books for Pop Culture Classroom, Zenescope Entertainment, and more.

Klean Photography

D.L. CORDERO is a sci-fi fantasy author, occasional poet, and horror dabbler working out of Denver. As a nonbinary, queer, Afro-Latinx and Taíno person, Cordero aims to write intriguing stories that center around characters from marginalized communities, without making identity the crux of the tale. Their work can be found on dlcordero.com and they can be followed on Facebook, Twitter, and Instagram (@dlcorderowrites).

Amy Drayer

AMY DRAYER grew up a free-range kid on a charming island in the Pacific Northwest. A graduate of Scripps College and the Lighthouse Writers Workshop Book Project, she published her debut novel, *Revelation*, in 2020. She also pens short stories, is an enthusiastic member of Sisters in Crime, managing editor of the *museum of americana*, and editor of the 2022 Rocky Mountain Fiction Writers anthology. Learn more about her work at makahislandmysteries.com.

Peter Heller

PETER HELLER is the author of the best-selling novels *The Dog Stars, The Painter, Celine, The River,* and *The Guide.* He holds an MFA in poetry and fiction from the Iowa Writers' Workshop, is a former longtime contributor to NPR, and has been a contributing editor at *Outside, Men's Journal,* and *National Geographic Adventure.* Heller is also the author of four books of literary nonfiction.

Lorena Martinez

TWANNA LATRICE HILL is a writer, actor, educator, and activist. She earned a BA in Russian from Princeton University with minors in creative writing as well as theater and dance, an MA in Soviet Studies from Harvard University, and a masters in nonprofit management from Regis University. Hill was awarded a Lighthouse Writers Workshop Book Project Fellowship for 2019–2021 and lives with her service dog, Roxi.

Trystan Photography

BARBARA NICKLESS is the Amazon and *Wall Street Journal* best-selling author of the award-winning Sydney Parnell crime novels. Her essays and short stories have appeared in *Writer's Digest, Criminal Element,* and elsewhere. She also teaches creative writing to veterans at the University of Colorado in Colorado Springs. Nickless is often in the Rocky Mountains where she loves to hike, cave, and drink single-malt Scotch—although usually not at the same time.

Florence Hernandez Ramos

MANUEL RAMOS has published eleven crime fiction novels and one short story collection. His books have been awarded the Colorado Book Award (twice) and the Chicano/Latino Literary Prize and short-listed for the Edgar and Shamus awards. He is a cofounder of and regular contributor to the award-winning Internet magazine *La Bloga* (labloga.blogspot.com), which is devoted to Latinx literature, culture, news, and opinion. He lives in Denver's Northside. His latest novel is *Angels in the Wind.*

Tom Sandner

MARK STEVENS is the author of the Allison Coil mystery series—*Antler Dust, Buried by the Roan, Trapline, Lake of Fire,* and *The Melancholy Howl. Trapline* won the Colorado Book Award and the Colorado Authors League Award in 2016. *Kirkus Reviews* called *Lake of Fire* "irresistible" and *The Melancholy Howl* "smart and indelible." Stevens was the 2016 Rocky Mountain Fiction Writers' Writer of the Year and president of the Rocky Mountain chapter of Mystery Writers of America.

MATHANGI SUBRAMANIAN's novel *A People's History of Heaven* was a finalist for the Lambda Literary Award and was long-listed for the PEN/Faulkner Award and the Center for Fiction First Novel Prize. Her middle-grade book *Dear Mrs. Naidu* won the South Asia Book Award. Her essays have appeared in the *Washington Post, Harper's Bazaar,* and *Ms.,* among others. She lives in Denver with her husband, her daughter, and way too many picture books.

CYNTHIA SWANSON writes literary suspense, often using historical settings. Her debut novel, *The Bookseller,* was a *New York Times* best seller, an Indie Next selection, and winner of the 2016 WILLA Literary Award for Historical Fiction. Swanson's second novel, the *USA Today* best seller *The Glass Forest,* was noted in *Forbes* as being one of "Five Novels with a Remarkably Strong Sense of Place." She lives with her family in Denver. Find her at cynthiaswansonauthor.com.

DAVID HESKA WANBLI WEIDEN, an enrolled citizen of the Sicangu Lakota Nation, is the author of *Winter Counts,* nominated for an Edgar Award and winner of the Anthony, Thriller, Lefty, Barry, Macavity, and Spur awards. The novel was a *New York Times* Editors' Choice, an Indie Next pick, and named a Best Book of 2020 by NPR, *Publishers Weekly,* and *Library Journal.* He lives in Denver, Colorado, with his family.

ERIKA T. WURTH's literary-horror novel *Whitehorse* is out with Flatiron/Macmillan. She's a creative writing professor at Western Illinois University, is a *Kenyon Review* Writers Workshop Scholar, attended the Tin House Summer Workshop, and is a narrative artist for the Meow Wolf Denver installation. She is of Apache/Chickasaw/Cherokee descent and was raised outside of Denver where she lives with her partner, stepchildren, and extremely fluffy dogs.

Also available from the Akashic Noir Series

LAS VEGAS NOIR
edited by Jarret Keene and Todd James Pierce
320 pages, trade paperback original, $15.95

BRAND-NEW STORIES BY: John O'Brien, David Corbett, Scott Phillips, Nora Pierce, Tod Goldberg, Bliss Esposito, Felicia Campbell, Jaq Greenspon, José Skinner, Pablo Medina, Christine McKellar, Lori Kozlowski, Vu Tran, Celeste Starr, Preston L. Allen, and Janet Berliner.

"The writers do such a great job of layering, creating depth, building suspense and weaving in the histories of different characters that even readers who prefer their literature without violence and warped characters, derailed and teetering through social land mines, will likely enjoy *Las Vegas Noir*." —*Las Vegas Sun*

SANTA FE NOIR
edited by Ariel Gore
264 pages, trade paperback original, $15.95

BRAND-NEW STORIES BY: Ana Castillo, Jimmy Santiago Baca, Byron F. Aspaas, Barbara Robidoux, Elizabeth Lee, Ana June, Israel Francisco Haros Lopez, Ariel Gore, Darryl Lorenzo Wellington, Candace Walsh, Hida Viloria, Cornelia Read, Miriam Sagan, James Reich, Kevin Atkinson, Katie Johnson, and Tomas Moniz.

"Readers, if you like noir and you like Santa Fe, this is a must-read!" —*Eldorado Living*

"There is a real charm to the local specificity of *Santa Fe Noir*, and it's a pleasure to discover how different imaginations can channel the chiaroscuro energy of well-known places." —*Santa Fe Reporter*

PHOENIX NOIR
edited by Patrick Millikin
270 pages, trade paperback original, $15.95

BRAND-NEW STORIES BY: Diana Gabaldon, Lee Child, James Sallis, Luis Alberto Urrea, Jon Talton, Megan Abbott, Charles Kelly, Robert Anglen, Patrick Millikin, Laura Tohe, Kurt Reichenbaugh, Gary Phillips, David Corbett, Don Winslow, Dogo Barry Graham, and Stella Pope Duarte.

"'Nobody looks good soaking wet and dead.' That's Diana Gabaldon's line, but what she doesn't say is that you'd look even worse if you were wet and dead and left to stew in the furious Phoenix sun. The stories in this book are a collective treat, and you can read them in any order you like." —*Arizona Republic*